THE ABANDONED QUEEN

Berengaria of Navarre
Book Two

Austin Hernon

SAPERE
BOOKS

THE ABANDONED QUEEN

Published by Sapere Books.

24 Trafalgar Road, Ilkley, LS29 8HH

saperebooks.com

ISBN: 978-0-85495-207-6

For my little friends, Ellie Megan, Daisy Amelia and Connie Elizabeth.

CHAPTER ONE

Cyprus, June 1191

My wedding night had not gone as planned. As I eventually embraced sleep, having shed many tears, I reflected on the past few months.

As Princess of Navarre, I had been sought by the formidable Eleanor of Aquitaine — Queen Dowager of England — as the bride for her crusading son, King Richard. Though we had met only once before, back when I was a girl of twelve, I had fond memories of him and so I agreed to become his queen. Since Richard was on his way to recapture the Holy Land from the Saracen forces, he had been unable to propose to me in person. Therefore, together with my favourite ladies, Alazne and Arrosa, and a large entourage, Eleanor and I rode and sailed across Europe to catch him up. We were all finally reunited in Messina, where I was also introduced to Richard's sister Joan, the widowed Queen of Sicily. She had recently been rescued by Richard after Tancred — the bastard cousin of her deceased husband, King William II — had seized Sicily and placed her under house arrest.

After spending some time with Richard and Joan, Eleanor left for England, where her youngest son John was reportedly reigning poorly as Regent in Richard's absence. The remaining party set sail, got caught in a storm, and then headed for Cyprus, intending to gather supplies. However, since Cyprus proved hostile to us, Richard invaded and captured the island from its ruler, Isaac Comnenus. Much of our party — including me, Joan, and our ladies — then moved into

Lemesós Castle, Isaac's erstwhile abode. Isaac and some of his men subsequently went into hiding in the hills. Richard was not inclined to let him get away so easily, but he paused his pursuit long enough for us to get married.

I was dismayed to discover that Richard had taken a vow of chastity, to be upheld until he recaptured the Holy Land. However, on account of our need to produce an heir to England's throne, he had secured one day's dispensation from the Bishop of Evreux, to be used after our wedding. In the event, we proved unable to consummate our marriage, and our night together was cut short when Richard was called away on military matters. I was therefore left alone in the private tent that had been erected specially for our first night together, wondering how I was to produce an heir with no husband beside me. After all, his priority lay not with me, but with capturing Isaac Comnenus and driving Sultan Saladin's army out of the Holy Land.

'Berengaria, Berri, wake up, it's almost midday.'

I opened my eyes. It was Joan, with Alazne and Arrosa hovering in the background.

'Midday!' I cried. 'Where's Richard?'

'He went off in the dark, so I'm told,' said Joan. 'I looked in at dawn, but you were still asleep.' She sat on the bed beside me and took my hand in hers.

'Did he say aught about last night, Joan?'

'No, not to me. How did it pass?'

I looked at Arrosa and Alazne. 'Leave us, please. I'll see you up in our chambers.'

When they had reluctantly left, I leaned against Joan.

'Odd. It seemed odd. We tried together — you know what I mean — but it didn't seem to work.' I lowered my voice still further. 'I'm not sure he entered. And he said something about his vow.'

'His vow? Couldn't he forget that for one night?'

'No. And his dispensation runs out today.'

'Quite,' said Joan. 'I did not want to remind you, but you will remain unvisited until Jerusalem is free.'

'Does this mean that he doesn't like me, Joan?'

'No! Who could not like you? I think it means you need to pray more. When he seizes the city, you will gain a husband. Come on, Berri, time to face the day, what's left of it. I'll help you dress.'

'What am I going to wear?' I was looking at the crumpled wedding gown lying on the floor, my netherwear scattered about on top of it.

'You stay here. I'll go to our bedchamber and get something, and I'll ask Hugo to fill the king's tub for you. Then you can decide in peace what to do next. I didn't drink much yesterday, with all those men gawping at me.'

After I had returned to the castle and bathed and dressed, we found our ladies at table in the guard hall. There was plenty of food, as we were the only ones eating. Richard and his men were long gone; I was told that they had set off after Isaac Comnenus, who had been sighted the previous night. Only the garrison troops were left behind to guard us.

'Hugo's found some glass goblets. He says that they're ancient. They certainly make this fine wine taste better.' Joan's eyes were already a bit shiny.

'That's as may be,' I retorted, 'but I am still short of a husband. How long is this campaign likely to last, I wonder?'

'Until Richard skins Isaac of all he owns, if I know my brother.'

'Has Javier gone with them, Arrosa?' I asked. After a short but intense courtship, Arrosa had recently married the captain of my escort.

'No, Your Highness,' she replied. 'Actually, I wanted to ask you something, if I may.'

'Ah!' I said. 'Arrosa has a plot stewing.'

'Javier has had an offer of employment,' she began hesitantly. 'As you are now under the protection of the King of England, you might be thinking that his — our — services are no longer required.'

I was surprised. It had not occurred to me that as a queen through marriage, I was able to make my own choices in such matters. 'I had not considered this. Joan?'

'You are now the responsibility of Richard and you are Queen of England. Of course things must change, for you have exchanged your duties in your father's kingdom for those in my brother's. We should go into more detail about this together, Berri. I'll happily become your mentor.'

'Thank you, Joan. What is it that Javier wants to do, Arrosa?'

'Hugo carried a message from some lord in the king's entourage, asking whether Javier would like to become Captain of the Guard here in Lemesós.'

'I see, and you would like to stay here?'

'It is very nice. It's warm, and the people seem pleasanter than their leaders. We should do well here … and … and I am with child.'

'Oh, Arrosa! How wonderful! Come here, let me give you a hug.'

We celebrated a little before going to the privacy of our bedchambers, and the discussion about babies lasted all afternoon. Joan stayed quiet, and I took her to one side and apologised for the direction of the conversation. I was aware that her own child had not survived.

'Don't be silly. People will go on having babies, regardless of my fortunes, or yours. Don't forget why you are here, Berri, if your husband manages to visit you now and again.'

'I know. If only he could have said goodbye, or sent word. We are lost as to where he is or what he is doing. That is the worst part, not knowing.'

She kissed my forehead. 'Go on, go and talk about babies. I am tired after yesterday; I'll take a nap. We'll talk later.'

'Thank you,' I said, returning her kiss. 'Joan, can I speak to your confessor? Mine died at sea.'

'Certainly. Father Francis is always willing to listen. Is something troubling you?'

'A bit. I find some emotions rather exciting — perhaps a bit too enjoyable.'

'Do you not believe that sex is for procreation?'

'It's what the Lord ordained, Joan, is it not?'

'So Mother Church has decided.'

'It has also decided on the vow of chastity; is the Church not wise?'

'Is it? It is based only on men's ideas, after all. When were you ever asked?' Joan held my gaze and a light dawned in her eyes. 'Are you saying that you would like Richard to repeal his vow?'

'Yes.'

'Be careful with that one; Father Francis will not like it. Never let him know that you discussed it with anyone else.'

'So I am to remain a near-virgin until Richard takes Jerusalem?'

'Try it. What will you do now?'

'I'm not sure. I need to find out more about this vow. He took it in England at his coronation, before our marriage — yet it still applies.'

Joan squeezed my hand. 'I'll speak to Father Francis for you. I'll be careful what I tell him, as he might not understand the fullness of your love, or desire.'

'Thank you, Joan. I'm grateful.'

That evening, a horseman trotted into the yard with news from Richard's camp. He came into the guard hall to find Hugo de Mara, Richard's scribe and the temporary warden of Lemesós Castle. We hung around until he had divulged his information, whereupon Hugo came over to us and sat down at Joan's invitation.

'Thank you, Your Highness. I am no longer the castellan here, if I ever was. I am returned to clerk's duties.'

'Oh,' said Joan, 'does that upset you, Hugo?'

'No, I look forward to once more being an observer and recorder of the events of the day. Being in charge of something like this is quite wearying, and somewhat thankless.'

'Here,' I said, 'hold this goblet. Alazne, fill Hugo's pot; we are celebrating.'

'Yes! Another fest,' she said, before calling on a servant to bring wine over.

'So what is my brother doing, Hugo?' asked Joan.

'There are some negotiations to take place some distance away. He has invited Isaac to meet and see if they can reach some kind of agreement.'

'So can we get on with the Crusade soon?' I asked.

'I believe so, but my instinct tells me that the king will not leave here before he has the island under his full control,' replied Hugo. 'It should be noted that if an army wanted a strategic base to operate from to support its operations across the water in Outremer…'

'We are sitting on it,' I stated. 'Is this a plan? Did he intend to land here before we left Sicily?'

'I cannot answer for the king's thoughts, Your Highness, but it has occurred to me that the great storm we came through did not alter his plans much. Duke Robert of Normandy did something of the sort during the First Crusade, and King Richard reacted to Isaac's moves without much ado, as if he had planned this for some time.' He turned to Joan. 'You know him best, Your Highness. What is your view?'

'I might not know him as well as you assume, Hugo. We were separated a long time ago, and his situation has altered as much as mine. However, I can say that deviousness runs in our family. You may make of that what you will.'

'So we have to wait here while Richard plays games with Isaac,' I said indignantly, 'instead of besporting himself with his new wife?'

'I'm afraid that he has been known to prefer warfare to the bedchamber, Berri. But we must not question his commitment to his vow,' said Joan.

I looked at Hugo, for it was time for him to leave.

He bowed and said, 'I'll bring news as fast as I receive it, Your Highnesses. I believe that the king prefers the poet Ambroise to record his doings, and I am to remain with you.'

'Really!' exclaimed Joan. 'And what will you scribble, Hugo?'

'Events, Your Highness, only events. If you wish me to add your words or thoughts, then say so, otherwise they will remain unrecorded.'

And with that, he bade us a goodnight and left.

We lapsed into silence for a while, until I posed a question.

'So is Richard uncertain, Joan? On our wedding night, he treated me kindly but did not mount me with any ardour.'

Joan looked up. 'Leave us now, ladies, if you please.'

Our ladies left politely and, although in the guard hall, we were in a corner, and the few people still in there left us alone.

'You have not had much experience in the bedchamber, have you, Berri?'

'No, I told you, I haven't had any. Pass that carafe.'

'Yes, it is very palatable, this local wine. To your health, sister-in-law.'

'Yes, and yours.'

'So he didn't refuse to let you touch him, or push you away?' asked Joan.

'No, but something was holding him back. I am frustrated yet safe, I suppose. I just wonder if his ardour is all that it should be, or if he didn't like what I had to offer.'

'How odd, Berri. You lack naught. But you should know that all men are different. I cannot describe to you the constant man, for he may not exist. My experience with William confirmed that.'

I nodded sympathetically. Joan had told me how she had been devasted to discover that her late husband had kept a secret harem in their castle.

'I believe that Richard wears impatience as a cloak. It may be that it conceals something else, something he would not wish to become known — a struggle between his natural desire and his given vow, or perhaps something deeper.'

I gazed into Joan's green eyes, wondering if she knew more about her brother than she cared to admit. 'How many women has he bedded?'

'Honestly, I do not know. He acknowledged his son, Philip of Cognac, and the mother is well cared for, although she is no one of note. But he has never bragged of bedding anyone else, although of course there are rumours. All princes might expect favours.'

'To sire a child requires a degree of, er, intimacy, does it not?'

'Obviously. It will not work from a distance.'

We both descended into laughter at the thought.

'I'm certain now that he did not complete,' I said. 'He tried, but then it ended before we'd really started. He seemed to receive the military summons as an excuse to get away. What does that signify?'

'A problem, which time and circumstance may cure. Be hopeful and pray, Berri. Come near — this is delicate.'

I moved around the table to sit next to her, and she whispered in my ear.

'He can't concentrate on you at the moment. He needs to get over his guilt, or whatever it is — perhaps a concoction of frustration brought about by his vow and worries about managing the Crusade, not to mention King Philip and the other leaders. It's a powerful disincentive to desire. After Jerusalem you must take charge. Do all you can to draw him to you.'

'God, how difficult will that be?'

'That, dear Berengaria, is what you are going to have to resolve for him. And if I may say one more thing: play it as something normal. Don't make it serious nor cast it off as a jest. He must not be embarrassed by this, or it could spark his anger and might even lead to a rejection.'

'Of me?'

'Of you. Someone will need to take the blame for a king without an heir.'

'Mother of Christ, what have I got myself into?'

'A delicate matter of state and Church, sister, one which needs managing with skill. Pass that carafe, please, and calm your desire. You'll get nowhere until he has Jerusalem in his grasp.' Joan poured some wine into her goblet and took a swig. 'Did you discuss how you might feel about your impending marriage with your confessor?'

'No, not directly, but he died on the way here, and might not have had the answers,' I said. 'He was too remote from earthly matters, I feared. God bless him.'

'Did he comment on the matter?'

'Well, we discussed love, not relationships.'

Joan laughed and some men at another table looked around curiously. We were in the light of braziers now, and the hall had a more intimate atmosphere about it.

'So what was your confessor's response?'

'That love was eternal, and that we should pray for it.'

We were both silent for a moment.

'Queens and princesses do not seek love, Berri,' said Joan. 'They seek liaisons of state. But you should know that.'

'Sadly. But I have my king — will you find one?'

'For Sicily? I doubt it. Even as we speak there will be whispered discussions in Rome. The Pope and Emperor Heinrich will be carving up my realm to suit the Church.'

'But if they upset you, will they not upset Richard? He seeks the liberation of Jerusalem on their behalf. What if he saw you disadvantaged?'

'I am not such a fool as to think that I will come first in that equation. Richard sees dynasties in marriage, not families. I am but an asset in his affairs. If I find love, he will only approve it if it suits his plans, be assured of that. We are in the same position, dear sister: prime flesh and prime assets.'

I was too stunned to reply.

Joan took me by the hand and led me up the stairs. Outside the bedchambers, she kissed me gently and whispered, 'Sweet Berengaria, enjoy your love while you may. I must plot my own course. Goodnight.'

The king did not return to us after his reported meeting with Isaac. The messages that evening spoke of an early agreement, in which Isaac conceded everything Richard demanded.

The next day we were escorted to visit the nearby salt flats — as a diversion, I supposed. Rising early to make the most of the cool air, we found the site fascinating. The workers let the sea roll over some embankments until it became a lake, and then closed off the entry points. The water disappeared in the heat and what was left was salt, which was raked up and despatched all over — a very profitable gift from God, I thought.

That evening, we received the news that Isaac had disappeared from the negotiating ground and run off to Famagusta, a fortified city further along the coast. This seemed like a big mistake, given the presence of Richard's fleet in the harbour. We thought that Richard was certain to winkle him out. But apparently, when he had arrived, the gates were open and Isaac had fled.

Around our castle there were orchards full of olives, oranges and lemons, and meadows replete with sheep and goats. That evening, we enjoyed the local cuisine: goat stewed in herbs, along with the local wine.

There was also the daily bounty from the sea. Every morning, we were taken to the harbour to watch the fishing boats landing. I had a new kind of fish taken to the castle every day to try for the evening meal. At the same time, the daily messenger rode into the yard and we gathered to hear of Richard's progress, and Hugo sat to write it all down.

At the end of the week we heard of the landing of some French diplomats. They had been sent by Philip of France to hurry up Richard, since the war in the Holy Land was going badly for him. He was now stuck in an impasse outside Akko, and he wanted Richard's army to land and give aid as soon as possible.

Richard refused, especially since Philip's emissaries also demanded a share of the spoils won in Cyprus, even though he had not been present.

Two weeks after the reporting of the pursuit of Isaac, news came to us that Richard had despatched two fleets of war galleys to ensure the encirclement of the island. Richard split his fleet. Taking charge of one half and with Robert of Turnham commanding the other, they set off in different directions to meet at the well-guarded harbour of Kyrenia on the northern shore.

When Richard landed, he headed for the walled town of Nikosia, which surrendered without much ado, whereupon Isaac fled from there to the mountain range that towered above Kyrenia, named the Pentadaktylos.

'This name means "five-fingered", Your Highnesses,' Hugo informed us, 'so called after the highest peaks. The range also holds a number of castles built at the very tops of mountains: Saint Hilarion, Buffavento and Kantara, these being the most impossible to attack. Then there is a very large castle sitting with its feet in the sea at Kyrenia, guarding the harbour. Isaac was there for a while, but then he came out for the failed meeting. It is also difficult to attack. If Isaac hides within any of these, it will take months to winkle him out. Our friend, King Guy de Lusignan is in charge there.'

'King! Mother of God, let's pray that he has better fortune than hitherto,' exclaimed Joan. We all knew that Lusignan, the erstwhile King of Jerusalem, was hoping to win back his throne by allying himself with Richard. 'Does my brother ever mean to get on with this Crusade?'

'He might remember it one day,' I moaned, 'along with his new wife.'

At the end of the third week of the king's campaign, a troop of knights appeared in the castle yard.

Hugo panted his way up from the guard hall, crying out, 'Your Highnesses, the first of Richard's men have returned!'

I was idling on the bed, staying out of the heat with Alazne brushing my hair. She rushed to look out of the window as Joan emerged from across the corridor.

'Come down, Your Highnesses,' said Hugo. 'There will be news: Robert of Turnham has arrived.'

'Who?' asked Joan.

I looked across at her. 'One of Richard's fleet commanders — a likable man,' I replied.

Hugo, on his way back down the stairs, shouted back, 'He is an Englishman appointed to govern the island. He will be the new castellan of Lemesós Castle. Come down, Your Highnesses, and meet him.'

Emerging into the blinding sunlight, from the top of the main gate steps we could see a group of tired and dusty cavalrymen being questioned by a throng of cheering onlookers.

Hugo was at the side of the man who appeared to be the leader. He looked scruffier and more bloodstained than the rest — clearly he had been in the thick of it. His men were all drinking from gourds of water or wine, passed to them by castle servants.

Hugo spotted us. Tugging at the arm of the leader, he led him across the yard and up the steps.

'Your Highnesses, Robert of Turnham.'

The ruddy-faced man of middling age removed his chain coif to reveal wispy blond hair. He bowed and smiled. 'Your Highnesses, I have come straight from the king. He sends his regards to you both, and his love to his queen.' He looked at me.

'You and I have met before, but briefly,' I said. 'Cannot he bring his love directly, Robert?' I was a bit irritable, and he may have struggled with my accent, but he got the message.

'Ah! Your Highness, there is something you should know. The king is not well. He did not make it to Kyrenia, and he is waiting to board his war galley at the ancient city of Famagusta, some way along the coast.'

'What ails him, Robert?' asked Joan.

'Some recurring weakness and inertia, sweats and sickness. With his armour off and some regular food, he was soon up and about, but he remains near his tent, enjoying some sunshine.'

'Why were we not informed?' I demanded. 'There have been enough messengers back and forth.'

'We were under strict instructions from the king himself not to mention it, Your Highness. He did not want you to worry.'

Joan put her arm around my shoulder and I felt Alazne's hand grasp mine. I was upset but said naught.

'Famagusta? Where is it?' queried Joan.

'It is the best part of seventy miles away, Your Highness — more than a day's ride, I fear, if you thought to go there.'

'So what are we supposed to do while the king waits to board his ship?'

Robert looked at me warily. 'I am to prepare the fleet for sea, and set it off to rendezvous with the king off Famagusta in three days' time, Your Highness. The king's baggage is following me. Most of the army is marching on to Famagusta, where we will join them … and then sail to Akko.'

'But what is a seaman like you doing fighting on land, Robert?'

'I am a soldier carried to battle by sea — the Norman art of war.'

I smiled at him. He was quite personable, and if he was to escort me, then I felt we should become friends. 'Well, Joan, off to sea once more. Alazne, start packing. Which ship are we to voyage in, Robert?'

'The one you came to Cyprus in, if that is to your satisfaction, Your Highness?'

'It will do,' I answered. I had some fond memories of the good ship *Dione*, in spite of the storm that had hit. 'How far is Akko from Cyprus, Robert?'

'About three days, Your Highness, given a fair wind.'

'And given another storm?' asked Joan.

'That will depend upon which direction the wind blows in, Your Highness,' said Robert. He then addressed both me and Joan. 'There is something else that you should know, Your Highnesses.' He waved across to one of his men, who was standing by a palfrey with a young girl mounted upon it. I had not noticed her before, for she was small and had been obscured by the throng of men.

'Who's that?' asked Joan.

'She is Isaac Comnenus's daughter. She is named Eirini, I believe, and she's a titled princess.'

'So what is she doing here?' I asked.

'Guy de Lusignan captured her in Kyrenia Castle, after which Isaac capitulated to secure her release. He is presently in chains, awaiting the king's pleasure.'

'And?' I pressed.

'The king would like you to care for her, raise her in courtly ways and accustom her to our lives. She speaks little sense, but she is quite angry, for one so small.'

The girl was placed in front of me, so I smiled at her. I received a scowl in return as she tugged at her captor's arm.

'Mother of God!' gasped Joan. 'How old is she, Robert?'

'Twelvish, Your Highness. The king says that Isaac will behave himself as long as we hold his daughter, as she is very precious to him.'

'How cruel,' I said. 'We must take good care of her.'

I held out a hand. As we were of a similar height, our eyes were almost level and she seemed reassured. She took my hand in hers, which was warm and clammy. I could feel her trembling.

'This child is terrified,' I said. 'I will take her inside while we pack.'

'One more thing,' said Robert. 'The king proposes to lease or sell the island to the Knights Templar, for a goodly sum. They will occupy and govern it while we are over the sea. It will act as a base for our operations in Outremer. I am to wait here until they arrive to take control.'

'Oh!' I said. 'Am I not the Damsel, or Lady of Cyprus anymore?'

'Of course, and the king is still Lord of Cyprus,' he replied.

'Did you think to lighten your burden of so many titles, Berri?' laughed Joan.

'It might have been an opportunity. Come along, Eirini.' I smiled at her and she seemed to become a little happier. 'I must see Hugo. I've thought of a letter that I must write. I'll be with you shortly, Joan.'

No matter how busy Hugo was, I needed a letter with the seal of England upon it. After I had found him — and used my new powers of persuasion as Queen of England on him — I scurried back to our chambers and sat down on my bed, inviting Eirini to sit next to me.

My French had improved since I had left Olite, my birthplace, but I didn't know any Greek.

'Do you understand me?' I asked the girl, trying to keep things simple.

Her face was blank.

I pointed at the ladies. 'Alazne, Pavot and Torène.' Lastly I placed a finger on my chest. 'Berengaria.'

Her face brightened as she laid a finger on her chest and said, 'Eirini.'

'So, what's next?' asked Alazne.

'I think that we should get on with packing and speak normally. She will pick it up as we go along.'

'She seems bright enough.'

'Point at and name everything that you touch, and let her help with the packing. And Alazne, go down to find a seamstress. I think she has been too long in that dress — get her some small wear made up.'

We only had three days to prepare to set sail.

'What if Richard has already crossed the sea and is at war in Outremer?' I fretted.

'Don't be silly, Berri,' scolded Joan. 'Did not Robert say that it would take at least a week to organise and embark at Famagusta? We will probably set off at the same time, and

Robert will no doubt receive instructions sent by a fast horse before we leave here.'

While we slept, a horseman did indeed arrive, and it was not long before everybody in the garrison was heading off down to the harbour, both those about to embark and those who were to remain behind.

My main chests had been sent down to the harbour the previous day. We just had to dress in our seagoing wear and pack the last of our clothes into one small chest. Once we had done so, we sat on the bed, waiting to be escorted to our ship.

Eirini was in a sulk. She had gathered that we were leaving Cyprus and refused to move, sitting on the small truckle bed I'd brought into my room for her. Her arms were folded and the new clothes we'd had made for her were still lying on the floor.

'What should we do?' asked Alazne. 'Apart from getting some man to pick her up and carry her down to the ship, of course.' Alazne had taken to Eirini and they were becoming closer.

I had a thought. 'Alazne, go and find Hugo. Ask him to see if there is a Griffon woman in the castle who would come with us as an interpreter and friend to Eirini. Why did we not think of it earlier?'

'A very good idea, Your Highness. We have been too busy to think of such things,' said Alazne.

'You've got used to not calling me Princess?' I said with a smile.

'Since you married Richard, I could call you by any title imaginable and I would be correct. Your Highness, Princess, Duchess, Countess.'

We laughed, and then I thought of the perils that might await us at sea.

'Embrace me, Alazne. I'm feeling vulnerable again. Arrosa, join us.'

We sat entwined for a few moments, while Eirini watched us curiously.

Arrosa began to unlace me and Eirini began to pay more attention, fascinated by my gown. Then I pulled on a pair of breeches and a shirt: minimal, practical clothing was best for going to sea.

Then Alazne reappeared, followed by a young woman. She was a very handsome creature with black hair and an attractive smile and figure.

'This is Amynta, Your Highness,' said Alazne. 'She was married to a local man, but he died. She is looking for a new life.'

'Greetings, Amynta. You are a Griffon, and speak Greek?'

'Indeed, Your Highness. I also speak French, and some English. My father was a pedagogue and taught me to be interested in other folk and their tongues.'

'And you would come with us to Outremer?'

'Gladly, Your Highness.'

'What did your husband die of?'

'Curiosity, Your Highness. He went down to the strand when your ships arrived and stepped out from behind a tree when your archers let fly.'

'He was not a warrior?'

'No, Your Highness. He was a tutor like my father, a mild man. This is an opportunity for me, and the time is right to take it.'

'You are very direct. Good. Has Alazne acquainted you with our requirements?'

'Indeed. May I?'

Amynta looked beyond me to where Eirini was sitting, watching. On my nod, she went across to her and began a conversation in Greek. Soon they were sitting on the bed next to each other, deep in conversation.

'Your Highness, Eirini says that she is not going to take off her clothes with everybody watching,' said Amynta.

'I see. But will she wear the seagoing clothes? Will you?'

'I'll wear anything to get away from my memories of this place, and so will Eirini, in the hope of being reunited with her father.'

She had another conversation with the little princess.

'She asks if her father is safe, Your Highness.'

'Tell her he is safe. And that he is leaving the island with King Richard.'

A few more words were exchanged before I was informed, 'She will wear the clothes, but she wants to change in private, Your Highness.'

'If you would stay and help her, Amynta, that would be useful. Come on, Alazne, let's see if Queen Joan is ready.'

We crossed the corridor to find Joan's chamber in chaos.

'Oh God, Berengaria!' she cried. 'We're not nearly ready. The seagoing clothes were buried deep in the last chest we opened.' She turned to her ladies. 'Pavot, Torène, do hurry.'

'Sorry, Joan, I thought that you had lists. Shall I tell you about Princess Eirini while you are waiting?'

'Oh, do. Does she understand you? Who is that woman you have in there? Tell me everything.'

We sat and chatted until Pavot and Torène began to cast off their gowns in favour of breeches. Amynta walked in when they were near naked and apologised.

'Don't worry, Amynta. It gets worse; at sea there is no privacy. How are you doing with Eirini?'

'Very well, Your Highness. I think that I might have a new friend. I have got her into the clothes you prepared for her — shall I change too?'

'Yes, please, and hurry. We must be running out of time.'

We were, but within the hour our party were gathered in the castle bailey, waiting for Hugo to escort us down to the ship to begin our next voyage. He approached us from the direction of the harbour in company with someone I recognised. It was William of Harfleur, the master of the ship that had carried us to Cyprus.

'Master William!' I greeted him. 'Are you to take us to Akko, master?'

Hugo had stopped several paces back and was staring at our attire.

'Do you like our sailors' garb, Hugo? It suits us, don't you think?' teased Joan.

Hugo's face turned red beneath his tan and he coughed, struggling for words until he handed a vellum roll to me, complete with Richard's seal.

'What's that?' asked Joan.

'You'll see shortly,' I replied, grinning. I turned to Hugo. 'He approved?'

'The king said there is no need for you to seek his approval for such matters, and he will have a seal made for you to use in future.'

'Are you readied for another storm, Your Highnesses?' asked William. He looked at me. 'Talking of which, may I offer my services to a new queen?'

'You may, Master William. We have been improved since we left you. We are now two queens and one imperial princess.' I indicated Eirini, who was hiding behind Amynta. Both were now also clad in breeches.

'The young girl is Princess Eirini, the daughter of Isaac Comnenus, who is in the safekeeping of my husband. She is the guarantor of his good behaviour,' said Joan.

Eirini's eyes focused on Joan at the mention of her father's name, but I was not certain how much she understood. I decided that I would instruct Amynta about how much she should know until we got her off the island. We needed to keep her calm.

'Well, well, a cargo of queens and a princess,' said William with a smile. 'We have made some improvements while we have been in the harbour. There is a new garderobe hanging out over the stern, if it is not too dizzying for you to use, Your Highness.'

That raised a few titters.

'So we take the buckets into this garderobe?' asked Alazne.

'No, you sit on a bar and hang over the water, madam.'

'What if this … garderobe falls off? We'll drown,' Alazne protested. 'You expect two queens to hang their bare behinds out of the ship?'

'That's the point of it. It's like a little privy chamber,' said William. 'No one will see … anything. And it was constructed by my ship's carpenter, so it will not fall off, madam.'

I stepped between them. 'Alazne, see to the baggage, if you please. Master William, we will be privileged to inspect our new facility. Now, ladies, can we get embarked? The light is fading already.'

'Well handled,' said Joan as we moved towards the harbour. 'I suspect that the palace of Olite was very well managed while you were in charge.'

'Believe it, Joan. And that was a lifetime ago, so it seems.'

'Excuse me, Your Highnesses,' William interrupted. 'My instructions are to take you as far as Famagusta, where you are to transfer to the king's ship, his war galley. That will be a new experience for you.'

I took Joan by the arm. 'Come on, Joan, we're going to war.'

The *Dione* was not in harbour; she was waiting outside at anchor. We, along with our baggage, were going to embark on a small galley to be taken out there, but first I had a duty to perform. Arrosa and Javier were watching, feeling a little guilty at not joining us, perhaps.

'Come near, you two. You have been the best of my friends and served me well. I am sorry to part, but the fates dictate, and it will be better for you both to remain here. If I return, perhaps you would honour me by re-joining my service?'

'We would love that, Your Highness, wouldn't we, Javier?' Arrosa replied at once.

'We would,' Javier agreed. 'It has been a privilege to serve you, Your Highness.'

'Well, Javier, at least you got that right, and you've served Arrosa just as well,' I quipped, looking at her stomach.

She blushed as I embraced them both. When we broke apart, I turned to Javier.

'I have something for you,' I said, offering him the scroll. 'This is a commission from me, as Queen of England. It is for Sancho, my brother, and it guarantees you employment within his household if you ever decide to return to Olite.'

'Oh, Your Highness,' gasped Arrosa as she seized me by the waist and planted a kiss on my cheek. 'I love you so much. Will we ever meet again?'

Javier spoke next, as I was overcome and couldn't answer.

'Yes, Your Highness, I pray that we will meet again. And this is an honour,' he added, waving the scroll. 'We will pray for your safe passage. Thank you.'

I turned away before the tears could fall and waited for Joan, who was also embracing them both. We then scurried along, hand in hand, to board the waiting galley.

CHAPTER TWO

The next two days were surprisingly pleasant, with light winds. Passing Larnaca, we spied marching troops along the shoreline.

'That helps things, Your Highnesses,' said William. 'The king can't leave until they arrive in Famagusta, which will be after us.'

'Oh, good,' I replied, and went forward to join Joan and the ladies at the front of the *Dione*.

'Cyprus is a lot bigger than I knew, Berri,' said Joan, looking at the distant mountains.

'Look!' cried Alazne, pointing ahead. 'Ships!'

'Famagusta!' shouted Master William from the stern.

As we closed in on Richard's fleet, the full extent of their power became frighteningly clear. There were ships of all shapes and sizes: dromons for troops and cargo and *hippagōga* for horses, as well as warships.

William saw me watching. 'The warships are of Roman design, Your Highness, fashioned from ancient Greek vessels. There are up to fifty rowing places for speed and power. The beak protruding from the bottom of the bow is cast from bronze, and the protruding walkway above it, sticking out from the foredeck, is a platform. Men may run along it to board an enemy ship.'

'So how is it deployed?' asked Joan.

'The ship will be brought up to full speed and they will crash the beak into the sides of their target, penetrating the hull so that it may sink. At the same time, soldiers will run along the top platform and board the unfortunate vessel, so the crew of the enemy ship will need to fight — or drown.'

'What about the rowers, are they slaves?' asked Joan.

'Not in King Richard's fleet, Your Highness. They are also paid soldiers and will provide reinforcements to board the enemy ship once it has been transfixed by the beak. They row in chainmail, ready for battle.'

'They will surely drown if they fall overboard,' gasped Joan.

'Indeed, Your Highness, indeed. And now I see the royal vessel; excuse me while we deliver you safely into the king's care.'

William began to shout his orders, and soon the vessel was alive with seamen once more. Some were at the ropes controlling the sails, while some tended the mooring ropes fore and aft. Great bundles of interwoven rope were dropped over the side opposite the steersman.

'To cushion the impact and prevent rubbing when we go alongside the king's ship, Your Highnesses,' explained William, seeing our puzzled faces.

Our ladies appeared from where they had found places to rest, the noises having woken them.

'Your Highnesses,' called Alazne, 'you've not been in your berths.'

'There's too much going on up here to lie idly down there,' I told her.

'Well, there's a lot going on down there too,' she said. 'Master William's new garderobe is very popular. Thank you, Master William — it was a good idea.'

'I'm busy, madam. Pray stand well back,' William replied.

'Jesu! Look at the size of that!' Joan exclaimed.

I looked to where she was pointing. A great war galley lay at anchor, and we were heading directly towards it.

'It's the king's,' said William. 'Observe the fluttering banners.' He carried on issuing orders.

Watching, we saw the mainsail being brought round as the bow of our ship was seemingly headed for a collision. Then the steersman pulled manfully on his great oar, and the ship slipped sideways in the water as its momentum brought us to nestle alongside the king's vessel. Order followed order: the sails slid down the masts to rest on the deck, and sailors with throwing ropes hurled them towards the rail of the king's ship, where they were taken up by its crew and secured. The rope buffers along the side were adjusted as we nudged against the mighty craft.

A face appeared over the rail of the galley's afterdeck.

'Well done, master, a fine piece of seamanship. Are the queens aboard?'

'They are, my lord. There they stand.' William pointed at us and grinned.

'What, those boy sailors? Do you jest?'

'No, they are queens dressed for the sea journey, my lord.'

'Jesu! I'll inform the king; he is in his cabin, plotting as usual.'

The face disappeared. After a few minutes, a canvas chair on the end of a rope hanging from the galley mast appeared, and William invited Joan to sit in it.

'Hoist away!' he called, and Joan was lifted into the sky. The empty chair soon reappeared, and it was my turn.

The sky rushed by, and a tilting sensation made my palms sweat and my stomach lurch. Mercifully, it was over quickly.

'Phew, that was a thrill,' I gasped as I stood on the deck of my husband's ship.

'I shall have one made, once I find a home to settle in,' said Joan.

Now we were aboard, I could see that the design of this galley was very different to that of the *Dione*. The wide platform down the centre above the rowing benches, where the crew might run along unhindered, loomed over us. It was even stranger to see it continue beyond the bows, jutting out over the sea. The oars were inboard, and the rowers were resting under the central decking or beneath the rowing benches.

Soon all our women were on deck, followed by our baggage, a breathless Hugo and a terrified Father Francis. As we gazed about, some grand fellow came to greet us.

'Your Highnesses, welcome aboard the *Thor*. I am Guilbert of Harfleur, master of the king's vessel.'

Just then, a stentorian voice cried out from the doorway beneath the afterdeck. 'Who are those people? Why do they crowd my deck, what, what?'

'Good morrow, brother! How nice to see you well again,' called out Joan, raising a few titters from the bolder members of the galley crew.

'Jesu, Joan? Come along, and bring those urchins with you. They are boys, are they not?'

He had a smile on his face as we neared, and applause began among the crew.

'Sister, wife,' Richard exclaimed, gathering the pair of us into his arms.

I pushed back to take a good look at him. 'Richard, you are the palest man in the fleet. You have been ill and not thought to tell us.'

'Ho! My feisty queen, you think to scold me, eh?' he said with humour. 'It was but a small thing — an attack of sweats and sickness. Beneath this pallor I am hale once more, and ready to pay the land of God a visit which it will not forget. So, how are you two? Good, I trust. I see the Comnenus girl — is she obedient?'

'She isn't very happy, my king,' I replied.

'Have you not a kiss for your two queens, brother?' asked Joan.

Colour flooded his face. 'Oh, come inside, out of the sun.'

He guided us into his space beneath the afterdeck, and we left our ladies with Amynta and Eirini above. It wasn't much more private than outside, it being full of nobles, but we did get another round of applause. I received an uncertain peck on the cheek from a king more at home with his men than his women.

'Oh, well,' said Joan, quietly, 'that's some improvement. Who are all these lords, Richard? Pray introduce us, for they were not all at your wedding, I can see.'

'No, no, Joan, but you met them at Messina. Here are Richard de Camville and Robert de Sablé, two of my fleet commanders. Robert of Turnham is still ashore, as you know, Berengaria.'

'Quite,' I replied, before turning to the two nobles. 'Nice to meet you again.'

'Good, good,' said Richard. 'I and Robert Turnham are responsible for the governance of Cyprus, but Camville and Sablé are here to conduct some business with the Knights Templar, when we have secured Akko. The small matter of the lease price for the island is to be discussed. Guy de Lusignan is over there, and here is my ship's master, Guilbert of Harfleur.'

'We've met. Master Guilbert has a way with ladies — a chairlift of dizzying properties,' I quipped, and they all relaxed a bit. I turned to Joan and whispered, 'There seem to be many sailors here from Harfleur; it must be a busy port.'

'Quite, and there's money to be made here for good ships and seamen who are willing to make the voyage.'

There were other men, of course, most of whom I forgot. They mostly seemed to be concerned with the duties of the army and how to storm a city — a tricky affair, I gathered.

There was a buffet set up under one side of the afterdeck, and soon we were in conversation. I was particularly assailed by men who were eager to tell me their histories. Joan was cornered in a similar fashion by Lusignan, as were our other ladies. Alazne had her usual fun with hopeful men, they not knowing that she preferred the company of women.

The sun was high in the sky when Richard called for attention. 'Time to leave now — be about your duties. We will be off the coast of Outremer by this time tomorrow. God be with you, and let's pray for an easy crossing.'

'Aye to that!' the men cried in response.

'Where's your confessor, Joan?' asked Richard.

'Over there, in that corner.'

'Give us a prayer, priest, for our voyage and our venture!' Richard bawled across the space, and Father Francis nearly fell overboard as the sound assailed his ears.

He began a prayer, but when he attempted a sermon his audience rapidly faded away, and the sound of orders being issued around the ship drowned the poor fellow out.

'How far is it, Richard?' asked Joan.

'About one hundred and fifty miles. We shall sail all night and be off the coast by this time tomorrow.'

'What shall we do?' I asked.

'When we get going, I shall take you round the ship and tell you of my plans.'

'You asked about the Comnenus girl, Princess Eirini. Where is her father? She has asked.'

'Tell her that he is safe. He will travel on another ship. She does not need to know any more. I will talk to her when I have time.'

'Very well, I'll tell her.'

Richard's tone made me suspect he was holding something back. I remembered Joan's warning about deviousness in her family and resolved to return to the subject later.

'May we go up, Richard?' asked Joan. 'To see the fleet cast off?'

'Yes, yes, of course. I'll come with you. I have an interest in this too, you know.'

Richard was in good spirits, and whatever else was on my mind was soon gone as we watched the largest gathering of war galleys that I had ever seen getting underway. What an endeavour: so many men, and ships bursting with arms and horses, all to recover the lands of God.

'Who is this man Saladin, Richard? What do you know of him?' I asked.

'He is the Saracen Sultan of Egypt and Syria, the first such.'

'Is he Egyptian or Syrian? I know of both from the Bible, of course.'

'Neither; he is Kurdish — from further east. That is where I shall defeat him.'

My eyes returned to the fleet, and I prayed that such a sight would deter this sultan from engaging with Richard and his allies.

Famagusta was our last sight of the island of Cyprus. It was now the fifth of June, in the year of our Lord 1191. I pressed against the rail beside my companions, watching the mighty Crusader fleet finally make its way to the Holy Land. We were somewhere along the coast of Outremer, trying to sight land.

A short while later, as promised, Richard gave us a tour of the ship.

'You could see the mountains if you were at the top of yonder mast,' claimed Guilbert as we were conducted to him.

'No, thank you,' Joan replied. 'I prefer the deck.'

'The way you are dressed, you should be up there, yes, yes,' laughed Richard.

'Tell me about where we are headed, and tell me how you are this day,' I said. 'I heard that you were unwell again.'

'Oh, it was nothing — one of those fevers which affect folk hereabouts. It will not halt our progress, my queen. Pray do not fuss. Now we are heading for the Crusader county of Tripoli, then Akko, further along the coast, to relieve Saladin of his prize and please Lusignan.' He waved across to the frustrated King of Jerusalem, who managed a half-hearted grin in return. 'If you will excuse me, I have briefings to conduct. Guilbert will show you the ship.'

'Thank you, Richard. Where are we sleeping tonight?' I asked, as an afterthought.

'We have brought some straw palliasses aboard, and strung a canvas beneath the afterdeck. You will all be very comfortable, I'm sure.'

'What about me?' I pressed him.

He seemed surprised. 'What, what, we will find you another palliasse, if you want. Two for a queen, and you, sister, if you require it.'

'Er, I'm not sure that Berengaria meant —' spluttered Joan.

'It's good,' I cut in. 'We'll be very comfortable, Richard, all women together. And it's only for one night, you say?'

'Yes, yes, one.' With that, he stomped off the afterdeck and went into his briefing chamber beneath our feet.

Guilbert stood in thought for a moment and then came to me with a conspiratorial look on his face. 'Your Highness, may I speak privily?'

I nodded. 'You may.'

'It is the vow of the cross, you see, and the chastity of the knights. Richard has forbidden women in the fleet. He struggled to bring you with him; his conscience would have you left in Cyprus, but he'd rather have you near so that he can keep you safe himself.'

I looked at Joan.

'He is a very complicated man, Berengaria,' she said. 'Get used to more surprises.'

'The ship, Your Highnesses?' ventured Guilbert hopefully.

'The ship, Guilbert. Keep us diverted, if you please,' I responded.

'I will. The king is discussing sieges and the like; that is none of my immediate concern. This galley has both sails and oars. The sails are mostly to keep the crews rested, but we may need the oars if the wind is unfavourable.'

He began to walk along the gangway down the centre of the ship and, as I followed Joan, I became aware of dozens of male eyes watching us. They were mostly sitting below us, with a good view upwards. Then I became conscious of the fact that my breeches were a little near my skin. I could see Joan's backside moving, and I was certain that it had not escaped the notice of the crew. I decided to brazen it out and began to smile and wave at them. That attracted more cheering — but at least it gave me the courage to keep moving. I could feel a flush on my face as I hurried after Guilbert and Joan.

'Twenty-five oars on each side,' Guilbert was saying. 'We can have one or two rowers at each oar; that's one hundred rowers, all men-at-arms. They wear the lightest of mail when action is near, so that they can row and move quickly to attack the enemy vessel over that bridge at the bow. In addition, we have thirty archers — or rather, some archers and some men with arbalests — and some slingshot specialists. Some of the galleys can send out Greek fire. This is one of our assault ships, and if you look over there, you can see that they have great rams at the front, which can penetrate a ship's side without much ado.'

'It all seems very dangerous, Guilbert,' mused Joan. 'Are we likely to see anything of that?'

'I doubt it. The Saracens have not got much in the way of ships. The leader, Saladin, seems to be more of a land soldier than a mariner, so we do not expect to meet much resistance at sea. We'll go back to the afterdeck now, if you don't mind, Your Highnesses. I have work to do. You can stay up there and watch the fleet follow us.'

'Of course,' I said, thinking that we would be retracing our steps for the benefit of the crew.

'What's wrong with you, Berri? You seem somewhat flustered,' said Joan when we were safely on the afterdeck.

'I realised that all those men were watching us as we paraded in our breeches.'

'Heaven's blessing, what can we do?'

Alazne rejoined us at the rail. 'I saw them watching you too, Your Highnesses. They're a lecherous lot. And I had an idea that might please the king.'

'What?' Joan and I chorused together.

'Wait here. If I can get at one of our chests, I'll be back with a solution.' She went off to our quarters.

I looked at Joan, but she merely shrugged her shoulders.

'Go with her, Pavot, and see if she needs any help,' she instructed, turning to one of her ladies. Pavot obeyed.

By this time, the sun was well into the western sky. Looking behind, we could see the whole fleet following on a southerly course. It was an astonishing sight.

We must be in the middle of the journey, I thought, *with Cyprus out of sight and Lebanon not yet in view before us.* I shivered as I gazed at the fleet.

'They seem as angels floating on the water,' said Joan.

'Angels of death, my sweet,' I said. 'We are not taking gifts of friendship to the Holy Land.'

She fell silent. I wondered about climbing the mast to see if I could see the mountains, but then Alazne and Pavot reappeared, wearing something new.

They were still in breeches but they had each added a short kirtle, which covered them from waist to knee.

'Where did you get that kirtle?' I asked.

'I made it from the dress I wore for your wedding, Your Highness. We won't be going to any more weddings, I suppose.'

'You supposed correctly. What have you got for me?'

'One of your gowns. Come below and we'll fit it. Pavot has one for you and Torène, Your Highness,' she told Joan.

'You are a pearl, Alazne,' said Joan. 'What an idea. Come on, Berri, let's hide our assets.'

We preened for a while beneath the afterdeck until a call came from aloft. 'Land, master, land on the bow.'

With everybody facing forward, it was still another hour's sailing before the mountains of Lebanon could be seen from the afterdeck. Richard did not bother to come out from his planning table under our feet until Master Guilbert called him.

'In sight now, Your Highness.'

Richard made an appearance in all his military glory. He wore black breeches and a red tunic embellished with three lions —

his coat of arms. His hair blew in the wind, his magnificent sword was strapped to his side, and he held his crown-topped helm under one arm. I was so impressed that I stumbled. Joan grasped one arm and Alazne the other.

Richard found my gaze and smiled, but he did not cross the deck to greet me. Instead, he called out to Master Guilbert. 'Where away, Master Guilbert?'

'Slightly off the port bow, Your Highness.'

'And where is our landfall?'

'Too early to say, Your Highness.'

'Let me know when you can, yes, yes,' he ordered, and returned to his consultation with his commanders beneath our feet.

It was not long before another cry came from aloft. 'Margat! Margat Castle, master. On the port bow.'

'Your Highness!' shouted Guilbert in response to the call from the masthead.

Richard came bursting out of his den, clutching a map. 'Where, master? Point it out, point, man.'

Guilbert stood in front of the king, holding out an arm. 'On the right of those three peaks, there's a dormant volcano. That's it: Margat, in the county of Tripoli. The greatest of the Knights Hospitaller strongholds, as impregnable as Crac des Chevaliers, many have said.'

'Got it. Is there a harbour?'

'Indeed, Your Highness, but not large enough to accommodate the whole fleet. The castle is about one mile away, not far if on the level, but it will be quite a climb.'

'Right.' Richard turned to Richard de Camville. 'Richard, hold the fleet outside. I'll go into the harbour and see if we can get the war galleys inside and then get the men off. They can take some exercise — do some sword drill.'

42

'Your Highness, is the prisoner to be lodged up there?' asked Camville. He pointed to the top of the silent volcano.

'Indeed. He can enjoy the hospitality of the knights and contemplate his mistakes. Right! Ladies, do you want to go ashore to stretch your legs?'

'Indeed — perhaps we'll find a bed that doesn't move about,' said Joan.

'Don't know about that. I'll see how the land lies when we get there. I'll start with a trip up that mountain.'

Richard went into consultation with Camville and various others, then came across to speak to me. I was gazing at the mountainous shoreline and the silhouette of the castle in the distance. Amynta had Eirini by her side by the far rail, and they seemed to be content. Joan was by my side.

'Berengaria, Joan, can you do something for me?' asked Richard.

'Certainly,' I replied, with some surprise.

He moved forward, away from the stern of the ship, and began to speak conspiratorially. 'We've got Comnenus chained up on another ship. I want to get him ashore and into yonder castle, to prevent any nonsense back in Cyprus — you understand?'

'Really?' I gasped. 'You've kept that quiet. I didn't know the former ruler of Cyprus was travelling in secret with us.'

'We've kept him out of sight. It's better if his daughter knows nothing. Keep her quiet too, will you?'

'Yes, she would make a fuss if she knew,' I said.

'I've been told she was named Eirini after her grandmother — Eirini Komnene, of the Doukas family of Romania.'

'So the girl is Romanian?' asked Joan. 'And you want her kept out of the way?'

'No. Eirini's mother, Isaac's wife, was Armenian. But if you can manage it, avoid the subject. Keep her distracted, and she should believe that her father remains in Cyprus.'

'Agreed, if you wish,' I said, and Joan nodded.

When the ship was lodged alongside the jetty in the small port, we took Eirini into our curtained-off chamber under the afterdeck and engaged her in conversation, helping her learn Joan's *langue d'oc* French. Joan left us there until the business was done. She came back and gave me the nod, thus ending the lesson. I took the young Byzantine princess up onto the deck to view the sights. Richard, his guest, and their escort were by now mere specks on the long, steep road leading up to Margat Castle.

We went ashore for a brisk walk, Hugo accompanying us, and then watched the men exercising. I would have thought that rowing was exercise enough, but there had been little of that for the larger galleys, which had managed mostly by the power of their large sails.

'They need to practise their fighting skills,' said Hugo. 'The day when they are called to action can't be far off.'

I also questioned him about what he knew of Isaac Comnenus' fate, as no one else had thought fit to mention it.

'As far as I am aware, Your Highness, he surrendered because he believed that his daughter was in danger, but he set a condition.'

'Which was?' asked Joan, looking around to make sure that Eirini could not hear.

'That he would not be confined in irons.'

'But he must have been confined while aboard the ship, and surely he will be confined within that castle up there.' I pointed up the hill.

'The king kept his word. He confined Comnenus in chains made of silver.'

'Unbelievable!' I gasped.

'I told you that this family is devious,' said Joan with a grimace.

'That's not all of it,' continued Hugo. 'He had the Griffons who joined him shave off their beards. He said that they looked too much like Saracens.'

I gazed at the scribe. There was a hint of hair on his chin, but nothing that could be described as a beard.

He smiled. 'I'm not a Griffon, Your Highness, and therefore I may remain unshaven. But look, the king is on his way back down the hill.' He pointed at the dusty slope. 'We'd better re-embark; we need to be in Akko.' Then, shouting some orders, he escorted us back onto the ship.

'How far to Akko, Joan?' I asked.

'I don't know. I think that I shall sit on the afterdeck and enjoy the sights. Will you join me?'

'I will. Alazne, see if you can get some food sent up. We are setting sail once more.'

The rail was above the quay that we were moored to, and I watched as Richard rode up to the small wooden bridge set between the ship and the pier. He dismounted and threw the reins to a wrangler to take care of his horse. It was a magnificent white destrier, as befitted his status.

Guilbert joined me. 'The beast travels in one of the cogs, Your Highness,' he said. 'It will be loaded separately when we clear the quayside.'

'Thank you, Guilbert. Do you think he is pleased, or not?'

'He seems calm. Go and smile at him, Your Highness. That would cheer any man.'

'Come with me, Joan,' I said. Richard had a special place in his heart for his sister, and I intended to make use of it.

We skipped down the steps and on to the main deck. Some sailors had fashioned sandals for us in the Roman style, but with rope soles. They made getting around the ship much easier, and we were feeling quite at home now. In exchange, we listened to tales of their wives and families back home in Normandy.

'Ha!' shouted Richard from the bottom of the bridge. 'Are we ready for sea once more?' He bounded up towards us.

'You are feeling better, my lord?' I asked as he joined us on deck.

'I am. Better for that gallop up the hill. You ready, Master Guilbert?'

'Ready, Your Highness.'

'Off we go — off to Akko. We might call at Tyre on the way and get the latest news about Saladin. Yes, yes. Hello, Berengaria,' he added somewhat belatedly. 'You two look fit.' He put an arm about Joan and me. 'Is sea life agreeing with you?'

'It is interesting, brother,' answered Joan.

'In small doses,' I added.

'Where is Tyre?' Joan asked.

'Down the coast, in the Kingdom of Jerusalem. It's about a hundred and fifty miles away. We'll be there on the morrow, won't we, Guilbert?' He looked up at the master, who was now busy on the afterdeck, getting the ship underway. 'Will we arrive at Tyre in the morning?'

'In the afternoon, Your Highness,' replied Guilbert. 'We'll see how the winds blow.'

'Good, good. Must go, ladies, got some planning to do.'

We both received a peck on the cheek. Married life was turning out to be quite different from the tales I had heard. Richard was more of a monk than a husband.

Suddenly, I felt exhausted. 'Alazne, help me get ready for bed. My day is done.'

'You look a bit tired, sweet Berengaria,' said Joan. 'Let's pray for a steady voyage, and you should feel better in the morning. Look after her, Alazne. She is very precious to us all.'

'Of course, Your Highness. I'll do my very best. Please excuse us; we'll try to get some rest now.'

A ship was never silent, even when sailing in a gentle breeze. What wind there was made music in the ropes and sails, the mast creaked, sailors shouted out to each other, birds squawked, and the sea beat against the bows and rippled along the sides of the vessel. It was a more diverse cacophony than the greatest band of musicians could ever hope to make, and tonight it lulled me to sleep.

When morning came, we continued our voyage in peace. Light winds and a calm sea meant an easy passage, and we arrived, as forecast, off Tyre in the late afternoon. Richard instructed his commanders to prepare for a night ashore to rest the men, and he called for a small galley to take him there to visit the garrison commander.

After the evening meal, we took our positions at the rail of the afterdeck and gazed at the city. We were joined by Robert de Sablé, Master of the Order of Knights of the Hospital of Saint John of Jerusalem, although I had never heard all of its name spoken in conversation. Usually, the order was referred to as the Knights Hospitaller. There had been no sign of Richard, and I was concerned for his safety. Robert was a man of middling maturity, but due to his experience he was a trusted and reliable commander within the king's inner circle.

'What do you know about Tyre, Robert? It seems quite small from where we are anchored. I thought we were to spend the night there?'

'It is a possession of Philip's friend, Conrad of Germany, Your Highness. We will soon know more: here comes Richard's galley. As you see from the sun, we are on the northern side of what was once an island, until Alexander the Great built a causeway linking it to the mainland. It was an important trading post of the Phoenicians once. Now, it is an important fortress in Outremer, and easily defended. There are many Roman buildings still standing.'

The setting sun was in our eyes, and it was difficult to see the approaching galley in detail. I certainly could not see Richard.

'What's he up to now?' said Joan.

'A change of plan, perhaps, Your Highness,' offered de Sablé.

The craft came alongside, and we looked down into it to see the master.

'Ho, the boat,' called de Sablé. 'What news?'

'Lord de Sablé,' the master called back, standing by the steersman. 'Not good.'

'Where's the king?'

'Ashore. He's staying the night. I'm to take him a tent.'

'Are we not landing?'

'No. The castellan says that there is not enough room. The king thinks that he is acting under instructions from the French king, Philip.'

'Oh. Is Conrad not there? Why is our king staying the night?'

'Because he can, Lord de Sablé. He is making a point: nobody refuses Richard.'

'We are not short of entertainment with your brother around, Joan,' I said. 'What now, Robert?'

'Guilbert,' he called, 'get a tent for the king into this galley, sharp as you like, and get another six men-at-arms in there too. We'll not risk the king's well-being for the sake of his making a point.'

'As you wish, Lord de Sablé,' replied Guilbert, and he called out the necessary instructions.

Soon the galley was on its way back to the shore so that Richard could shake a fist at his supposed ally, Philip of France.

'Oh, well,' said Guilbert, 'I suppose we'd better feed the crews, Lord de Sablé.'

'Aye, Guilbert. Make the arrangements; they'll not be so grumpy if we feed them and get them some early rest. We'll be off again in the morn.'

'As soon as the king decides to come back, we'll set sail. Ladies, I'll feed you out of the king's larder.'

'Thank you,' replied Joan. 'Then we can talk tittle-tattle all night, if we wish.'

I laughed. 'Let's concentrate on Eirini. When she's not angry, she's a quick learner.'

When I awoke the next morning, I was alone in the screened-off sleeping area, and I could hear new noises coming from outside.

There was a drumbeat, a splash, a squeak, and the sound of many men grunting in unison. I soon realised that the ship was being rowed.

Sitting up, I saw that buckets had been left for me and quickly put them to use, although I felt very vulnerable with only a canvas screen between me and a ship full of men. I

49

cleansed myself and dressed, ready to face the day. I knew that the sun was high, and I caught glimpses of the oar blades through the side openings of the ship as they flashed back and forth to the beat of the drum. I could sense excitement in the air, and suddenly I wanted to be on deck to witness this activity.

Drawing back the curtain, I saw that no one was at Richard's great planning table, though it was still covered in maps and lists. I emerged from under the afterdeck and was immediately faced with a big drum, which was being beaten by a very large man who was naked to the waist.

A further shock came as my eyes accustomed themselves to the sunlight and I observed two banks of rowers, stripped down to their loincloths. The aroma of sweat hit me; the men were so wet with perspiration that they looked as if they had been oiled.

The craft was churning through the water at speed, and I was wondering why when a voice called from above my head. It was Alazne.

'Your Highness, come on up. This is exciting; we are chasing a Saracen ship.'

I looked up. She was hanging over the forward rail of the afterdeck, pointing ahead.

'You let me sleep!' I called up accusingly.

'You needed it, Your Highness. Do come up; the king is here.'

I walked across to the ladder and paused to look at the rowers. There were twenty-five oars on each side, with two men on each. The effort showed on each man's face as he bent forward, dug his oar into the water and pulled with all his strength. The ship leaped forward with a jolt that I could feel through my feet. They were all working as one to the beat of the drum, and I wondered how fast this vessel that we were pursuing was moving. I climbed up to see.

'Berri!' cried Joan. 'Come and look.'

'Berengaria!' Richard's voice reached me above all the other noises. He was standing next to Guilbert by the steering oar, smiling.

He waved at me to join him. He wore his mail hauberk with canvas breeches and a helm with his crown, and he actually put his arms around me and gave me a peck on the lips.

Beside him, Joan was standing with Torène, Alazne was holding hands with Pavot, and Amynta and Eirini were also clasping hands; these two seemed the most disturbed by the events unfolding before them.

'See, Berengaria,' said Richard as he pointed ahead at the target. Our sail was down, useless, so fast were we propelled by the oars. I spied our quarry not far away.

'What is it?'

'A Saracen supply ship, a big one; it must be bound for Akko. If it escapes into the port, it will prolong our siege. I must stop it, yes, yes.'

'Is that why we are rowing?'

'Indeed. We are fortunate that there is little wind to propel yonder ship; I must catch up with it before any breeze comes along. It might out-sail us, for we cannot row at this pace for very long.'

I looked down at the rowing benches. 'Yes, the ship will fill up with sweat and drown us all before long.'

'Ha! Hear that, Guilbert? The queen has spotted our Achilles heel. Drowned in sweat — ha!'

'Yes, Your Highness. The water carriers are on their way among them now.'

'Don't lose the rhythm; pour it over them. I'm going forward to direct the action.' Richard galloped off down the steps and along the central gangway to take up a position on the forecastle with some archers.

'What's he going to do there, Guilbert?' asked Joan.

'He will control the fleet through signal flags. See his signaller standing next to him: he has flags of different colours and shapes, and his hand positions will send messages to the other vessels.'

'How clever,' I said. 'He wouldn't be heard above the noise.'

'Indeed, Your Highness. Ah, here come the war galleys.' He pointed astern. The slow cargo cogs and busses were falling behind us due to the lack of wind, but four of the smaller galleys were racing ahead and had begun to overhaul us. Faster and lighter, they held the foaming waves in their teeth. They were full of oarsmen-cum-warriors, who were encased in mail hauberks. Surely they could not keep up this pace? Then the bigger craft began to pass us; the kind with prows like birds' beaks and wicked rams protruding, ready to do damage.

Richard was waving his arms at them and shouting, exhorting more effort, and soon the first of the small galleys was alongside the great Saracen ship. I had expected it to be boarded and to surrender at once. I was wrong.

There was sudden activity at the rails of the Saracen ship, and a hail of death rained down upon the heads of our crews, forcing the vessels to veer away.

'It's carrying soldiers; they will not give up so easily!' shouted Guilbert. A few archers, slingshot specialists and men throwing rocks were all along the rails; there would be no boarding that ship without penalty until Richard thought of a different approach.

'He looks angry, Guilbert,' I ventured, watching Richard stomping about on the forecastle.

'He can rage as no other, Your Highness. He spits venom when he does not achieve his aim. Watch closely, and listen.'

We were among the failed galleys as they returned to the *Thor* for further instructions, keeping pace with us. The ships with the beak-like prows kept station further away. From the afterdeck, we could hear Richard clearly.

'Such language!' said Joan. 'He is a man possessed by devils. Hear him.'

Threats, exhortations and pleadings all tumbled out as the king demanded that the galley masters return to their task, with Peter des Roches, the senior galley master, particularly targeted. They were reluctant to get underway again, but help arrived as the ramming vessels steered alongside the *Thor*. Robert de Sablé, despite his mail, clambered down the side and got himself aboard one of them.

'What's he doing? Is he leaving us?' exclaimed Joan.

'The king has sent a steady head to command those ramming vessels. His next plan must work, Your Highnesses,' said Guilbert.

Still close enough to hear the king, de Sablé received his final orders from his new position on the other ship. We watched as he in turn instructed the ramming vessel masters, who listened to him and then backed away their craft.

'What are they going to do, Guilbert?' I asked. I'd heard but did not fully understand the king's instructions.

'Just watch, Your Highness. The Saracen ship is about to receive some unwelcome visitors.'

The ramming vessels backed off before splitting into pairs, heading away from us on opposite sides of the Saracen ship, which was near stilled in the miserly wind. I could hardly make out any detail, so far away did they row, but then they turned towards the Saracen ship, their sails came down, and they were solely under oars.

Richard watched, a proud figure standing at the prow of his flagship, waiting to see if his new tactics would work. I dreaded to think how he would react to failure this time.

Richard gave his signalman, who was standing beside him, a tap on the shoulder, and he raised two flags, one red and one green. The galleys were still on the water as Richard shouted back to Guilbert. 'Move closer!'

Guilbert gave the orders for the *Thor* to creep closer as more archers were summoned to the foredeck.

'I'm frightened, Joan,' I said. 'Something horrid is about to happen.'

Alazne came to support me, and Joan grabbed the hands of Pavot and Torène. Amynta and Eirini huddled together. The atmosphere was tense.

The whole fleet must have had their eyes on the king as he watched his ramming vessels. Then his hand slapped the signalman again on the shoulder, and the two flags dropped.

I could see the splash as the oars dropped into the water, and the blades flashed as they came out. The ramming vessels and the smaller galleys gathered speed quickly, and, as they neared, both the drums and the grunts of the men could be heard.

Four metal beaks were now aimed at the hull of the Saracen ship, two on either side. There was no way back from this; the outcome would be death, and Alazne tightened her hold on me. The smaller galleys under the command of Peter des Roches moved in closer and gathered like carrion crows, waiting to see what damage the ramming vessels would inflict before falling on their prey.

Both rails of the target were lined with men screaming insults and sending volleys of various objects towards our rapidly advancing ramming vessels. Richard gave another order, and our archers standing near him on the foredeck nocked their bows and rained death down upon the Saracen sailors.

They were trapped by a deadly pincer manoeuvre as the ramming vessels struck the helpless cargo ship almost simultaneously, with a crash that must have been heard back in Cyprus, and buried themselves deep in the timbers. As the ships came to a halt, our men-at-arms, who had been hanging on tightly along the centre gangways, ran across the foredeck and began to board the stricken Saracen vessel while the marine soldiers from the small galleys hurled grappling irons and swarmed up the sides.

There was fierce resistance. The first of our soldiers to cross the bridge were hacked at and tossed into the sea, but then Richard's archers began to thin out the enemy so that some of our brave or foolish men could make landings on the deck of the Saracen ship. The crew were forced back, and two lines of battle formed: one with their backs to the steering deck at the aft end, and another which was pressed forward towards the bows.

The battle was joined in earnest, but those aboard the Saracen ship were not as skilled or as determined as our men, and so began to fall back. The cries of the wounded filled our ears as our archers began to take a toll on the Saracen commanders, now huddled around the steering position.

The smell of blood grew stronger as the *Thor* drifted closer to the action. Eirini was sick over the side and then hid in Amynta's arms as she too gagged at the sight and smell.

The foredeck was almost cleared now, the last of the Saracens hurled over into the bloody waters. My attention now turned to the final resistance at the rear of the stricken craft, where the commander and his officers were hacked down by our frenzied soldiers. Those who survived — some of whom had cast down their weapons — were also hurled over the side, crying for mercy.

Then there was a silence, broken only by the moans of the wounded and the laughter of seabirds circling overhead.

I heard Robert de Sablé as he issued orders, and our men began to return to their ships. Richard grabbed his signalman and held some different flags aloft.

'Back off, Master Guilbert!' the king shouted. 'The Saracen ship is sinking.'

The men who had boarded the enemy ship were now hastening back to their ramming vessels, some carrying our wounded. One pair slipped and were condemned to the sea. As the Saracen ship slowly sank, the soldiers from the galleys were able to step back into their crafts. Soon, with their oars flashing, the ramming vessel masters made every effort to extract their ships from the shattered timbers.

As the ramming vessels broke free, the Saracen ship went under quickly. The remaining men jumped, fell or crawled over the sides, but could not save themselves — not even those trying to get rid of their armour. They went under in the turmoil.

As the waters washed over the deck, air gushed out through open hatches and churned the sea into a red foam. Watching, horrified, I heard Richard chuckle and then shout out as the top of the last mast disappeared beneath the surface.

'See, Saladin, see that? Richard is here, what, what!' My husband was triumphant in the carnage of war.

A cheer resounded across the waters from within our fleet, and then there was another silence, save for the cries of the seabirds and the clatter of debris against the sides of our ships. Barrels, planks, chests, bodies and ropes crowded the surface of the sea.

Guilbert coughed apologetically. 'Nearly fifteen hundred must have gone down. Let's pray that God is content with Richard's work this day.'

I was not, and felt sick. Torène retched over the side, and the other ladies were silent. How could this be a good day for God?

Richard came trotting back along the deck, smiling and acknowledging the cheers of his men. He grabbed me and lifted me aloft. 'You see, Berengaria, that's how to deal with them. This war will soon be over, once Saladin hears about our success, yes, yes.'

'Richard, please,' I complained.

As he slid me down his body, my stomach bumped over something below his waist. He was hard; I felt it. He was clearly impassioned by violence. When my feet touched the deck, I took a step back into Joan's arms. I could feel I was blushing.

Joan spoke to break the awkward silence. 'I should have thought that some respect for the dead might have been a proper reaction, Richard. This celebration is indecent.'

He looked at her. There was a peculiar look in his eyes — a madness of some kind. Then he seemed to subside, and laughed nervously. 'I don't normally watch, Joan. I'm usually at the front of things; it's easier somehow. You might be right about the dead, but it is a sadness for somebody else. Now, onward, Guilbert. Are the ships gathered in?'

'The cargo ships are on the horizon. They'll follow us as we resume our voyage to Akko; we'll be underway shortly.'

'Good, good. Is there anything in the water worth saving?'

'Not a lot.'

'Wonder what they had in their holds? It's not going to Akko anymore, that's for sure — it's all gone to their God. Summon my commanders. There's knowledge to be gained from this.'

'Aye, Your Highness, as you command.'

Richard went into his briefing chamber without another word.

'You seem disturbed, Berri?' said Joan gently.

'Yes … something has disturbed me.'

'I saw, when he lifted you up, he was…?'

'I think so. I was shocked.'

'I thought he was about to ravish you on the spot.'

'I'd prefer somewhere less public, if at all.'

'If at all? Come, let's sit by the rail and pray. If this was God's work, then I like it not.'

'It is what we came for,' I said softly.

'Would not words help, some negotiation? Killing men rarely alters their minds.'

'No, I wondered about that. Perhaps Richard could have offered them a surrender?'

'All those stores in the hold could have been saved.'

'And many widows.'

'I know.'

I paused, lost in sadness. Then something occurred to me, and I went below deck and approached Richard. Joan followed.

'Who cares for our wounded, husband?' I asked.

'Wounded? Ah! The Knights Hospitaller. They're on our vessels; they aid pilgrims and soldiers alike.' With that, he called for Guy de Lusignan to join him at his planning trestle and summoned his scribes. 'Hugo, write it all down, and Ambroise, make it pretty. We'll have a record of the day's doings.'

I felt dismissed, and Joan took me by the hand to join my ladies.

'It's none of our business, Berri. Let's leave them to their task.'

As the fighting men stripped off among the rowing benches to wash the stench of blood from themselves and their equipment, we retired to our quarters under the afterdeck.

Richard came in later. He had removed his mail and seemed calmer. 'Enjoy the battle, ladies?' he asked with a laugh.

'Reminded me of a slaughterhouse,' said Joan.

'Will there be much more of it, Richard? Is this God's work?' I made my displeasure known.

'Where next, Richard?' asked Joan quickly as Richard gazed at me in surprise.

'We should reach Akko before morning,' he said. 'We'll find Philip. I'll go ashore and see what's going on.'

'That usually means trouble for someone,' said Joan.

'Quite. Where's that Comnenus girl, Berengaria?'

'She's hiding behind the curtain, very disturbed by your battle.'

'Get her out here. Don't want to scare the girl, do we? I'd like to talk to her.'

Amynta poked her head out from behind the canvas curtain. 'She's asleep, Your Highness. Perhaps I can bring her to you later?'

'Asleep? Right, I'll see her later. I'm off now — things to do.'

Joan and I gazed at each other. This was not going well.

'We might just be in his way. Perhaps he doesn't want us to know what his business is going to be here. That sea battle might be a precursor,' muttered Joan.

'Those praying in Rome for the relief of Jerusalem from the Saracens are separating their vision from the actual means of achieving it. I can see that now. Joan, we are on our way; let's take each day as it comes. It might not be all bad.'

She shook her head sadly. 'Let's go up top and see what's happening. It's gloomy down here.'

With the crews now dressed, the fleet was re-formed. Although the battle had delayed us, we ploughed on into the sunset and then through the darkness. Richard had taken to hanging lights from the mastheads of all his ships after the storm that had cast us onto Cypriot shores.

Joan and I retired to our little canvas enclave beneath the deck and got ready to settle down. If we reached the anchorage of Akko during the night, so be it. I did not intend to stir before the sun came up, if my restless mind would let me sleep.

CHAPTER THREE

Awakened by the silence, I opened my eyes to find Alazne hovering above me. 'Good morning, my queen.'

'It's very quiet, Alazne. Has the wind dropped?'

'No, Your Highness. We are at anchor off Akko.'

I struggled to sit up; the straw bed was not good for my back. 'You let me sleep.'

'I wondered if you would ever go to sleep, Your Highness, after that dreadful slaughter.'

'Where are the others?'

'Some are up, and some are still abed.' As she spoke, those still prone began to stir.

'Joan and I will wash and take some wine,' I said, 'before we view this new city.'

'I'm going up top,' said Alazne. 'Are you coming, Eirini?'

The girl nodded. Her understanding was growing by the day.

When Joan and I were ready, we emerged into the sunlight and greeted our cheerful shipmaster.

'Good morrow, Master Guilbert. Are we at war yet?' asked Joan, scanning the city walls across the water.

'In parts, Your Highness, in parts.'

'What do you mean, in parts?' I responded.

He guided us to the rail and pointed at the Saracen banners flying about the city ramparts. 'There, it needs some explanation. The city is a bit like Tyre, encircled by walls rooted in the sea and stuck out on a promontory. It's still held by the Saracens, but it's been under siege for a while now by Guy de Lusignan's men. Look further inland and you may see the banners of France fluttering: King Philip has the city cut off from the land. We are working to isolate it from the sea; that ship we sank yesterday was probably full of relief stores, so now the city will starve or surrender. And look yonder — those ships.' He pointed at some ships at anchor; they were not of a familiar design. 'Egyptians, caught when we entered the bay. That'll stop Saladin from supplying the city by sea.'

'Oh, how simple,' I sighed. 'Let's pray that sense prevails and no more deaths occur.'

'Amen to that,' added Joan.

'What now, Guilbert?'

'What now, Your Highness? Look beyond the French flags to yonder hills. Do you see aught?'

Screwing up my eyes against the sun, I tried to see to the far horizon. On the hills, something moved. 'There's something there, Joan,' I said. 'In the shadows in those hills.'

'I thought so. What is it, Guilbert?' she asked.

'Saladin's army. As Philip has the garrison bottled up inside the city, Saladin has Philip trapped between his army and the city walls. They are at an impasse.'

'Mother Mary! What now?' I cried.

Father Francis joined us. '*Domine conserva in nobis*,' he intoned, appealing to the highest authority.

'Now, Your Highness,' continued Guilbert, 'we will wait until the king returns, and he will tell us what next.'

Joan and I whiled away the day in conversation, and we also spent some time with Eirini. Her attitude was changing and she showed a desire to learn new languages: Basque with me and *langue d'oc* with Joan, an hour in the morning and another in the afternoon.

That evening, the sun took on a red hue as it dropped towards the horizon.

'A portent of something, according to some people,' ventured Joan.

'I don't like it,' added Alazne. 'It reminds me of the sea around that poor ship yesterday. Or was it the day before?'

'I'll be very surprised if this ends without more blood being spilled,' I said.

'My brother seems to like spilling blood,' murmured Joan.

'It has given him more cheer than I have,' I responded.

'Give him time; this is hardly the setting for lovers,' said Alazne.

I hadn't mentioned to her the king's ardour after he had destroyed the ship. Joan looked at me, and I shook my head and motioned towards the opposite rail.

'Give me a moment, my sweet,' I said to Alazne. 'I want to discuss something with Queen Joan.'

I watched as the sun cast our shadows on the water below, then Joan coughed. 'Well?'

'I didn't tell her about the king's excitement after the slaughter.'

'Really? But why should she not know? She shares most of your secrets.'

'Yes, but I can't have the idea that there is any chance of an annulment going around. You know how tittle-tattle spreads. If there's no consummation, there's no marriage — as I understand it. I trust you, though, Joan.'

'I honour you, Berri. Worry not, I'm thinking.'

'I must give him time, and Alazne must not begin to hope that we can go back to Navarre together before I can try to make this marriage work.'

'You could live elsewhere,' Joan said hopefully.

'Where?'

'I don't know. I expect they'll find someone suitable for me one day; perhaps I'll be able to go back to Sicily. You can live with me … with whomever you want.'

'They'll need to get rid of Tancred before that happens.'

'He will only be tolerated if Rome wants him there.'

'Who else is there, though? He is of the family.'

'True. Illegitimate or not, he is the son of the late King Roger — king before my husband William.'

'God bless him,' I laughed.

'God rot his bones,' Joan retorted. 'Fornicating devil.' She paused. 'The German emperors have long eyed that island. It would not surprise me if Heinrich found some connection to exploit, some vague relative.'

'Are you resigned to giving up your title?' I asked.

'Probably, especially if Tancred is involved.'

'He kept you close.'

'Yes. I was not quite a prisoner, but neither was I free. He did not harm me, but I suspect he was working hard to wring some advantage from keeping me on the island.'

'You can please yourself now that your brother has claimed you.'

'I doubt it, and no more can you, my sweet.'

I sighed. 'We are sisters in so many ways. We have nothing except what we are allowed to have. But returning to Navarre as a spurned bride will send mutterings across all the courts of Europe, and I have the blessing of the Pope to contend with, not to mention your mother.'

'Oh God, Mother!' Joan said, covering her mouth with her hands.

There was a shout from the sentry on the forecastle. 'What boat? Identify yourself.'

The response came from the gloom now draping the sea. 'The king's galley. We are coming alongside.'

'Master Guilbert, the king,' was the sentry's call.

'Thank you. Man the side; the king is coming aboard.'

The deck was suddenly busy as the crew came tumbling out of the shadows and lined up at the rail to attend King Richard. Robert de Sablé, back on board now, also appeared out of the dark.

Richard dragged himself up from his small galley and cast a leg over the rail, spurning any help, then planted his feet firmly on the deck. He was not smiling, and my heart sank.

'Where's Camville?' he asked.

'At your planning table, Your Highness,' replied de Sablé.

'Good, good; that's where we are all going. Come along. Sister, Berengaria, you should both hear this. The French scoundrel is playing games.'

'Philip?' asked de Sablé.

'Yes, yes. Get some more light in here. Where are those maps, Camville? Berengaria, help me out of this hauberk; the strap's on the back. Joan, is there any wine?'

A few moments of chaos ensued while the king's demands were met, and then he called us to the table and began his briefing.

'You ladies need to hear this, because we are going to be very busy tomorrow and you'll have to fend for yourselves. Philip has got himself deep in the mire. You've seen his banners? He's got the Saracens trapped in the city, but beyond the coast sits Saladin and his army. He is besieging the besieger's camp. The only way in and out is via the beach, which we have secured. We hold the sea approaches outside the harbour to deny the city reinforcements.'

As he spoke, he pointed out the salient features on the map, stabbing the table with his dagger. I wondered if he was going to explode with rage.

To try to calm him, I asked a question. 'Cannot we send to Saladin? This suits neither of us — are we to wait until the city runs out of food, Richard?'

'Yes, yes, a very good question, my sweet Berengaria,' Richard said, 'but that will not work. I want to draw the Saracen army onto my sword; the fate of the city might just do that. But I favour my other solution.' He stabbed the table again. 'A full-scale assault.'

'Our siege materiel is still far behind us, stuck in these light winds, Your Highness,' said de Sablé unnecessarily.

'Indeed it is,' added Camville. 'On the cogs, together with the horses, are the trebuchets and other missile-hurling machines, dismantled climbing towers, thousands of arrows and all the other paraphernalia of war.'

'Quite. I will not move against the city until all my soldiers and their equipment are landed, no, no. And that's that.' Richard looked up at me and Joan. 'You'll need to stay on board Master Guilbert's craft, my queens. I cannot risk you going ashore as long as the camp is threatened. Besides, it is not fit for a queen's eyes. Do you understand?'

'If you say so, brother,' was Joan's response.

I was thinking that while Richard might have some diplomatic skills, his first thought was to attack and destroy, regardless of the fact that most of the people inside the walls might not be soldiers. Disturbed, I asked, 'What are you going to do now, Richard?'

He looked across the table at his commanders, captains and lords. Then he called for a chair; he had turned pale and suddenly did not seem his usual ebullient self, but he pressed on. 'We are going ashore. I want to inspect the city walls, spy out its weaknesses and find a suitable area to set up camp. By the time my cargo ships arrive, we will have eight thousand men ashore, and it needs some planning.' He turned to Guilbert. 'Guilbert, I place my ladies in your care. You can be responsible for the welfare of the fleet while everyone else is grappling with Saladin. Hugo can scurry betwixt and between. I'll let you know what we're doing, but expect no fuss until the remainder of my ships catch up — then we'll have the means to wrest this city from its inhabitants. Take care to anchor the remainder of the fleet in accordance with this plan.' He handed over a map of what looked like the harbour area to Master Guilbert. 'Form a screen of ships to defend the harbour area, and unload the transport vessels in accordance with this list when they arrive.' He handed over a long list of ships and their cargoes to the doughty master. 'Happy, what, what?'

'Content, Your Highness. It is well planned. What if the vessels turn up in the wrong order?'

'Communication, Master Guilbert — send to me and I'll make a decision. We will not be idle for a moment longer than necessary. I'll allocate storage areas for everything once I am back ashore, and you can have all the cargoes sent directly to their proper places, however they turn up.'

'You've thought of everything, Your Highness.'

'Many a long hour, Guilbert. Now, if you will excuse us, ladies…'

It was time for us to go. I noted that Richard's face was sallow, and he trembled from time to time.

'Are you not well, Richard? What ails thee?' I asked with concern.

'Nothing that time will not cure, dear Berengaria,' he replied. 'Fret not; it is merely a repeat of that fever which has afflicted me before. They say that it returns from time to time until it eventually leaves the body. I shall be well. I need to go through more details with my commanders; they need to brief their men so that everyone in this venture knows their proper place. We are about to land an army on the enemy's shore. Ah, there is Herbert Poore.' He was looking at a clergyman who had boarded the *Thor* with him; I knew not which vessel he was travelling in. 'Perhaps you can bless our venture.'

'Who is he?' I whispered to Guilbert.

'The Bishop of Salisbury,' he informed me.

Herbert Poore was joined by Father Francis, and I supposed that this was our cue to depart.

As we left, Joan murmured, 'Richard is stubborn, and driven. The Lord will safeguard him if He desires it so.'

'Who am I to disagree?' I said churlishly. 'I am merely his wife.'

I awoke the next morning to the smells of cooking. Sitting up, I recognised that we were safely within our canvas cabin on the *Thor*.

'What's that smell?' mumbled Alazne.

'Someone's cooking,' I replied. 'I'm starving. Come on, get up.'

Untidily dressed, we stumbled out onto the open deck to be hailed by Guilbert. He was standing on the afterdeck with two of his crewmen and Hugo.

'Your Highness, Alazne,' he called, beaming. 'Welcome to our kitchen.'

Drawn by the aromas wafting about the ship, we climbed the steps to find a brick-built oven with a grill on top.

'You've made this, Guilbert?' I asked.

'Indeed, Your Highness, because we are at anchor and we carry all the necessary materials: the bricks, the metal grill, the metal oven box, and a few bags of charcoal. And *voilà*! Grilled fish for your breakfast, with freshly baked bread — and wine, of course.'

'I had never thought of that, Guilbert. What a truly excellent start to the day. Thank you. Why do you carry such things?'

'We never know where we're going to spend the night. It is only sensible planning, and experience.'

'Who's planning? Good morning, sweet Berengaria.' Joan, in good humour, together with Torène and Pavot, had clambered up to join us while I was admiring Guilbert's kitchen.

'Good morning, dear Joan. See what our shipmaster has for us: an oven, grilled fish, fresh bread and wine.'

'Jesu!' Joan exclaimed. 'Where is everyone, Guilbert? The ship is deserted.'

'They're all ashore, Your Highness. The oarsmen have converted into warriors, and the rest of my seamen have gone to see where the siege engines might be erected when they arrive.'

'Ooh,' I said in appreciation as one of Guilbert's cooks held out a platter of steaming fish.

'Ahem, there's something else first.' It was Father Francis, apparently attracted by the smell of food.

'Prayers for Prime,' he reminded us. It was a rare event — a duty which had been missed too often.

'Of course, how remiss,' I agreed. 'Please lead us, Father.'

We spent a few moments in contemplation, during which I asked for guidance for my new husband. I prayed for him to be gentle and considerate, and not only to me.

That done, Joan quickly returned to the subject of sieges. 'Why do they need seamen to help with the siege engines, master?' she enquired.

'All the engines are in the holds in parts, Your Highness,' said Guilbert, 'and they need to be assembled using ropes, chocks and pins. My ship's carpenter, sailmaker and seamen, who understand ropes and suchlike, are the experts in these matters. It is their task to make certain that the soldiers put them together properly.'

'How clever,' I said.

The air was still now, save for the cry of seabirds, the chomping of bread and fish, and the occasional slurp of wine.

Well-fed and curious, I began to question Guilbert about his knowledge of the goings-on in the siege.

'Why does the king not want us there, master? What do you know beyond what he told us last night?'

'It seems, Your Highness, that the Crusader camp, managed by the French, is a midden. It is unfit for decent folk, especially women … except that there are women in the camp, those of a certain kind who have drifted in to provide services for the soldiers.'

'Disgraceful,' mumbled Alazne.

'And the sanitation is dismal — pits all over the ground. Some have drowned in them at night. This is why Richard has gone to make a more detailed assessment of his army's needs; he does not want disease to bring down his men.'

'There are brothels?' I queried, to be certain of his meaning.

'In a Christian camp?' added Joan.

'Indeed, the beast within men arises from time to time, and I'm told that some Saracen men have been caught sneaking across the lines to sample the delights. Their gold is welcome too.'

'They are taking custom from the enemy?' I was astonished.

'You misunderstand the nature of chivalry, Your Highness. The soldiery and the leaders are not hostile to each other; only when they are drawn up in a battle formation to offer a challenge are they enemies. Indeed, Saladin has sent King Richard his greetings and looks forward to defeating him on the field of battle.'

'They're as mad as we are, Berengaria,' said Joan. 'And what are the bishops doing about such debauchery?'

'The bishops believe that all men are sinners and that they will make a few bezants from hearing confessions, Your Highness.'

'You are cynical, Guilbert,' I told him.

'If we are stuck out here,' said Alazne, changing the subject, 'we might as well make some improvements to our quarters.'

'That's a good idea,' said Torène. 'How long are we here for, master?'

'When the ships arrive, it will take a day or so to disembark the soldiers, a week to unload the stores and another week to erect the siege engines. Give it a month before Richard is ready to begin his war, if the French haven't gone home by then. It will take another month to breach the walls and occupy the city — then Richard and Saladin have the matter of the king of Jerusalem to resolve. Another war will be needed to settle that, probably.'

'Oh, yes,' I said. 'I forgot why we are here — the recapture of the Holy City. Is that now a side quest, Guilbert?'

'For the moment, Your Highness, for the moment. As for how long we'll be here, that's anybody's guess.'

Joan and I stayed on the forecastle for most of the morning, watching events on the land — or as much as we could see from out in the harbour. A pair of seamen came and asked if we would like a canvas shade erecting, which we agreed to. One of them then asked me if I wanted to climb the ladder up the mast to see further inland.

'I'll go up a little way,' I responded, 'but you'll need to stay close to me. And do not raise your head above my ankles. What's your name, anyway?'

'Henri, Your Highness.' He grinned. 'I wouldn't think to discomfort you, Your Highness, but if you become giddy I'm going to grab you anyway.'

'Very well, Henri. Let's do it. The longer I think on it, the less likely I am to go up.'

'Is this wise, Your Highness?' cautioned Hugo. 'What if you slip?'

'I'll fall into the sea,' I said.

Setting foot on the rope ladder was the first fright. I had to stand on the rail where the bottom of the thing was secured and grab hold of a rung — my first mistake.

'Hold the sides, Your Highness; it is safer.' Henri got up beside me. 'Just slide your hands up the sides and you'll always have a grip, see.'

'Right,' I said, doing as he instructed.

'Now, keep looking up; don't look down.'

I took a step upwards, and then, sliding my hands up, took another. Looking up, I felt steady, but then I looked down to see where Henri was, and nearly lost my hold.

Below where I was, halfway up the mast, were my companions' anxious faces. Then Henri's head came into contact with my backside, but I did not complain because I felt safer.

'Are you staying here?' he asked, his voice muffled by my rear end.

I looked up and didn't fancy going any higher, so I said weakly, 'Yes.'

'Well, take a goodly hold, wrap your arms around the outside and grasp the rung. And don't worry — everyone feels at risk the first time. Now, take a look around, Your Highness.'

I did as he suggested. The city walls had sentries posted all along, including those parts with their foundations in the sea. The watch towers and a small island nearby with a tower built upon it were also guarded, but most of the activity was on the land side.

'What can you see, Berengaria?' called Joan.

'Most everybody is on the landward side. You can't see that from where you are. Then there is a space, and then there are lines of soldiers. They're too far away to see any details, but there seem to be one or two of those rock-throwing devices — '

'Trebuchets, Your Highness,' offered Henri.

'Trebuchets,' I repeated, 'then lots of tents and smoke from burners — they must have kitchens. Then there are perhaps two miles or so before there is another line of soldiers, banners, and tents. Jesu! Is that the Saracens' camp, Henri?'

'Yes, they're all across the horizon, Your Highness. My neck grows weary; can we climb down, please?'

'Very well, I have seen enough of this bloodied land. What do we do?'

'Get hold of the side ropes again. I'll drop down a bit and guide your feet, one by one. And do not be tempted to rush; we'll soon be on deck safely, Your Highness.'

One step at a time, my feet guided by a secure hand, we reached the bottom and I swung onto the deck, beaming with pride.

'What was that like, Berengaria?' asked Joan. 'Was it frightening?'

'It was like sitting on a hot rock,' I replied, pointing at Henri's shaven head. That caused some merriment, but I caught his eye to let him know I was grateful. 'Thank you for your help, Henri.'

He smiled. 'I'll remain at your service, Your Highness, should you wish to…'

'No, I will not, thank you.'

'Then I'll go about my other duties now, Your Highness.'

The ladies pressed close to me and began to ask more questions.

'Tell me, dear Berengaria, what's to be seen?' demanded Joan.

'It's a mess. Those walls nearest to the sea are almost empty of men, because they are all at the far end of the city wall, nearest to the land. The French are outside the gate there, but there are banners of many colours. It would be difficult to pick out Richard's. All of Europe seems to be there.'

'And the Saracens are beyond them. Our army is cut off, to all intents and purposes, and the only route into our camp is from the sea,' interjected Guilbert, who had now joined us.

'But why do the Saracens not attack?' I asked. 'They clearly outnumber us.'

'Rumours I heard can explain that, Your Highness,' responded Hugo. 'If he waits long enough, Saladin hopes that the Crusader camp will collapse through disease or desertion, and he'll be able to walk right into the city unopposed.'

'I see,' I said.

'What now?' asked Joan.

'We'll wait for our cargo ships. The equipment they are carrying should turn the tide,' answered Guilbert.

'What is that island called, the one with the tower on it?' I asked.

'That's marked on the chart map as the Tower of Flies, Your Highness. It was believed to belong to the devil in ancient lore. The name Baalzebub means "lord of the flies" in Hebrew.'

'Devil's island? I'll take care not to go there.'

'Or anywhere else in this unholy land,' said Joan.

CHAPTER FOUR

It was another two days before Richard bothered to send us news. We watched as one of his fast small galleys left the shore and moved towards us. A dusty captain of cavalry clambered aboard and greeted us.

'I'm sent to speak to the queens, madam,' he said to Joan, who was still in breeches and did not look much like a queen.

'Then I am Joan of Sicily, and this is Berengaria of England. Are we who you had in mind?'

'Indeed, Your Highnesses. An honour.' He bowed and introduced himself. 'I am Geoffrey of Anjou, and I come from the king. I have here a parchment for Her Highness Queen Berengaria, and I am instructed to answer all of your questions, if I can.'

'I have one,' I said. 'Why send a cavalryman?'

'We have few horses, and it seems to be an infantry war at present, Your Highness.'

'His horses are catching up, I hope,' said Guilbert.

'Have you any news of our ships, master?' the horseless rider asked eagerly.

'No, but if you have news, you'd better tell it,' said Guilbert.

'Come and sit over here,' I said. 'We'll have some wine sent over; this may take some time.'

Guilbert issued instructions, and we all sat down on the afterdeck steps to listen to Geoffrey of Anjou.

'Firstly, Your Highnesses, the king is suffering with a fever and has taken to his bed to rest. He says it is not serious and you are not to fret.' He looked at me and I nodded.

'In the meantime, King Philip has continued to attack the city with a pair of small trebuchets — hopeless, and this in spite of King Richard's opinion that they should wait until his siege engines arrive. Philip's efforts have been repulsed with heavy casualties, as predicted. Guy de Lusignan has had some success, and the leaders of the Pisan army have pledged to join with Richard.' Geoffrey paused for a slurp of wine. 'The surprising news is that Saladin and Richard have opened communications. Saladin has sent the king some fruits and his wishes for a good recovery. It seems that a solution may be obtainable through negotiation, or...'

'Or?' I pressed.

'Or Saladin's envoys may have been sent to spy on the Frankish camp, because they keep assaulting the ditch.'

'What ditch?' I asked.

'The camp is defended by a ditch right across the front, facing Saladin's camp. It's deep enough to protect us against their cavalry, but they keep trying to fill it up with earth to cross it. Guy de Lusignan made a spirited defence against one such attack; he is a very brave knight. Then the defenders on the wall threw Greek fire at us. It is a horrible death.'

'What now?' asked Joan.

'We still wait for the engines of war,' said Guilbert.

'And I must return to the king. Are you Hugo?' Geoffrey asked, looking at our scribe.

'Yes.'

'You can come with me; the king has need of you.'

'Oh, good. Not that I am not enjoying your company, Your Highnesses, but it sounds very interesting ashore. What am I to do, Geoffrey?'

'Make notes, then come back here and brief the queens from time to time.'

'That sounds like a task which I will undertake gladly.'

Hugo disappeared for a moment and reappeared with a small bag — his personal items and writing things, no doubt. Then he flung a leg over the rail and dropped down into the waiting galley.

A week later, we were still anchored in the bay of Akko.

'Richard still hasn't sent for me,' I complained.

'He is up and about, though, recovering from his illness,' said Joan, 'and I don't want to sleep in their smelly camp, anyway.'

'No, we are quite comfortable, that's true, but I am his wife.'

We were sitting in a circle on the afterdeck with the other ladies, enjoying the sunlight. We had turned our quarters on the deck beneath us into something passably homely, and now we were busy turning some gowns into pantaloons, baggy but narrow at the ankle, in the Eastern style. Amynta had advised us on their construction.

'Sail, master!' the lookout cried.

Dropping everything in the dash to the rail, we scoured the horizon.

'There!' cried Alazne. 'There are three.'

'Are they ours?' Guilbert called up to the top of the mast.

'Can't tell yet, master,' came the unhelpful response.

Guilbert called out to the other crewman still on board. 'Henri, go in the dinghy and get us some soldiers back on board until we know who these vessels belong to. Your Highnesses, down into your quarters, if you please.'

We scuttled down the ladder and took shelter as Henri sped off across the water.

Soon a galley full of marine soldiers left the shore and, bypassing us, stationed themselves between Guilbert's *Thor* and the steadily oncoming fleet.

'The siege engines!' I shouted. 'It must be Richard's machines.'

'About time,' said Guilbert, and we watched as the lumbering cargo ships dropped anchor one by one.

That small galley was speeding around, giving out instructions as to where to go to each of the encroaching vessels. They must have been stationed on the beach for just this purpose.

'Is this Richard's plan, Master Guilbert?' I asked.

'Indeed, Your Highness. I have a copy here in my hand; everyone to their place. We'll begin unloading soon and then you'll see some action, I'll warrant.'

By the time it was dark, the ships were safely anchored and the harbour was alive with lights.

'I wonder what Saladin thought when he spied this fleet coming over the horizon.' I was at the rail, staring in wonder at this demonstration of Richard's power.

'Are you dreaming, Berri?' It was Joan.

'I seem to be married to a very powerful man.'

'Yes, he can cover the sea with ships.'

'But he won't let me near him; he won't let anybody near him who is not dressed in armour.'

Joan put her arms around my waist. 'What to do? We are but two lonely queens.'

'True, but you comfort me. Thank you, Joan.'

'Let that not change, Berri.'

Alazne came over to us with a cloak, and Joan stepped back a little to let her stand alongside me. 'Hello, my queens. Are you cold?'

I accepted the cloak. 'Thank you, Alazne. The shore is alight with campfires; do you think that all the soldiers are ashore now, Joan?'

'I should think so. Guilbert said that he was happy with the ship count: eight thousand men and whatever equipment the ships are holding. That should satisfy Richard.'

'Now he has the means to enact another slaughter.'

'Yes, his new machines are within range of the city walls. He frightens me at times, so reckless can he be. One way or another, I might not leave this place with a brother, Berri.'

'And I might lose a husband.'

Joan grasped my hand. We went into our quarters, but no sleep came to us that night as the unloading of the cargo ships went on unabated. We heard the shouts of men, the bangs and crashing as equipment was moved, the creaking of rigging and rope slings as the men unloaded more cargo, and the faint sound of horses in the holds as they smelled land. It was now July, and the next phase of the war was upon us.

When the first light of dawn came I had heard enough, and decided to go up top and watch.

'Come on, Joan. Let's see what's moving up there,' I called, and dashed out onto the open deck. Because the vessel was swinging round the anchor, the shore was behind us and the afterdeck offered the best view.

'Look,' called Alazne, who'd had no sleep either. 'Over there, they're landing the horses.'

One of the giant cog ships had been beached sideways onto the sand, and the great door in its side was open. We could see the figures of the wranglers, tiny from a distance, leading their steeds onto the beach. Soon they were trotting the freed horses around and getting them used to moving once more.

'Over there.' Joan was pointing at other cogs, likewise against the sand, but these had carts emerging from the loading doors.

'That'll be the parts for the siege engines, Your Highness,' said Guilbert. 'Watch while they hitch up those palfreys to drag them towards the city walls. Ever since William the Conqueror, the Normans have constructed siege engines so that they can be unmade and remade somewhere else. It is a sight to behold; they can raise a castle in two days, one of those trebuchets in one day and an onager in hours — that's a machine for hurling spears.'

Unconstrained by fear now, I ventured some way up the rope ladder and called out my observations to the eagerly awaiting ladies below. 'There are very few Saracens left on the city's sea walls now; all the activity is at the city gate. The Crusader camp is alive with men, but further inland the Saracen hordes stretch from horizon's end to horizon's end. That is very worrying.'

'Can you see Richard's banners?' shouted Joan.

'I think so. He appears to be at the centre of things.'

'Come back down, please, Berri,' she said. 'The wind is getting up.'

I did as bidden. Although my palms were wet with perspiration, it was exciting, and I thought I might go higher next time.

Guilbert came over to the ladder. 'You're a mighty brave one, Your Highness, that's for sure. But I'll lose my head if you fall; the king isn't one for forgiving.'

'Of course, Master Guilbert,' I said, humbled by the pleading look on his face. 'How thoughtless of me. You need not fear. But let's pray that we'll not be cooped up on the *Thor* for much longer, though we enjoy your company.'

'Well,' he said, 'take a look at the beach. The cogs are light enough to un-beach now that their cargoes have been unloaded; we will be at the climax before long. I wonder how much longer the defenders can hold out. Time for some negotiations, I should think.'

There was one note for us the following day. 'It's from Hugo,' I revealed as I unrolled the parchment on Richard's planning table.

'Good, good. Read it, Berri,' said Joan.

'He says that Richard is now very busy and that he, Hugo, is to keep us informed daily.'

'Well, that's an improvement,' retorted Joan.

'He also says the walls are in a parlous state and will not withstand a battering from the new engines. Saladin keeps sending envoys, but Richard will only parley with him face to face; he wants to negotiate with him directly. But Saladin has refused because he believes that it would not be seemly for two kings to wrangle over the table; he wants the outline of a peace treaty settled before they meet.'

'That would be better than more killing,' said Joan.

'Indeed, and Richard says that lots of the armies have transferred their allegiance to him from Philip of France. They consider Philip weak and prefer that Richard leads the siege now that he is here. And the leaders are arguing over who should be King of Jerusalem.'

'But Lusignan is king,' protested Joan.

'Not in everyone's eyes, it seems. He was only king because he married the widowed, and now deceased, Queen Sibylla. There are those who prefer her half-sister, Isabella, and her new husband, Conrad of Montferrat, over Guy.'

'That will cause trouble when this siege is over,' said Joan.

'It already is, by the tone of this note,' I replied. 'Still, that's for later. Never a dull moment around your brother, Joan.'

'That's true.'

A renewed clamour reached our ears from the shore. Richard's trebuchet-carrying wagons were rolling towards the

Frankish camp, greeted by cheers from the soldiers encamped near the beach. Saladin should worry now.

Henri and others, even a cook or two, made repeated trips up the mast now, leaving the cooking to the one other seaman left on board: Anton of Barfleur, he was called, and he was happier at the stove than up that precarious rope ladder.

Three or four times a day someone called down observations, and we all gathered beneath the mast to listen.

'Lots of activity between the trenches and the Saracens. They keep sending raiding parties, but they are all repulsed at the moment. The gate wall is the busiest; the Saracens have a trebuchet inside the city walls and are throwing rocks over the wall, and Greek fire from the top. Our troops are returning three rocks to their one, so we will win that battle; it is very impressive.'

That was an early report, but it changed over the next couple of days.

'All the activity is from the camp into the city; the defenders are being worn down. Saladin's attacks on the trenches are increasing, but we are winning.'

After the second day, the din went on all night and the sky lit up with Greek fireballs.

'This must end soon, surely,' I said to Joan.

'The defenders are very brave not to have surrendered under that continual shower of missiles,' she responded.

On the next day, the fifth of July, Hugo's note told us that an important tower had been collapsed by mining beneath it, that the main gate was in a state of ruin, and that both the garrison commander, named Mestoc, and the city governor, named Kara-Kush, had emerged under a flag of truce to sue for peace. King Philip was minded to accept, but Richard refused.

The Saracens wanted free passage to join Saladin on the far side of the Frankish camp, but Richard wanted a city full of potential hostages.

I was shocked, but Guilbert was in favour of the cunning decision.

'It's very wise, Your Highness. If the Saracens hold any Christian prisoners and threaten the city after it is taken, hostages give us leverage.'

This was an outrage to me. 'So innocent folk are now bargaining assets in a game of kings?'

'It is war, Your Highness. To win is everything; to lose is a disaster.'

'I like it not.'

'Come on, Berengaria,' Joan said, 'you can't change it by not liking it. It is the way of men, politics and war. It was ever thus.'

On the twelfth of July, it was done. The defenders had taken enough punishment, and even though some Egyptian vessels had attempted to land relief stores and Saladin's men continued to probe the trench defences, Mestoc and Kara-Kush sued for peace and Richard entered the city. Every man, woman and child were now prisoners of the King of England.

The next of Hugo's notes was a cursory scribble. 'We are repairing the gate and wall, and the king will send for you as soon as suitable. You should be ready to occupy the governor's palace in due course.'

'A palace! We're going to have a roof over our heads,' I exclaimed.

Joan celebrated by dancing on the deck, joined by the rest of us ladies, much to the delight of Guilbert, Henri and Anton. Eirini watched for a bit, then joined us too. I took the opportunity to teach them a Navarrese wedding dance.

Guilbert brought out some Cypriot wine. Anton went off in the rowing boat, and after a tour of the anchored ships he came back with a chicken.

'Such high prices,' he moaned, 'but we'll eat properly this evening, Your Highnesses.'

We ate our meat with fresh bread from his oven. Then I was reminded of something.

'Alazne, have all my gowns been converted into pantaloons?'

'No, you still have gowns and kirtles. Why do you ask?'

'I would like a gown in which to go and occupy my new palace.'

'So would I,' agreed Joan.

'And me, please, Your Highness,' chorused Pavot and Torène.

'How long have we got?' asked Alazne.

'I don't know,' I answered. 'Let's get everything laid out on the deck and see what we have.'

As it happened, Geoffrey of Anjou and Hugo didn't come on board until the twentieth of July.

'Not writing today, Hugo?' enquired Joan, looking down into the galley, where she spied the pair.

'Your Highness, your moment has arrived,' said Hugo as he puffed his way on board and faced us on the deck, smiling. 'We'll take you ashore on the morrow.'

'Everything is arranged and you are to receive a right royal reception,' added Geoffrey.

'How have you been, Your Highnesses?' asked Hugo. 'You've had a good view of the war, I suppose.'

'You suppose right, Hugo, although it isn't the entertainment that I would have chosen. We are more taken with troubadours and the like in Navarre.'

'Ah well, that's all there is on offer at the moment. Perhaps you can change things when you are installed in your new palace. It is furnished in the Saracen style. I think that you will find it quite comfortable.'

'We will, Hugo,' said Joan, 'and we have been preparing for it. Are we to ride or walk?'

'The king will meet you on the beach at mid-morning. The rubble has been cleared from the gateway and the road to the palace is clear. He wants you to ride with him — a statement of his authority, you see. Have you suitable clothing, Your Highnesses?'

'We have,' we chorused. Alazne, Pavot, Torène and Amynta, helped by Eirini, had put together some startling new pantaloon-cum-gowns. They were all-in-one garments that would be suitable for walking or riding.

'So, Geoffrey,' I said, 'what else is happening in yonder chaos?' I nodded in the direction of the Crusader camp.

'Squabbling — the usual thing when treaties are signed. Everyone reads them differently. Richard and King Philip of France are arguing over who gets what share of the spoils. Richard has offended practically all the other leaders, including Duke Leopold of Austria. Our king cast down the duke's banners from the walls of Akko, "because it was Richard's victory". Yet Leopold was first to enter.'

'Corpses are not yet cold and they're quarrelling over the spoils? What manner is this for Christians to behave?' I was furious; there was no decency here.

Joan faced me. 'Are you going to quarrel with Richard over this, Berri? He will not be pleased — he's hot from the fight, you know.'

'He can be as triumphant as he likes; he will hear my thoughts on the matter. This is a Crusade to take back God's city, not a melee for spoils.'

'Well, wait and see what he has to say tomorrow; there may be more to it.'

'Perhaps I should, dear friend. What would I do without you for guidance?'

'Go back home, I shouldn't wonder,' said Alazne. She did not smile, and I wondered — not for the first time — if she wasn't happy about my friendship with Joan.

'Come on, Alazne, let's finish preparing our queenly attire. I might as well look the part.'

The next morning, we all trudged up the steps onto the afterdeck to watch the sun rise.

It was quiet, suspiciously quiet. There was no movement on the horizon. Saladin must have been considering his next move. The sea was calm, and only a few sentries trudged back and forth along the sands. It was such a peaceful sight, and yet I knew that in and around the city walls, bodies lay awaiting their final resting place — a task that needed to be considered, however jubilant the successful attack on the city had been. Who would send the Saracens to their god?

Before long, Anton and another sailor came up to light their oven, and Guilbert poked his head out of the hold and waved a skin of wine in our direction.

'Go on, then,' said Joan. 'Let's celebrate the new day.'

Freshly grilled fish and Anton's bread soon disappeared, washed down with some rich red Cypriot wine. It was a grand morning, but the walls of Akko, glowering nearby, were sufficient to turn thoughts away from any pleasures that might lie behind them.

'Tell us what you think,' I commanded our audience. Geoffrey, Hugo, Guilbert and the two seamen were standing in a line, inspecting our new outfits.

'That's a risky command, Berengaria. Who knows what they'll come out with?' Joan laughed.

'I have never seen anything like it,' offered Geoffrey.

'It is, er, different,' said Hugo, who seemed a trifle disturbed.

'It is somewhat European, and somewhat Egyptian, and a bit of something else — I know not what.' Guilbert, the most travelled of our inspectors, expressed his view.

'Call it what you like,' called Henri, unasked, 'but it is the prettiest sight that I have seen for many a day.'

'Thank you, Henri; we don't need to know what you think,' I retorted with a laugh.

Anton just stared without comment.

Joan and I each wore rope sandals, baggy pantaloons made from the finest silk gowns, a short branc made from the same material, belted at the waist, and an embroidered sleeveless jacket over the top. We were modestly buttoned up with our hair suitably pinned and covered in fine headdresses, atop which our crowns sat precariously. We had decided to wear them to declare our status, although I had become unused to mine and felt as if it would come off at any moment.

Alazne, Pavot and Torène were now wearing my ladies' wedding outfits, Amynta was very Byzantine and little Eirini had insisted on her own design, which was different from all the others, and she wore a contented expression.

'Well, if Your Highnesses are ready, your galley awaits,' said Geoffrey. He held out a hand to help me hop over the rail.

'Upon my soul,' said the steersman when we were all aboard and seated, 'this is the prettiest cargo I've ever had the pleasure of carrying.'

'Just take us to the shore, man,' scolded Hugo.

They had left the benches nearest the steersman vacant for us, and we chose to sit facing backwards rather than staring at the rowers.

'The king is waiting on the sand, Your Highnesses,' said the steersman. 'He is on his great white charger, all done up in red and with a sparkling crown on his head.'

The galley soon grounded on the beach.

'Joan! Berengaria!' Richard called cheerily as he got off his horse.

Joan was first out of the galley, and she jumped into two feet of water, quickly followed by our ladies. I, being stuck in the middle of the bench, was last.

Richard, beaming, had Joan in his arms and was twirling her around, laughing. I lifted my pantaloons up before stepping carefully into the sea and trudging ashore.

'Berengaria!' Richard called, as if we had parted only yesterday. He dropped his sister to charge down the sand and grab me for a vigorous twirl.

'How are my queens, what, what? Have they taken good care of you? How do you like Akko?'

'We are well, Richard.' It was hard to breathe with him squeezing me, and my feet were way above the sand. 'And thank you for sending us the daily news; it was a bit frustrating, sitting out in the bay and not knowing what was going on. But have the sweats returned?'

Dropping me onto the sand, he pulled off a gauntlet. 'Not so bad, but look. Some of my nails have disappeared, and I've lost some hair — I'll keep my crown on, but you can have a look later.'

'How odd. But you are much recovered in spirit; you seem cheery.'

'I am. But there's lots to do, yes, yes. Let's get you to horse and we'll process through the city — a Roman Triumph for my ladies.'

I had a better view from atop a horse, and to my surprise, during our voyage from ship to shore, companies of soldiers had been lined up from the top of the beach towards the city walls.

I called over to Joan. 'It seems that we are going to be on display, Joan.'

'Heavens above!' she exclaimed, after looking up from arranging her attire. 'Richard, are we to ride through that lot?'

'Indeed you are. Two queens in a procession of possession; it is a rare event, and we are going to make the most of it.'

Hugo, who was on the ground, holding my horse's head, looked up and grinned. 'The king is right: this is rare. Make the most of it, and smile, Queen Berengaria. Smile as if you own the place.' He gave my mount a slap on the flanks, and we set off in the wake of the King of England.

Eirini was sitting safely in Alazne's lap, her mouth agape. I doubt she had ever seen the like in her short life.

The lines of soldiers did not hide the chaos which lay behind them. What I saw from the back of a horse betokened a lengthy struggle: scraggy tents laid out in tattered lines, malodorous pits — which by the smell were full of waste — rocks scattered everywhere from constant bombardments, and areas of scorched earth; this must have been where the dreaded Greek fire had landed. I could tell there were bodies among that devastation, not yet removed. The stench of death hung heavy in the air, along with something else.

'What's that smell?' I asked. 'It's coming from over there — it is like roasting boar.' I pointed towards some smoke drifting up from a deep trench. Some soldiers were standing at its side, looking down. 'What's going on over there, Richard?' I called ahead to him. He spoke to one of his escorts, who halted and waited until I caught up with him.

'That's where they've cast the poor souls set alight by Greek fire, Your Highness. It cannot be put out until their flesh is all consumed.'

Beyond the soldiers, tent lines and defensive trenches was the frightening sight of Saladin's army. It stretched from horizon to horizon, a solid wall of banners and tents. I couldn't understand how they had never succeeded in overwhelming our defences. I thought it must have been the will of God.

I observed all this as I progressed through the lines of cheering men. They were not bedraggled or tattered; these men were proud, shiny and triumphant. Richard had conquered, and his army was proud and had managed to put on a show in a short time.

Perked up by their enthusiasm, I returned the cheers with a smile and a wave. Soon Joan and our ladies were also waving enthusiastically as we approached the city, with its wall and gate on our left, or what remained of it.

Most of the the gatehouse was rubble, for it had been pounded until it fell apart. As for the wall, most of the crenels were level with the sliced-off merlons, and there were many places where it would be possible to run up the rubble and gain entry into the city.

Then we came to the gate — or rather, the largest gap of all, for little remained to keep anyone out. Richard's banners flew proudly on top of what remained on one side, and those of Philip of France on the other. There were men working on clearing the fallen masonry, but one door was missing, presumably buried, and the other was clinging to its last hinge.

Somehow a band of musicians had been gathered, and we were met by triumphant trumpet calls. I heard them, but my eyes were drawn to the rubble of what must have been an impressive entry into the ancient city, named Akko by the Egyptians and now chosen as a supply port by the crusading army.

A thousand years of history had been brought to dust by Richard's engines of war, and I suddenly felt a sadness fall over me. *At what cost, Richard?* I thought. *At what cost?*

Joan and I were riding close behind Richard and observed that he seemed mightily pleased, calling out, 'Well done!' and 'We showed them, good, good,' at every opportunity.

Those working stopped to cheer him on, and I heard a few exclaim, 'Cheers for the queen!'

As we progressed and moved away from the walls on the land side, the damage lessened and some fine, substantial buildings came into sight.

'Were these places out of range, Richard?' I called.

He half-turned. 'Yes, yes, good observation, Berengaria. We'll need to work on improving the range of the trebuchets.'

'Where are all the people, Richard?' asked Joan.

'Locked up in a compound,' he replied. 'They are hostages. I'll extract a goodly sum from Saladin before they see the light of day. Here we are.'

We had ridden though some iron lattice-work gates into a pleasant courtyard. Set within the far corner of the square was the palace itself, a solid building, more Norman and Byzantine than Eastern in style. In contrast, the courtyard was laid out in gardens in the Arabian pattern of such things, with fountains of running water.

Richard dismounted and came up to my horse to help me down. 'This has been much altered during the four years of Islamic occupation,' he explained. 'It serves as a secure palace.'

I remained seated and asked a further question. 'The women and children, Richard, the merchants and tradesmen, and the like — where are they?'

'I told you: they're all hostages until we reach an agreement with Saladin. Here, let me help you down, good, good.'

Sliding down to stand in front of him, I was reminded of how tall he was, and how small was I — a mismatch in anybody's eyes, I thought.

He bent down to kiss me on the forehead. I remained passive.

'I am conscious that we have not had much private time, Berengaria.' He was nervous. 'But Jerusalem is still far away, and there may be many a battle between here and there.'

He stood waiting for an answer, but I was more confused than ever. I had not taken to this Crusade at all, and evidently he was revelling in its carnage.

'I do not want any … private time, not in here, and I would not encourage you to break your sacred vow,' I replied, looking up at the looming outline of the palace. 'Besides, this place does not appear very friendly. What's it like inside?'

'Ah, now you're in for a surprise. Wait until you see what awaits within.'

Richard seemed relieved to change the subject and continued in his praise of his newly won buildings. 'It is familiar architecture outside, but very Eastern inside; it might be new to your eyes, I expect. It's well furnished, I think. See if you like it.'

We were led through a high doorway into an amazingly high, vaulted hall, to be greeted by the captain of the guard.

'All prepared, Captain?' asked Richard.

'Indeed, Your Highness, as you desired.'

'Lead on.' Richard stepped off and we were expected to follow, but our attention had been captured by the enormity of the place. I strained my neck as I stared at the fine Norman stonework.

'Come, come, ladies. No time to tarry; look later.'

I looked to Richard; he was many paces ahead, and the captain was standing in a second archway, waiting with a grin.

'How many halls, Richard?' I almost shouted after him.

'Several. Come along, tardy queens.' He laughed.

The second arch led us into a further hall, but this one was full of men sitting at rows of tables. They all stood, and silence fell when Richard entered. He waited to take Joan and me by the arms, then led us along an aisle in the centre, towards a great table set up at the far end.

'These are my finest men, Berengaria. Their first task was to take Akko by storm, and by the Lord's grace they did it.'

'They did, my lord. That is certain.'

Collecting my thoughts, I remembered who I was and began to look back at the rows of men standing in front of their benches, examining us. I started waving and smiling. Joan spotted me and did the same. Alazne blushed, Pavot and Torène giggled, and Amynta and Eirini gaped at the assembly. The place was awash with male sweat and steely power — it was frightening.

The guard captain guided us to our places.

'You have prepared well, Captain, so soon after the capture,' said Richard. 'Will the meal be as well prepared?'

'I am assured by the cook, a Kurd, that he will be pleased to serve Your Highness, as well as any other. I understand that he is anxious to return to his family in Baghdad unharmed, one day. Here's the hall, Your Highness. We have prepared for your arrival, my queen.'

They had indeed gone to a lot of trouble, the space being laid out with tables and all the wall sconces filled by glittering candles. Sunlight filtered through the narrow windows, high up in the walls. It was a pretty sight, but one which bothered me a little.

'They have worked hard, Richard, amid such chaos as war has brought.'

'Ah, yes, but there is work still to be done. Those drapes will come down and be replaced with something more suitable.'

The walls were indeed covered in Islamic symbols: flags and tapestry-like drapes all over.

'We shall eat and you can see your new quarters afterwards, if you desire. My men are anxious to see you once more, and there may be other visitors.'

I was quite content to stay. At least I had my husband by my side.

I turned around to seek out Joan. She was leaning on a table, inspecting the hall. Catching my eye, she shrugged. I had the feeling that she was as impressed as me.

'Let us eat, Richard, if you please,' I said. 'We must appreciate the labours of your people.'

'*Our* people, my queen. They are our people now, yes, yes.'

I took my seat and the hall sat with me. I turned to see that our ladies had been conducted to a small table immediately behind us, where some squires were positioned — waiting on the king, no doubt.

Richard stood, and the hall fell silent once more. 'My good lords, my skilled commanders and captains, and bishops, victorious all.' Waving his arms, he introduced us, as if no one knew who we were. 'My queen, Berengaria, and my sister, Queen Joan of Sicily.'

We received a goodly applause and smiled gracefully. I was being drawn into this military triumph, even though I had reservations. I reminded myself that it was for God.

The food presented was sparse, but for a city so recently under siege we could expect little else. Probably most of it had come from Richard's supplies anyway.

The conversation was polite, the Bishop of Salisbury and Robert de Sablé being closest to me. It became noisier after the Cypriot wine made another appearance. I was wary of that devil: smooth in appearance, smooth in taste and loosening of the tongue.

Richard engaged with everyone around me — Joan, de Sablé, his bishops, commanders and captains — but he said little to me, apart from an occasional, 'Are you well, my queen?'

He grew restless as conversation became near impossible. Everyone was shouting out their experiences of the siege, fallen comrades were toasted with increasing frequency, and it all began to make little sense to us ladies, who had not been a part of this male-only event.

'Do you think we should retire, my queen? What, what?'

'They might be happier without ladies in the hall, my lord.'

'Good, good. We're off now!' he shouted at de Sablé.

'Don't blame you, Your Highness,' shouted Guy de Lusignan, who was sitting next to de Sablé and leering at me.

As we stood and went off through another great arch and up some steps, the chamber was drowned in a great cheer.

Once we were out of the hall, there were attendants standing at intervals up the three flights of steps, until Richard declared, 'Here, the royal quarters.'

He squeezed his bulk through a narrow doorway, of which there were several off a long corridor. I heard the squeals of Joan and the ladies as they clattered up behind us, but I was already fretting about the prospect of a coupling opportunity.

'There,' Richard proclaimed, indicating the chamber door. He threw back some curtains to reveal a chamber of sumptuous appearance.

It was all drapes, covers, cushions and oil-burning lamps. An enormous bed dominated the chamber, and it too was bedecked with gauze curtains and much decoration. There were two young women, wearing little and standing meekly in one corner with their heads bowed.

'Who are they?' I asked.

'I know not. They seem to come with the chamber,' said Richard. 'I wondered if you could use them. I don't know what else to do with them.'

'What language do they speak?'

'Arabic, I presume.'

'Joan!' I called. I could hear her further along the corridor.

'Berri?'

'Bring Eirini and Amynta in here. We might have found them a new task.'

Soon the chamber filled up with women. Somewhat taken aback, Richard kept quiet and watched.

I took Eirini by the hand and walked across to the Arabian women. I smiled and gently lifted their chins. 'You are familiar with the Arabic tongue, Eirini,' I said. 'See if they will tell you their names.'

'Yes, Your Highness, I will try.' Eirini spoke gently. She had been more expansive of late, but it did not take much for her to clam up, and this might be a good opportunity to help her in that regard.

'Alya,' replied one of the girls.

'Nabila,' said the other.

'How old are they?' I asked.

'Fourteen,' came the translated reply.

'Why are they here?'

The two looked at each other before replying, and when they did it brought a blush to Eirini's cheeks.

'Er, they say that they are here to keep the governor comforted at night.'

'Really? Tell them there'll be no more of that. Tell them I'll find a place for them in my household.'

That was more complicated to express. By the time Eirini had exhausted her Arabic, Richard had become restless again, but the girls were all smiling, Eirini included.

'Is that settled, then, Berengaria?' he said. 'You've added to your court?'

'I have, my lord,' I replied, beaming. 'They will be taken care of and introduced to our Christian ways.'

'Ah! Yes, I was going to ask about that. You and me, you know, husband and wife?'

'Oh dear, bedding arrangements?'

'Er, yes, that sort of thing.' He reddened and I gave him not an inch, staring back up at him. Whatever he expected, I was not his for the taking.

'I'd meant to talk about that when we were alone,' I ventured.

'Oh, no, I meant that I wanted to speak generally — about the vow. But it can wait. I've plenty to do, yes, yes. I'll leave you ladies to get on with it. I expect that you will want to tidy the place up and re-arrange everything.' He went to leave, but then something else occurred to him. 'If those two girls need husbands, I can probably find someone for them, what, what.'

'They'll be quite content for now, Richard. There's plenty of time for that sort of thing.'

'Right, I'm off. Ho, it is Hugo. He has found you, my queens.'

Richard went off as Hugo entered, smiling.

'Hugo!' we cried, and he was enveloped in queenly hugs. Now we band of adventurers were complete once more.

'Well,' he said, noticing the Arabian girls, 'who have we got here?'

'This is Alya, and this is Nabila; they are additions to our court,' I informed him, and Alya whispered to Nabila.

'What did she say, Eirini?'

'She wants to know if he is her new husband.'

I smiled. 'Tell them that only prospective husbands who meet their approval will be paraded for them.'

'Oh, thank you, Your Highness. Very kind, I'm sure,' added Hugo, somewhat relieved.

I grinned. I had worked out Hugo's preferences a long time ago.

'Hugo,' said Joan, 'if we are going to set up here, then we need all of our chests off whatever ships they are on. Do you know where everything is?'

'Yes, Your Highness,' he answered emphatically. 'I have a list and I can trace every last one of them. I'll go and arrange things now.'

'Berri,' said Joan as he left, 'come with me. I want to show you my bedchamber.'

Pavot moved as if to come with us, but she was stilled by a slight movement of Joan's hand, and we went out alone.

It was quite a nice chamber: not as large as mine, but well decorated in the Eastern style. After she had drawn the curtains, Joan held me at arm's length to look into my eyes.

'What was that about? Did he propose anything?'

My eyes dropped and I pulled her in close. 'He has made his priorities clear. I come second to his great game and, at times, I'm thinking that even God does not figure in his calculations. This business with the prisoners — what possesses the man to treat folk as negotiating assets? It distresses me, and I have little inclination to go to bed with such a man.'

'Oh, Berengaria, dear sister, what have we come to?'

I looked up into her eyes, which were filled with sadness. 'Sister?'

She grasped me tighter. 'That's what we are, sister queens, and that's how I feel about you. I share your disappointment. We are pawns in a king's game.'

'Then answer me this, sister. Did your mother know about Richard taking the vow of the cross at his coronation? Was she there?'

'She was there, but I went to Sicily in the year 1177. As Richard's coronation was twelve years later, I know not. Why do you ask?'

'Work it out, Joan. If Eleanor knew that he had taken the vow, then they both conspired to bring me here under false pretences. They knew there would not be a consummation — except that Richard arranged a dispensation in Cyprus. But then he missed his chance. Now we must wait until he has taken back Jerusalem, and we are a long way from that.'

A light dawned in her eyes, and then she looked embarrassed. 'I told you that we are a devious lot.'

'I'm going to face him and ask.'

'I counsel against that; it might not help things along. They are a breed apart, these kings; I've had enough of them too. But he is still my brother — so if you talk to him, would you keep me and my advice out of your discussions?'

'Of course.' I kissed her forehead. 'You know nothing. Let's return to our ladies. I want to find Hugo again.'

Hugo was still in a good mood after we had tracked him down in this labyrinthine building. Richard called it a palace, but the fact that it had suffered the building activities of European, Byzantine and Islamic architects showed through in its complexity.

Hugo was very busy, organising everyone, but I wanted his ear.

'I take it that you've sent for our chests?' I asked, and he nodded. 'Tell me, Hugo, what would keep the king from attending his ladies? What other business claims his time?'

'Ah, it is a sorry tale, Your Highness. You should all listen. The Austrians are going home and taking the few Germans with them, because Richard had Duke Leopold's banner taken down. And now King Philip wants to leave and has asked for Richard's agreement, but he wants the worth of half of Cyprus and Akko.'

'Why does he want to leave after this success?' asked Joan.

'He says that he is not well enough to be of any use, but Richard thinks he has no stomach for the campaign.'

'Keep going, Hugo,' I pressed. 'No point in keeping us in suspense.'

'Philip of France received an inheritance back home from Philip of Flanders, who died in the battle for Akko, and he is anxious to go back to secure his new holdings in Artois. But Richard believes that the relationship between himself and Philip is now so bad that he suspects Philip might try to dispossess him of some of his holdings back home while he remains here.'

'But does not my brother, John, rule in his stead?' asked Joan.

'That's something else that worries Richard: John,' answered Hugo with a sad smile.

'But Mother will care for Richard's possessions. She is well capable of that, surely,' retorted Joan.

'She is nearer eighty than seventy,' I reminded her.

'There is something else, Your Highnesses,' Hugo pressed on. 'King Philip needs Richard's agreement to leave or else he will be branded a coward, and that will upset the Pope. Not to mention that quite a few of Philip's men want to remain with Richard, and Richard says that Philip will need to fund them, because he will not.'

'And there is you, dear sweet Berengaria,' said Joan, taking my hands in hers.

'Me?'

'Yes, Your Highness,' said Hugo. 'Philip has not forgiven Richard for repudiating his sister, Alys, in favour of you.'

'Oh,' I replied. 'Well, at least I have a part in something.'

Joan tittered. 'Give him time, Berri. He is a bit occupied, after all. Where is the king now, Hugo?'

'He's gone to see Philip. Just as Richard holds the governor's palace, and the garrison commander, Mestoc, prisoner, Philip has as his main prisoner the governor, Kara-Kush. And he occupies one of the city strongholds, now held by the Knights Templar, who were part of the early siege.'

'What do you think will be the outcome, Hugo?'

'I think that Richard will extract as much as he can out of Philip, then let him go, and be glad to see the back of him. He has done little except moan about the campaign and his lascivious sister's fate, in spite of the splendid efforts of his lords, knights and barons.'

'What now?' I asked.

'You have much to arrange, Your Highnesses,' said Hugo. 'These young ladies and Amynta, for instance; what position are they to have? Which quarters? You have your bedchambers, but what else do you want in there? Where are the ladies Alazne, Pavot and Torène to be accommodated? All this can be decided while you await the return of the king.'

'Oh, yes, that requires little thought. Lady Alazne is to have the chamber next to mine. Joan's ladies should be as close to her as possible.' I looked at Eirini and the two Arabian girls. 'Joan?' I beckoned her over and took her into the corridor for a moment in private. 'Does that trio have the appearance of a princess and her maidens?'

'Oh, of course. I think it would be ideal. Where's Amynta?'

'She's in one of the smaller bedchambers, snoring,' said Alazne, who had followed us. 'She has found the excitement overwhelming.'

'Wake her. She now has three charges to care for. They are to be brought up as a princess and her companions. Then you can attend me; we have arrangements to make.'

'As you command, Your Highness,' said Alazne as she went about her duties.

Later that evening, there were only women sitting around the table in the hall that I had designated for ourselves. Hugo had fussed around all afternoon, but I'd listened to his excuses for the king not being there more than enough, so I asked him to cease and prepare the evening meal for what was now my court. I knew how such things should be arranged, for I had organised my father's court back in Olite.

I had Hugo rearrange the tables in the refectory hall so that we were separated a little from the men through the arch in the next hall. I noted that they had formed groups — captains, sergeants, bishops and priests — but it was well ordered and there were not too many there. Most had duties to perform, I suspected.

I was pleased with Eirini's increasingly positive attitude. She seemed to like the idea of being recognised as a princess, and the Arabian girls were no doubt relieved to avoid the fate of too many females as a consequence of war. It was a convivial evening until the noises coming from the courtyard announced the arrival of Richard. He seemed to have some guests with him.

'Berengaria, Joan — well organised, I see. Brought some fellows for you to meet. They're Frenchmen from Philip's camp, and they've decided that he is a waste of space and want to continue to win with me — good, good, eh?'

He moved behind me and planted a kiss on the top of my head. Joan received one too, and then so did our ladies. I watched him, wondering if he would dare to approach Eirini and Amynta, sitting at a separate table with the Arabian girls in attendance. I could not smell any wine on him, so I assumed that he was simply in one of his rare good moods.

'This is Hugh of Burgundy,' Richard boomed across the hall, gesturing towards one of the men. 'This is William des Barres, and here comes Eudes, Duke of Burgundy. Welcome, my friends. Come and meet my queen.'

The last in, and the youngest and most handsome, was Eudes. He caught my eye and came straight over.

'Queen Berengaria,' he exclaimed while claiming my hand and kissing it, 'how could we leave the Holy Land without meeting you? King Richard, you have here a desert orchid in a sea of sand. How delightful.'

'Well, you can hand her hand back. This is Hugh of Burgundy.' Richard guided the man forward while Eudes went after Joan's hand. 'Hugh is in command of those of the brave Frenchmen who have cast their lot in with me.'

'Indeed, Your Highness. Queen Berengaria, we will do better for your king than we might have been allowed to do for ours.'

'I'm sure, Lord Hugh. This is all something of a surprise. Forgive us if we are slow to understand all this, er, politicking.'

'Indeed, dear Berengaria. Mind us not,' said Richard. 'We are blowing in the winds of fate. Meet also William, a most respected ship's master who is joined to our cause.'

William, a middle-aged man, seemed to be cut from a gentler cloth, and he greeted me quietly. 'My honour, Your Highness.'

'Well, Hugo, is there anything to eat? See that these lords get a drink; we'll all sit and have some discourse.'

William plonked himself down next to me, which I was pleased about, but Joan got Eudes. He should have been paying attention to Richard and Hugh as they discussed army formations, or something equally arcane, but he preferred to nod at the right times while casting his eye over Joan. I wondered if Richard would notice.

'William, you are English?' I asked.

'Indeed, Your Highness, and probably too old for all these shenanigans, but I brought some Englishmen from my domain to help in the Lord's cause.'

'Then the Lord's blessings upon you. These halls are a surprise, are they not?'

'Indeed, Your Highness. I had not expected such magnificence outside Europe. Built after the First Crusade, I believe.'

'Yes, I find the vaults above quite fascinating. How do they do it?'

'They're very clever, the masons. I have been to many a grand church and a few cathedrals, and this rivals anything I have witnessed in England or France.'

'I'm looking forward to seeing the ceilings in daylight. The braziers and candles are playing tricks on my eyes.'

'Indeed, Your Highness. It will be good to see some sunlight outside too.'

We laughed, for the skies seemed determined to stay grey.

William was a family man and interested in my life back in Navarre, so we chatted for quite a while until, abruptly, Richard called an end to the proceedings and announced that we were to retire for the night.

I bade our guests a safe night and Richard held out a hand to guide me up to our quarters. Alazne followed us up and I sat on the bed while she began to attend to me. Then I stopped, looking at Richard.

'Ahem, Richard?' I knew not which way his wind was blowing.

He stood. 'Give me a hand with this surcoat and mail, Alazne,' he instructed. He sat on the bed and waited while Alazne unbuckled his surcoat and then the mail. 'Ah! What a relief,' he exclaimed. 'It is easier battering down walls than getting Philip to see sense.'

I looked at his back. 'You wear mail under your surcoat, Richard?'

'Don't trust anyone. The city is probably infested with assassins and the like. Two fellows are outside the door. They'll be there all night. God, I'm tired.'

He lay back on the bed, and long before Alazne finished with my hair he was asleep.

'Oh,' she said. 'You've lost him again. Should we wake him?'

I gazed at the sleeping form of the most powerful king in Christendom. An assassin would have no trouble here, and neither would I.

'Should we shuffle him under the covers?' asked Alazne.

'Do you think that we could move his bulk? Jesu, look at the size of him. Leave him there and help me out of this gown. I'll slip under the covers.'

'Oh, my queen.' Alazne kissed me on the forehead and left the chamber.

I lay awake for a long time, wondering what I was doing there, but finding no answer.

Richard and I were both awoken by a great clamour outside the chamber.

'God! What's doing?' Richard sat up, trying to make sense of the candlelit surroundings.

I too shuffled up. 'Good morning, my lord.'

'Jesu, Berengaria. Did I sleep here?'

'You did, all night.'

'Sorry, what? You should have woken me. What's that kerfuffle?'

'Your Highness?' a familiar voice called through the curtains — it was Mercadier, Richard's guardian.

'What's doing? Captain Mercadier, is it day yet?'

The bearded knight poked his head through the curtain. I pulled up the cover, realising that I was near naked, but it was still gloomy in the guttering candlelight.

'There is a host of petitioners waiting outside the hall, Your Highness. Some Frenchmen, some of your commanders, some envoys from Saladin; it might be a busy day when you begin it, Your Highness.'

'Mercadier, never mind them for now, what, what! Is there food?'

'Waiting here for you, Your Highness.'

'Send it in. Where's Hugo? I want a bath.'

Some squires burst in, propelled by Mercadier's foot. They dropped their trays onto a table and chair and then ran back out, trying not to see me.

Richard grabbed a chicken and tore at it while trying to down a goblet of red wine — he was up and at his usual speed. I abandoned the idea of a husband-and-wife conversation.

'There's a Roman bath off the palace yard, Your Highness,' Hugo informed him through the curtain.

'Good, good, let's go. Mercadier, tell the men I'll see them when I've scraped the filth of battle off my skin. Get them into some order, will you? I'll begin with the envoys from Saladin. Must go, Berengaria. See you later; we must talk, yes, yes.' He kissed my forehead.

The privy quarters of the palace went quiet when Richard departed, for a few moments, at least. Then the ladies, followed by Joan, slipped into the chamber. I sat up, letting Alazne plump the pillows, and then leaned back.

'Nothing?' asked Joan.

'Naught!' I replied.

'Does he not know what he's missing?' asked Alazne, eyeing me up as she dressed me.

'Behave, Alazne. Ah, well, let's find Father Francis and offer more prayers for the relief of Jerusalem.'

'There's another boring day coming up. Would you like something off one of those trays, Berri?' asked Joan kindly. 'We'll have breakfast in bed.'

'Don't take too long, Your Highnesses. I saw Father Francis hovering out there,' said Alazne.

'We should let him say a few prayers,' I said.

'If it will help my brother to bed his wife,' quipped Joan.

'Better not let the priest see those,' added Alazne, tying up my bodice.

CHAPTER FIVE

Richard went about his business, and wherever it was, it was not in the governor's palace of Akko. He did call in for a short while a couple of times, but we mostly occupied our time teaching French to Eirini and her new companions.

Then, one day at the end of July, Hugo came in with the news that Philip had indeed departed for France with his court, in galleys lent to him by Richard. Richard had despatched his own spies — including Roger of Howden, an English annalist he trusted to record events accurately — to watch Philip's doings whenever he got back home.

'The king has also extracted a lot of money from Philip to pay for the French troops remaining, and they've settled who should be King of Jerusalem,' Hugo added. 'Guy is to remain the king in name until he dies, then Conrad and Isabella will share the throne. They are all granted some domains hereabouts. Guy has been given the governorship of Cyprus in order to extract as much money from the island as possible; some he will repay to Robert de Sablé and some he will send to Richard to aid the Crusade.'

'Until he dies?' I asked.

'An assassin's charter,' laughed Joan.

'What else, Hugo?' I asked.

'Er, something that might upset you, Your Highnesses. The king has given Saladin a set period in which he has to release his Christian prisoners and pay the ransoms for those Saracens held here by Richard.'

'And what happens if the ransom is not forthcoming?'

'Who knows?' replied Hugo, although I suspected that he did know. I wouldn't press him on that point today, although I might return to it later. 'We have heard that all is not well in the camp of the Saracens. Saladin himself is not well…'

'Quite like my brother,' said Joan.

'Indeed, but Saladin is near sixty years of age, and some of his emirs seem to be eyeing the prospect of a dynasty change in the near future.'

'He is vulnerable?' I said hopefully.

'Indeed, Your Highness. The winds of fate blow in all directions. Let us hope they favour us.'

Within days Saladin had moved his men back from their confrontational positions, and Richard took to reinforcing the city defences, which left me feeling abandoned once more. He slept on top of the bed, went out at dawn and returned at night, and we exchanged nothing more than pleasantries.

'I never feel his hand upon me, Joan.' We sat on the edge of the bed, with Joan's arm encircling me.

'I know not what to say.'

'Has he ever mentioned me to you? What his intentions are?'

'No, although I have tried to get him to talk. He just diverts me in some manner, changes the subject or finds some new urgency.'

There was a cough outside the door.

'You are hovering, Hugo. What do you have for us today?' I asked.

He entered nervously. 'Highnesses, they have begun to dismantle the siege engines and load them back onto the ships. The king wants the fleet ready to sail within a week. I have not received any orders to prepare you to move. I'm sorry.'

'Where are they going?'

'Ashkelon, the port for Jerusalem,' he answered.

'Are we to remain here?'

'I believe so, Your Highness.'

'For how long?' demanded Joan.

Hugo's shoulders drooped and he didn't answer.

'Joan, Hugo has not been told; that I can see.'

The situation needed clarification, and scolding our precious messenger would not help.

'Go back to the king or grab the ear of de Sablé, or one of his lords or a bishop — there's plenty of them — and get us some proper information,' I urged. 'I'm not packing until I know what's what.'

'Typical of my brother, leaving us in the dark!' spat Joan. 'What are we doing here, Berri? We have no part in his plans. We may as well go home, wherever that may be.'

'You may be right, but going home may be too drastic a move. At least he is now heading towards the Holy City; if we hang on a little longer, we should be able to visit there. Think of it: the tomb of Jesu, the Holy Sepulchre — we can see them and all those other places mentioned in the Bible. Apart from that, I am the Queen of England; I have responsibilities.'

Joan gazed at me, and then with a sigh she stepped forward and enveloped me in her arms. 'Dear Berengaria, what would we do without your wisdom?' Looking over my head, she instructed Hugo, 'Heed our lovely queen, Hugo. Off you go; find out what our fate is to be.'

It was two days later that Hugo returned. We had not been left unguarded — that at least was comforting — and the palace was now a fortress, with a captain of the guard and sentries galore to protect us. But as busy as we made ourselves, we were kept in suspense by the lurking question: were we to remain here, or were we leaving with Richard?

Hugo brought the answer to us in the Islamic central garden, where we occupied ourselves tending the plants in the evening cool, much to the annoyance of the gardeners who had returned after things had settled down. The clatter of hooves on the paving warned of the approach of someone.

'Hugo's here!' shouted Alazne, she being the nearest to the entrance.

'Lady Alazne, where are the queens?' I heard Hugo asking.

'Over here, by the oleanders,' I called back.

Hugo dismounted to walk around the rills to attend us. 'Good evening, Your Highnesses. The king will be with you before long, but I can brief you before he arrives.'

'Thank you, Hugo,' I said. 'Sit here on this garden wall and tell. Alazne, see if you can find a cooling sherbet for him, please.'

'Well, it is as I feared. You are to remain here, but the reasons are complex, so if you will indulge me a little, Your Highnesses?'

'Don't we always?' said Joan.

'The king has removed all of his troops from the city. They are enjoying the, er, facilities inside too much.'

'You mean wine and women?' said Joan.

'Indeed. He has moved the army back into their camps outside the walls and allows no harlots there. Only aged washerwomen are allowed in to work.'

'How long will the men put up with that, I wonder? He has paid them, I suppose?'

'Yes, Your Highness. That is the problem: the vintners and harlots were queuing up to relieve the soldiers of their well-earned coin, and the king wants the army ready to move at the earliest opportunity.'

'What about Saladin? Do we know what he is doing, or plotting?' I had heard enough about the aged yet cunning sultan to know that he would not take the loss of Akko without responding.

'They have opened diplomatic channels, but Richard feels that Saladin is dragging things out, so he has threatened the lives of the prisoners held here in the city.'

'Threatened?' asked Joan.

'Yes, the king has given Saladin an ultimatum: pay the ransoms, or he will execute the prisoners.'

A shiver ran down my back. This was unbelievable: a Christian king using lives as bargaining pieces? These were not soldiers; these were the common folk who lived their lives as their masters decreed and had little choice in the matter.

'I like this not, Joan. When will the king be here, Hugo?'

'As to that, Your Highness, he is expected soon, but we must await him. He is beset with problems. It would appear that most of the other leaders have now accepted him as the *de facto* leader, and he is expected to provide answers for all their ills.'

'I see,' said Joan. 'We might have moved down the list of Richard's priorities, Berri; we shall await his appearance with impatience. Go and get some rest, Hugo.'

'Your Highness, thank you.'

As we sat at the table in the hall after the evening meal, having squeezed every last morsel of information out of poor Hugo, our ears were assailed by the arrival of Richard in a jolly mood.

'Who's been put to the sword today, I wonder?' I whispered to Joan.

She shrugged. 'We'll soon find out.'

Richard filled the hall together with his closest commanders, including the ever-present Mercadier at his back. The noise levels increased, and all of a sudden I felt very small and threatened by all the metal, swords and male aggression. Our moods changed in an instant: I felt vulnerable, and annoyed because of that.

'My queens, I've just come to say goodbye; going to get off to Jerusalem. You stay safe here. It's for the best — there's no room on the war galleys for passengers.'

'You're leaving for Jerusalem, my lord? Sailing?' I asked, unsettled by his bluster.

'Marching the army along the shore. The fleet will escort us offshore and carry our supplies. Always ready for an attack, unencumbered by supplies, see.'

'I see,' said Joan. 'And what about these prisoners? We've heard rumours.'

'Prisoners, yes. We're going to line them up along the defensive trenches, you know — we'll let Saladin see them and push him to come up with the ransom money. Anyway, must dash, yes. I'll send for you when we reach Jerusalem.'

He planted a kiss on the tops of our heads, then disappeared out of the hall. Once more, there was a silence.

'That went well, Your Highness.' Alazne's voice broke into my thoughts.

'Yes,' added Joan, annoyed. 'How did we let him get away with that?'

'Richard does what he wishes ... and we have no say in the matter. Hugo, where will you go?'

'I'm staying with you, Your Highnesses — if you want me. I've no instructions to the contrary.'

'Well, Hugo, you are now appointed treasurer to the queen's household. Consider yourself fortunate,' Joan said, saddling him with an additional duty.

'Your Highnesses, I consider myself fortunate to serve such dignified mistresses. Thank you. One prays that I'll also avoid a Saracen blade.'

'As do we all, my good man.' I smiled and felt more comfortable knowing that he would indeed take the best care of us.

'If you please, Your Highness, I'll go and see what troops the king is leaving behind to guard the city and what I can wheedle out of Captain Mercadier for your personal protection.'

'I hadn't thought ahead that far — good idea. And find Father Francis; we could do with some spiritual support here. Where does he spend his time, I wonder?'

'He is often alone on the battlements, Your Highness — talking to God, I imagine — and if not, then he's in the kitchen, talking to the cook.'

I suddenly realised that we would be isolated in a sea of sand and hostile Saracens — what a confusing day this had turned out to be. And behind it all was the whirlwind of my husband; no wonder the Saracens had fallen before him. Richard would not be denied by anyone.

Since we had met in Italy, Richard had bested Philip of France in all the skirmishes the two had engaged in. At Messina, he had repudiated Philip's sister, Alys; he had taken Cyprus for his own and refused Philip any benefit from that; he had taken over the siege of Akko and settled that matter within days; he had a sickly Saladin at an impasse; and he had gladly received those senior dukes and other lords, formerly part of Philip's army, and welcomed them as his own. All in all, the French king must have been feeling severely bruised by his dealings with the Lionheart King of England as he skulked back to France.

It was time for our evening walk.

'So now what, Your Highness?' asked Alazne as we wandered along one of Akko's sea walls, finding Father Francis already up there in conversation with God.

'There is to be a meeting in the morning,' the priest told us unhappily. 'Richard's envoys will meet with Saladin's to settle terms for the prisoner exchanges before he sets off for the Holy City.'

'Oh,' replied Alazne, 'I had not heard that. What terms?'

'Hugo related them to us,' I said. 'You and Pavot were nowhere to be found. This palace is quite big; it is easy to lose track of someone.'

Joan cast me a knowing glance before explaining further. 'Saladin has offered a piece of Christ's cross, all his Christian prisoners, and a ransom of two hundred thousand dinars in return for all of Richard's Saracen prisoners. Tomorrow our envoys are to go to Saladin's camp and witness the cross, to see if they believe it to be genuine.'

'The king must be satisfied that all will be well if he is planning to march to Jerusalem,' said Alazne.

Hugo found us and joined us on the wall. 'It is a little premature, Your Highnesses, but the king has been bridling at the delay which Saladin has wrought. He set himself a target to leave here two days ago.'

'Hugo, what news?' I asked.

'Philip has left. He says that he has taken enough insults and is going back to France. Richard is now the supreme Crusade commander.'

'I expect that will keep him content, Hugo,' I replied.

'It might have, except there is a problem. Philip has gone to Tyre, taking half of the hostages, and he won't release them to

Richard to hand back to Saladin until he has received half of the ransom.'

'He doesn't trust my brother?' exclaimed Joan.

'They do not trust each other, but if Saladin doesn't get all of his people back, the deal will sink into the sands.'

That disclosure was met with silence, broken only by the cry of seabirds and the distant sounds of an army preparing to go on the march.

'It seems that this will be our home for a while yet,' said Joan. 'We should make ourselves comfortable, ladies.'

'I'll be comfortable when the matter of the hostages is settled. I have a dreadful feeling that something horrible might happen,' I said. 'Oh, Joan, we are here for the love of God, not the hatred of the unenlightened.'

At that remark, Father Francis returned from his heavenly tryst and remarked, 'I see dark clouds, evil deeds; no good will come of this episode. Indeed, I see it as the ruin of all we have come here to seek: salvation, and the release of the Holy City. If ill will takes the stage, then no man will prosper and no venture will succeed.'

I had taken a liking to the gardens. The gardeners, realising that I was no threat, but eager to learn, had dropped their suspicious attitudes and now were learning to communicate with me. I was learning Arabic and teaching them Navarrese, something which would be of doubtful value if ever I was to leave this place.

'You enjoy being covered in soil and worms, and suchlike.' Joan was in the garden, sitting in the shade, drinking sherbets and cool water and being fanned by Alya and Nabila.

'It's vastly more rewarding than cultivating a marriage,' I said.

'Perhaps, although those two seem to be getting nearer than we are.'

I looked across the plant beds and between the spiky boles of the date palms to where Alazne and Pavot were lying in the shade, on two truckle beds. They were holding hands.

'They become closer by the day. Are you going to say anything, Joan?'

'I don't think so. I'm just envious. Are you?'

'A little. But I had prepared myself for the knowledge of a man — evidently not a desire shared.'

'No. What will you do?'

'Wait until Richard has Jerusalem in his grasp. Is there another path?'

'Not one that I am contemplating, Berri. I'll wait as long as you, then ... who knows?'

'Here comes Hugo; we might find out where Richard is today.'

Hugo had the appearance of a man suffering from some disappointment. I did not expect to hear of anything that would cheer me.

'Your Highnesses,' he said, obviously wondering where to begin.

'Just give us your news, Hugo,' commanded Joan. 'It is too hot to play games.'

'Very well, Your Highness. Philip has now fled. He left the hostages he was holding in the care of Hugh of Burgundy at Tyre, only twenty-five miles back along the coast to the north. But Hugh has refused to transfer them to Richard until he receives Philip's share of the ransom, and Saladin has refused to hand over any Christian prisoners as a result.'

'Men! Stupid men!' spat Alazne, and I couldn't disagree with her.

'What is Richard minded to do, Hugo?' I asked.

'He has already sent an envoy to Hugh with a short message: "Bring the hostages to me, or I will come and collect them".'

Joan tittered. 'That should beget a result.'

'It should, and any more delays will have unfortunate consequences. Richard's ships are loaded and ready to set off; it will not aid his temper if this drags on for much longer.'

'How long has Burgundy got?' asked Joan.

'Today is the fifteenth of August. Richard will wait another few days, but we hear that Saladin is having similar problems. His emirs are becoming restless with the endless demands for men and money that the Saracen leader is placing upon them; all is not well in their camp.'

This was interesting. 'If the leaders lose control or support, will this Crusade fade from the face of the earth, Hugo?' I asked.

'An interesting conjecture, Your Highness, but not one I would place much faith in if you are thinking of going home.'

'No,' added Joan, 'Richard will have the Holy City, despite any difficulties that he is having, and I do not expect the Saracens to loosen their grasp upon it. Saladin may well withdraw all his men from our sight and gather them together in defence of the walls of Jerusalem.'

'This is dangerous, Joan,' I said after some thought. 'There is instability in the air; anything could happen.'

Two days later, in the late afternoon, we watched from the walls as Hugh of Burgundy led Philip's hostages back within the confines of Akko's walls.

My patience was thin, and Richard never came near us for more than a few minutes at a time; he spent all his time with his commanders or doing the rounds of the ships and the troops left ashore to cheer them up.

'We don't know whether to pack or not, Your Highness, whether we're staying or going,' said Alazne irritably. 'And those poor wretches down in that hostage compound? Dying in the sun, they are. The king won't have any left to sacrifice if there's not a decision soon.'

I agreed. My feelings were certainly more Christian than my husband's. 'I know. They are all souls who could be saved; it is not fitting to keep them thus.'

'Shall we go and see the bishops, Berri? They will listen to two queens, surely?' Joan was also unhappy with the situation.

'I agree. Where's Hugo? We'll get him to arrange an escort to go and seek the ear of charity for those lost souls.'

Hugo's face was apprehensive when we explained what we intended. He stood before us in our receiving chamber, a room we had found during our explorations of the palace. It had been the receiving chamber of the previous governor, who now languished in chains somewhere within the city walls.

'Are you sure, Your Highnesses?' he asked tentatively. 'The bishops might view the intervention of women, queens though you are, as unwelcome.'

'They might,' I said bridling, 'but then we will find out for ourselves, won't we, Joan?'

'Yes, Hugo. Please don't answer for them; they can answer us directly,' agreed Joan, with some ill temper.

Hugo, realising that he had gone as far as he could, merely bowed and shuffled his way out of the room.

He reappeared later in the day with Father Francis by his side, seemingly as some kind of reinforcement. He let Francis stand to the fore, bowing to his superior position. Joan and I were engaged in our daily language class with Eirini, Amynta, Alya and Nabila, so I dismissed them.

'We'll resume this evening when it is cooler.'

Joan went on the offensive, having arrived at the same supposition as myself. 'Is this an escort or a delegation of refusal, Father?'

After a series of throat-clearing exercises, Joan's confessor confirmed the latter. 'May I know more about your proposal, Your Highness?' he began.

'More, Father Francis? What more do you wish to know? The fate of those poor wretches languishing in that compound — chained! — is obvious to see. How can a Christian witness such cruelty?'

'But they are committed heretics, by the grace of God. They will be martyrs to their beliefs and God will deal with them in his wisdom.'

'But you know not what is in their hearts, Father, nor how many would gladly accept the true cross.'

'They have been examined, I believe. The matter is decided.'

'And what if their fate decides the fate of Christians captured by Saladin?' demanded Joan.

'I cannot prophesy, Your Highness, but I'm certain that they would be received directly into heaven if they lost their corporeal lives here in God's Holy Land. The bishops will not hear you gladly, and may even question your own piety. I counsel against making your feelings plain in this matter, Your Highness.'

'Is this the wisdom you were seeking upon the battlements, Father? I thought you were seeking an honourable solution.' I was riled up now.

'I have had guidance on the matter, Your Highness; it is not for you to question the wisdom of God or His Church on earth, if you will forgive me for saying so.'

'It will not be my forgiveness you or the Church will need, Father, if you have gauged this wrong.'

I gazed at Joan, for she was clearly equally bemused. She bowed to her confessor and smiled gracefully, thanking him. Father Francis took the opportunity to scuttle out of the chamber and disappear from view. Hugo was left shaking his head while we stood in stunned silence.

'Did we leave Christian mercy, forgiveness and understanding on the shores of Cyprus?' I demanded.

'It may reside in Aquitaine,' responded Joan, 'for it certainly does not lie here in these bloody sands.'

We embraced in distress.

'I intend to discuss this further with Francis. I'm not sure that I want him as my confessor, knowing his views,' said Joan.

'And I intend to find out how much of this is under the direction of Richard,' I replied, 'for I truly do not know the man nor how much his obsession blinds his heart.'

The teaching of languages, some stitching and sewing, and the exploration of our different cultures took up our time for the next few days. But knowing about the horrors of the world outside made the atmosphere strained and uncomfortable.

Richard graced us with his presence a couple of times, but there was no place for a serious conversation. I grew weary of his visits.

The following week, on the twenty-seventh day of *Rajab*, a month during which battles were forbidden by the Islamic faith — or the twentieth day of August according to our calendar, during which they were not — the looming storm broke.

I heard a man puffing his way up the stairs. I was hardly dressed, and Alazne was the first to identify our early morning visitor.

'That's our dear Hugo. I can tell; he grunts at each step. Should I let him in, Your Highness?'

'He might be heading for Queen Joan's quarters. How's Pavot? Are you getting on well together?'

'We're fine. I pray for you, though. It isn't fair to come all this way and be ignored.'

'I know, but I chose my path. Perhaps I have too much curiosity.'

Hugo called outside Joan's quarters and we heard Pavot bid him enter. A short time later, Joan was shouting for us to cross the corridor and join her.

'They're marching the hostages out of the city in chains, Berri.'

'The wall — let's to the wall,' I responded immediately. I dressed hurriedly and dashed down the steps and out of the citadel, towards the city gates.

That caused some chaos, and the captain of the guard protested as we ran through the palace gates into the city. I held up the skirt of my gown, as did the others, and soon we came to a stream of bedraggled men, women and children. They included traders, artisans and some soldiers who had survived injury, and they were all chained together and heading for the city gates.

Soon the captain of the guard noticed me and tried to get us to leave.

'I'm going to the gates,' I insisted. 'I want to witness this.'

'The king will have my head off, Your Highness,' he said pleadingly.

'I'll deal with the king. Just get us on top of the gates.'

There were cries from the line of captives. Some were pleading, and others, from the tones of their voices, were cursing us as we ran into the shelter of the gatehouse.

'Jesu! Sergeant!' the captain called up to the battlement, his chest heaving with anxiety. I cared not; I wanted to see what Richard was going to do next with this human chain of misery.

'My God!' cried Joan as she lined up next to me. Our ladies, Eirini, Amynta, Alya and Nabila joined us.

Beyond the city walls stood a line of soldiers, lined up along the defensive ditches. They were facing a similar line of Saladin's troops on the other side of the ditches — a direct challenge. They were close enough to be able to spit on each other. Our troops were strengthened moment by moment as more of Richard's men poured off the ships in the harbour, joining the line to face the Saracen army.

Then, through the gate beneath our feet, the stream of wretched humanity tripped and stumbled its way towards the trenches of the Crusaders, where they were forced onto their knees and made to stay still.

'This is hopeful,' cried Joan. 'They are going to be handed over.'

'No, Your Highness, they are not.' Hugo had caught up with us. Panting, he shouted out, 'There has been a report in the camp that Saladin has beheaded all his Christian prisoners! This is Richard's response.'

A shiver ran down my back and my stomach churned. This was no prisoner exchange; this was retribution. 'Joan, he can't! In God's name, he mustn't. Where is he?'

I managed to scream out my protest, but the king, now visible behind his troops and in front of the hostages, sat proudly on his great destrier as he surveyed his design. He did not hear me.

There was shouting from the ditches. The Saracens were attacking, anxious to take back their people, but nowhere did they succeed in crossing the obstacle to break our lines. They were met by a hail of arrows and retreated, helpless and watching, as their compatriots continued to trudge through the gate and line up along the length of the ditches.

It took some time, but eventually there were no more treading that inglorious path, and silence fell as we waited in anticipation of Richard's next command.

There was no movement from the distant hills, where Saladin's banners flew, silhouetted against the horizon. No envoys, no messengers, and no pleas for mercy came from that direction. Then howls of anger came from the Saracen soldiers, now at a safe distance from our men's arrows.

'As I said earlier, Your Highnesses,' declared Alazne, 'the madness of men is on display in this arena today. God rot their souls.'

'The Saracens are manoeuvring for another attack, but Richard's archers remain lined up,' Hugo told us. 'They will see off those Saracens if they try to cross the ditches.'

It happened as he predicted. Whatever force Saladin hurled at the steadfast lines, neither infantry nor cavalry could come near our troops, for the sky turned black with their arrows. The Saracens were soon recalled, leaving the miserable hostages lined up to await their fate.

'They're splitting them into groups now,' observed Joan miserably.

'They are in groups of ten,' said Hugo. 'There are hundreds of them, and tens makes them easy to count.'

And so the citizens of Akko were arranged in lines, hundreds of paces long, still kneeling in their groups. There were three such rows, with a sergeant standing to the front, centre and back of each group, and another at the end of each of the rows.

Richard spurred his steed to take a position in the front of this display, and his signallers waved flags, probably to attract the attention of the centre of Saladin's lines, where presumably he was sitting on a horse.

When the flag-waving received no response, Richard dragged harshly on his steed's mouth and returned to the rear of his formation.

'He is angry,' remarked Hugo. 'I can tell; I've seen his actions before today. May God have mercy on their souls.'

'Have you finished counting, Hugo?' I asked, feeling numb.

'Not quite, Your Highness, but I reached three thousand.'

'Jesu!' cried Joan, wiping her eyes. The ladies clung to each other and I began to tremble. Joan put an arm about my shoulders, and we watched and prayed.

Richard held up an arm and his signallers raised their flags. We heard the sergeants shout, and the line of soldiers nearest to us turned away from the enemy to face the hostages. Swords drawn, they gazed into the faces of the kneeling doomed, waiting for the next command.

Richard dropped his arm, the signallers dropped their flags, and the slaughter began.

First a few heads dropped onto the sands. Then, as they realised what was going on, the remaining hostages tried to get up off their knees, but since they were restrained by their chains, it became a melee of the desperate.

Instead of cleanly beheading, the soldiers began to hack them to pieces, and their screams could be heard across the desert.

It did not take long before an unearthly silence spread across the land. The sands were stained red as they sucked up the blood of mankind. It did not recognise religion, only the cruelty of man upon man.

Joan and I clung desperately together, wanting to cast our eyes down in shame, but they were drawn back to this vision of hell before us.

Then there came a new noise: a rising tumult of howls and screeches from the Saracen army. Whatever discipline Saladin kept over his troops had disintegrated into a headlong dash towards the Christian lines as desperately angry warriors hurled themselves into the valley of death and onto Christian swords, spears and arrows.

This was the price of Richard's cruelty; many more were to die because of his anger and obsession.

'Jesu!' I shouted. 'If that monster thinks that I will carry a son for him, then he will wait until death, when God's revenge shall reach him.'

'Berengaria!' exclaimed Joan, shocked, but she could find no words to gainsay mine. We watched miserably as the chaos of battle unfolded before our eyes.

The sound of Hugo's sobbing reached my ears. Father Francis was on his knees, his eyes focused on the ground in front of him.

'Come,' said Joan, 'let us away from this shambles. We need Father Francis to lead us in prayer. We may all meet a Saracen sword before this day ends.'

But Father Francis heeded us not, so lost in his own miserable world was he, and we left him there.

'Is that the wisdom of Mother Church?' demanded Joan, shouting at the top of the kneeling priest's head as she passed him by. 'It has ensured the death of many by its wisdom. Pray on, Father, pray on.'

She stomped away down the steps. Father Francis lifted his head as she left, and I saw the tears in his eyes. I prayed for an end to this hatred. How could harmless folk be used as bargaining pieces in this game of faiths?

CHAPTER SIX

Next morning it was dark when we emerged from the tiny chamber we had designated as a chapel. An eerie silence hung over the palace, but we were still safe, still with our heads upon our shoulders. Richard's army had prevailed.

Father Francis had clearly been awake all night, reading some passages from the Bible, mostly about striking down God's enemies. I had seen enough of that yesterday. We left him on his knees, and Hugo joined us at the palace door.

'I have arranged for some food from your kitchen, Your Highness. We will have it set out in the refectory hall, if you wish.'

'I'm not sure that I want anything,' said Joan, 'but we'll sit a while. We ladies will all sit together, Hugo, if you will join us, please. We'll need to support each other, I fear.'

'Where is the king?' I asked.

'He is on the beach, organising his departure, Your Highness.'

'Organising his departure?' sniffed Joan. 'Why is he not organising the saving of his soul, or the welfare of his wife and sister? He would be better rewarded.'

'He'll receive no rewards from me,' I retorted.

'The king seems to have cleared his mind of the events of yesterday, Your Highnesses, and is full of purpose renewed,' said Hugo. 'He has caused the tents of harlots and wine-sellers to be thrown onto a fire, and they are sent on their way. He has set up a new military camp on the beach, and the soldiers are confined there until they march out. They will go to Ashkelon, Your Highness, and everything betwixt here and there will be swept to one side. His Highness considers yesterday's victory over Saladin to be a signal from God to get on with the task.'

'What victory? I saw no victory,' said Alazne tearfully.

'After the massacre, Lady Alazne, there were many more Saracen lives lost in the trenches. They assaulted our lines in vain and at great cost.'

'And my husband considers that a great day's work?' I demanded.

'Indeed, Your Highness, indeed — as does the Church.'

A new voice entered the conversation as Father Francis approached. The atmosphere cooled as the priest stood at the edge of the table. He was not invited to join us. He became aware of the hostility and had a sudden recollection.

'I should attend the bishops now, Your Highnesses. They are to brief the priests as to their duties during the great march, so I have no time to join you. Perhaps I will later in the week when the king has departed, if you please, Your Highnesses.'

'Indeed,' replied Joan, turning her face away.

The twenty-second day of August dawned inauspiciously, with me in my bed alone, awakened by our ladies toing and froing along the corridor. We had a wash-chamber at the end, next to the *komuna*. It was very convenient and busy in the mornings. Joan and I had forbidden the presence of men up here, apart from Hugo, who was no threat.

It was not until we had progressed down to the refectory hall for breakfast that things became interesting.

Settled with a selection of fruits, eggs and bread, I was ready to eat when I heard the clatter of hooves echoing through the great halls.

A sergeant called from the outermost doorway that led into the courtyard gardens. 'The king! King Richard is here.'

I looked at Joan, and she picked up a piece of bread and hacked off a lump of cheese. I helped myself to a delicious-looking fig and waited.

Richard ploughed into the hall like a ship in full sail battering its way through the waves. 'My queens!' he shouted. 'My breakfast, I spy.'

He sat down, edging Pavot and Alazne along the bench, not seeming to notice that we were eating together with our companion ladies.

'I'm not stopping — got all that nonsense sorted, yes, yes. Saladin has backed off; now I'm going to Ashkelon to secure a harbour before going to Jerusalem. No more obstacles. I'll get the job done, yes.'

Joan raised her eyes. 'You remember me, Richard? Joan, Queen of Sicily?'

'Yes, yes, what's wrong?' he asked suspiciously.

'Nothing much, apart from ungodly slaughter. And this is your queen, Berengaria.'

'Ah, of course. Did you witness the despatch of the ungodly, now you mention it, Joan?'

'*I* did,' I said with great hostility.

'You shouldn't have done, no. It was not for female eyes.'

He ate ravenously, seemingly impervious to our cold reception, and was soon finished to his satisfaction. No more conversation was offered as we sat quietly, waiting for him to try. I thought that it was up to him to say something about his actions, but naught came until he stood up abruptly.

'Hugo taking care of you, yes? I'll be off — going to march along the shore. Can't take you, oh no. You follow later. I'll send for you when it is safe, yes?'

He came around the table and planted kisses upon mine and Joan's heads. Then he ran his eyes up and down Eirini, Alya and Nabila, and without further ado, he stomped back out into the courtyard, calling out to his lords as he departed.

Hugo broke the silence. 'Saladin and his army have disappeared, but the king has left a guard. I'll introduce the commander later. Perhaps when you have finished eating, Your Highnesses?'

'Fine, fine,' replied Joan. 'I'm not hungry anymore.'

'Nor I. Let's go up onto the sea wall and watch the army leave,' I said.

'I expect that we'll find Father Francis up there,' said Joan.

'Yes, he has stopped communing with us very much; he seems to have found God up there.'

'I think that the bishops have strengthened Father Francis's resolve; he was seen on the beach, on his knees, with two bishops waving their arms at him.'

'We'll see,' said Joan.

As we puffed up the steep steps to the battlement, Joan continued to interrogate poor Hugo.

'Tell us what Richard has in mind, Hugo, because he seems unwilling to share it with his wife or sister.'

As we reached the top, she gazed from the battlement along the beach, taking in the view of an army preparing to march off. The sight of Father Francis on his knees once more had reignited the flame of her ire.

'Perhaps I can explain, Your Highness.' A kindly voice came from behind.

'Ah, Stephen of Turnham,' said Hugo. 'Welcome, Lord Stephen.'

'Their Highnesses seem surprised to see me again. Hugo, have you not explained?' Stephen asked, smiling politely.

'I was not certain that you would come up here, Lord Stephen.'

'Queen Joan, Queen Berengaria, I am one of His Grace's advisors, the elder brother of Robert, who you are aware holds Cyprus at the moment. Now I am your new garrison commander, temporary Castellan of Akko and Keeper of the City, and most importantly, I am responsible for your safety during the king's absence, together with those two knights yonder.' He waved an arm in the direction of two men standing at a respectful distance. 'They are Guy de Bernez and Stephen Longchamp, son of Hugh.'

'Oh, we wondered who would receive that onerous task,' said Joan, seemingly unimpressed.

'Onerous, Your Highness? I consider it a privilege, but if you consider me unsuitable I will find you someone else.'

'Forgive Queen Joan,' I interjected. I was not going to dismiss the man without some examination. We had not had much of a conversation, and Joan's temper might lose us an honourable guardian. 'She remains upset from the events of late, as do I. We will be happy if you could care for us, and the city.' I was assessing him. He was of middling age and clearly a soldier, but of a pleasing countenance, and he limped a little. I thought him suitable — if he didn't need to run around much. 'Are you injured, Stephen?'

'A minor blow. I'm not comfortable on a horse, but I'll recover.'

'Then join us. We'll pray for your recovery.'

'Thank you, my queen. I will do my best not to annoy you, Queen Joan.'

'I'm sorry, I should not chide you for my brother's doings.' She held out a hand and he took it as an offering of peace.

'Tell me, Your Highnesses, who are these gracious ladies? They are too lovely to remain in the shadows, I believe.'

Alazne, Pavot and Torène stepped forward, and I waved at Amynta to bring forth Eirini, Alya and Nabila.

Our tending ladies curtsied as expected, but when I brought forward Eirini, Stephen said a rather peculiar thing.

'The Byzantine princess; how delightful. No wonder Richard prattles on so much about her.'

He held out a hand to take hers and brushed his lips upon it, his eyes not leaving her face.

I looked at Joan, and she indicated that we would discuss Richard and Eirini later, in private.

'Bring your knights over. I would meet my guardians,' I said, looking at the pair shuffling about uncertainly.

'Of course, Your Highness.' Stephen indicated and the pair came over, bowing and making polite noises.

I asked what their duties involved, and to our relief they did not include standing at the bottom of our beds, but rather standing at the main gates, or beside us if we ventured out. They were happy to be dismissed by Stephen and moved away as soon as they could.

Stephen stood up to the crenels and pointed to the ships in the harbour.

'See, Your Highnesses, as Richard and the army march along the shoreline, they will be shadowed by the fleet, so there's no need for foraging in a countryside laid bare. Our scouts report that Saladin and his army are marching along the same shore, destroying or seizing such food supplies as Richard might have made use of. Richard will be re-supplied by sea; all his supplies will travel safely offshore.'

'What about us, Stephen? Are we to be abandoned here?' asked Joan.

'Indeed not, as this will be a central supply point between Cyprus and the army. There will always be ships in the harbour to maintain communications, and to re-supply the army, wherever Richard may be.'

'And to help us escape if needed,' I added hopefully. 'So, he is headed for Ashkelon — the main port nearest Jerusalem?'

'Quite, but there are many places in between, and they must be secured as the army moves along the coast.'

'They are off to shed more innocent blood?' demanded Alazne.

'Ah, yes. That's how wars are. See how they are ordered,' said Stephen. 'The men-at-arms are in lines closest to the land. Alongside them march the archers and crossbowmen, while nearest the sea are the cavalry and the baggage wagons.'

'Why is it so? I thought that the cavalry was the most dangerous to the enemy?' said Joan.

'It is in response to the nature of the Saracen cavalry that Saladin deploys. They ride loosely and fire arrows from horseback, so it is difficult for our heavy cavalry to get to grips with them face to face, whereas head on, our horsemen will ride straight over them without hindrance.'

'So the infantry are protecting the horsemen, Stephen?' I had begun to see the sense in it.

'Indeed. The Saracens cannot get to grips with the men-at-arms because of the arrows of our archers, and if they do they will be faced by a wall of shields and spears. It all makes perfect sense and shows how great a general Richard is.'

'Then why bring the cavalry, Stephen?' Joan asked.

'Richard's aim is to find a place to tempt them into battle. It is a principle of all good generals to seek battle in a place of his own choosing.'

'And if they are not tempted?' I asked.

'In that case, Your Highness, Richard and his army will march unhindered and reach their destination without harm.'

'So Richard has the best of it, whichever way it goes,' said Joan.

'I see,' I said. 'Cruel but clever — a difficult combination to beat, Stephen?'

'We are not here to make friends, Your Highness. We are here to wrest the Holy City from the grasp of the ungodly.'

'That remark places a different emphasis on things, I suppose, but why could not the cruelty be confined to the belligerents, the armed men? Why civilians?'

'The ungodly, the unshriven, the doomed to lasting fire,' wailed our unsettled priest.

Stephen inspected Father Francis, who seemed disturbed.

'Are peaceful citizens always victims of war, Stephen?' I asked, with little hope of a satisfying answer.

'Indeed, Your Highness. It was always so, and I cannot see it changing much. The passage of war rolls onward without much consideration of ordinary mortals.'

'The ships are moving now, Your Highness.' Pavot called our attention to the harbour.

'You say there will be vessels left behind for communication, Stephen?' said Joan.

'Indeed, Your Highness. It is about one hundred miles to Ashkelon, but fast galleys will ply between us and the king all the way. We control the sea, and there is no one to gainsay that.'

'If Richard thinks I am going to write to him, he can think again,' I muttered.

'Tell me, Stephen,' said Joan, 'why did you take this task?'

'I thought it would be a nice change to stay still for a while. My knee has gone awry; I do not fancy riding one hundred miles, and I'd be a hindrance. And the prospect of your company helped me accept the king's request without hesitation.'

'And you intend to go to Jerusalem?'

'Yes, with you by sea, when Richard has it safe and he calls for us to join him.'

I gazed into the distance as the last sail disappeared over the horizon and the cloud of dust denoting the marching army settled back onto the earth. We were women alone, once more.

'What if Saladin decides to re-take the city, Stephen?' No one else had mentioned it, so I thought that I should.

'The king knows that Saladin has decided to precede him and is likely to seek a place of battle before our Crusaders ever reach Jerusalem. Selecting the place is also Saladin's first priority. The king has left me sufficient soldiers and some artisans; we have some fast galleys, there are caretaker crews on the captured ships, and I have some money. Our means of escape, perhaps back to Cyprus, are secured. The city gates are near fixed, and I will direct further repairs to the walls in quick time. And, of course, we have Bernez and Longchamp to guard your persons, and twelve men-at-arms to guard mine.'

'Something has occurred to me, Stephen,' said Joan. 'Who is left in the city with all the fit young men slaughtered?'

He looked at Joan with sad eyes. 'Women, children and old men, Your Highness, who were better hidden away than most, fortunate souls.'

The palace was eerily quiet that evening. When we left the mumbling priest on the walls, the beach was deserted. The only movement was on the water, where the few remaining ships were anchored. It seemed as if the women of the city, now without their young men to guard them, would not venture out.

I had a thought. 'Tomorrow, Joan, we must bring life back into this city. We must get it organised — fed, at least — and then see about making it a place fit to live in once more.'

'I suppose that will be more interesting than sitting sewing until my brother decides to send for us. I'll help. What do we need to do? You have managed a palace before, and I had dozens of factotums to scuttle about, organising things. Tell me what needs doing.'

'First, Alazne, go and find Hugo and Stephen. Torène, get Father Francis in here. Pavot, take Eirini, Amynta, Alya and Nabila and shout around the city that all women are to come to the courtyard in the morning.'

As I lay in bed that night, I was adding to the initial lists that Hugo had scribbled down that evening. It had taken him a while to root out the means of writing, but once he had found the Saracen clerk's office, now deserted, he was fully equipped.

The next morning, Alazne surprised me with the news that Father Francis was waiting in the chapel for Prime prayers. I wondered if he would make any sense, but I travelled across an inner courtyard, with Joan on my arm, to find out.

The priest was lucid, but he avoided any mention of slaughter, instead concentrating on the miracles of bread and fishes — apt, considering that we needed to feed a city of lonely souls. Afterwards, we broke our fast frugally in the refectory hall: fruits, cheeses, bread and wine were on the buffet.

139

'Hugo has found the palace larders, together with the larderers, have you not, Hugo?' I said.

'Indeed, Your Highness — and the vintners, all hidden away behind well-shuttered doors. They needed some persuading to come out. And other palace staff have bravely emerged from their hiding places. I think that they will work for us.'

'Good. When all of you have finished eating, Hugo will have the tables cleared and we will get on with our day.'

'Indeed, Your Highness. I'll go and dig out Father Francis; he seems recovered this morning.'

'Be careful with him, Hugo. He may be fragile for a while yet.'

'Indeed, Your Highness. He told me that he has been to see the bishops; they seem to have brought him back from wherever he went to in his mind. I'll give him some easy tasks to do. But there is something else to see, if you can spare a little time?'

'Something else discovered, Hugo?' asked Joan.

'Indeed, Your Highness: something astonishing.'

Later, as bidden, Hugo led us along the foot of the city wall, passing a few people trying to restore buildings crushed by Richard's hurled rocks. We soon reached a mostly undamaged part of the city about three hundred paces or more from the Crusader halls, and we entered a different courtyard.

'The Caravanserai of Pillars,' Hugo explained, looking at the cloister-like architecture of an inward-facing square building. It had a walkway around it, defined by rows of pillars on all sides. 'The Khan al-Umdan.'

'Very nice,' said Joan, 'but what brought you here?'

'This is where the merchants bring their goods for sale, Your Highness. I have found their warehouses.'

'How clever,' said Joan admiringly.

'There's more,' added Hugo mysteriously. 'Follow me, Your Highnesses.'

He took us to a dark recess in the darkest corner of the building, and we entered a tall arch. Two old men stood waiting in the gloom, carrying lit firebrands.

'There, Your Highnesses, there.' Hugo stood back and left us to admire the gaping arch.

'It seems very deep, Hugo. How far does it go?' I asked.

He beckoned towards the two elderly men, and they stepped forward with their flaming torches.

'I wondered what they were doing,' said Joan, as they led the way into the tunnel. It was high enough to ride into on a horse, it seemed, and without an end in sight.

'Shall we follow, Your Highnesses?' asked Hugo.

'Lead on,' I replied. And off he ventured into the flickering gloom.

'The caravanserai,' he continued to explain, his voice echoing, 'lies at the eastern end of the city, overlooking the harbour where our ships lie. We are heading west to the outer harbour, where we captured the Egyptian fleet.'

Sure enough, we emerged inside the walls of a small fort. Three sentries looked down at us from the battlement in astonishment.

'Who are you?' shouted one fellow.

'She is Queen Berengaria,' replied Hugo. 'Let's go through that arch.'

I looked to where he pointed. Through an archway, I saw the sparkle of the sea, and as we passed under it, the western harbour was revealed, complete with the captured Egyptian ships lying peacefully at anchor.

There was silence, save for the cry of the seabirds, as we took in the sight.

After a few moments, Joan said, 'Hugo, why did the governor and his people not use this tunnel when Richard broke in?'

I answered for him. 'The sea, Joan; we have control of the sea. Our fleet was at the other end and the Egyptians were trapped in the harbour at this end.'

'Indeed, Your Highness. Saladin cannot match us in that regard,' said Hugo.

'Quite,' said Joan. 'How far have we come from the citadel?'

'About half a mile, Your Highness. Yes, there's lots to do. I need an inventory of warehouse goods and —'

I cut him short. 'There's more to do than assess our larder, Hugo. Let's go back.'

Soon we were back in the tunnel, admiring the work needed to create this architectural wonder: the brickwork, the pick marks on the walls and the sheer scale of it.

'The work of someone with vision,' said Joan as she gazed upwards.

Soon we were back in the refectory, with the tables cleared and Father Francis installed at a table with Hugo's lists, ready for him to begin allocating tasks.

Stephen was first, and although surprised to be ordered about by our factotum, he accepted with good grace, knowing how short of manpower we were.

'Lord Stephen, get one of those empty *hippagōga* prepared for sea. All the horses have gone with the king, so we can send it back to Cyprus for supplies. There is money in my treasury; tell me what you need.'

'There are faster ships in the western harbour, Hugo. One of those captured Egyptian ships would be better.'

'Do you know how to sail one, Stephen?'

'No, but I can put some of our seamen on board, and the Egyptians can sail it under orders.'

'Excellent; now we're thinking. What will we save with a faster ship?' I asked.

'A day per leg, Your Highness, given the wind and sailing all night. It is only one hundred miles.'

'Good. Do it, Stephen — put a few of our marine soldiers on board too, just to be safe. Thank you.'

'I will contribute,' said Joan. 'Torène, see to it: a bag of coins from my treasury for Stephen, if you will.'

'Yes, Your Highness. Should I go to Cyprus with it?'

Joan looked at Stephen for an answer.

'She should be quite safe; she has an escort with her. She can spend the money wisely, in the name of the Lady of Cyprus. Beware of Lusignan if he is there; he has a reputation for wandering hands.'

'We've met him. How long will it take, there and back?' I asked.

'About a week.'

'Good. Alazne and Pavot, you are in charge of the contents of the palace larders. I want a full inventory by the end of the day,' I said. 'Stephen, please provide an escort for Amynta and the girls; they are going to persuade the women of the city to cooperate in the matter of rationing once we know how much food there is within the walls. Then brief the sergeants of the guard: I want every Christian banner that you can find flying from the rooftops and wall towers. The Saracens should know that we are in residence here, and intend to stay. Hugo, you remain in charge of the palace staff. Have a list prepared for me, seek out interpreters from among them and get them up and working as normal. I especially want to see the head cook, and we will work out the rationing when we have an inventory of supplies.'

There was a buzz about the place now, and Joan was looking at me and laughing. 'Who are you?' she asked.

I grinned modestly as Alazne answered for me. 'Queen of England, Lady of Cyprus, Duchess of Normandy, Duchess-in-waiting of Aquitaine, Countess of Anjou and the owner of many towns and domains besides. Have I missed out anywhere, Your Highness?'

'Nowhere of note. This should be enough to get things done. If there are no more questions, let's be about our business, good friends, and God go with you.'

The chamber cleared except for Joan and Francis, who was scribbling at Hugo's lists. After a while, Joan went to the buffet and poured a couple of goblets of wine. Plonking them down on the table, she sat next to me on the bench and put an arm around my shoulders.

'That was an education, Berengaria. I now know how you came to manage the palaces of Palermo and Olite.'

'I had a loving father and brothers, and a good education. What excuse have I to get things wrong, eh? But it is all quite exhausting; why don't you take over for a bit? I'll have a lie down. I didn't get much sleep last night.'

'I will. It'll be my pleasant duty to sit in your absence and preside over your plans.'

'Indeed, Your Highness,' added Francis. 'I can manage under Queen Joan's kindness.' Then he bent his head to his lists, fully functional once more — I wondered what the bishops had said to him.

'Thank you,' I said, and picked up my wine, planting a kiss on top of Joan's head as I left.

The ladies left me lying on the bed, fully dressed and expecting a little rest, but I awoke in the dark. The only candlelight was coming from a sconce in the corridor. Jesu! What time was it? My senses returning, I got up and scampered down the steps to find everyone sitting around a table, beset with the remains of a meal.

'You let me sleep,' I said accusingly.

Stephen stood up. 'We had much to do, Your Highness. Your instructions were clear and have been set in motion. When I returned, it was dark and you were in the arms of Morpheus.'

'Is everything done?'

'Everything,' confirmed Joan. 'Come and join us, and we'll tell you all about it.'

Everything was working; the local women were glad to have some guidance, and the older men left behind were willing to work. They were tasked with clearing away the skeletons and corpses into pits and allowing the locals to perform some rites. Though it was an upsetting process, it was preferable to the fate that their sons and grandsons had met at Richard's behest.

The palace staff were also willing to be absorbed into our little community, and once they had handed over the keys to all their hidden rooms, our supply lists improved enormously.

Hugo found them to be a valuable asset in managing the palace and the small garrison; the crews from the ships left behind in the harbour also received sustenance from us for as long as they were there.

The first galley came back from the army after a week. On hearing the cry from a sentry, we gathered on the sand to

145

watch its progress carving though the waves. We arrived at the edge of the sea in time to greet the arrivals as their vessel ploughed into the shore.

'Good morrow!' cried a burly, sunburned individual as he leaped from the prow.

'Welcome,' replied Stephen. 'Have you come from the king?'

'I have. I am the ship's master, and these must be the queens. You were described to me, Your Highnesses,' he said, executing a parody of a bow, 'but the description did not do you justice. I am honoured, Your Highnesses.'

'You may well be,' responded Joan at her haughty best, 'but your sweet words belie your appearance. What's your name, rogue?'

'Oswald, Your Highness — Oswald of Dartford, in England.'

'You're a long way from home, Oswald.'

'Indeed, Your Highness. I like a good war, and this has the makings of one.'

I looked him up and down. He had a lot of hair and wore a ragged shirt that offered little protection from the sun, scarcely concealing a chest of impressive size. His breeches hardly fell below his knees, and at his waistband he carried at least two knives and a crescent-shaped sword.

He noticed my inspection of his sword. 'Saracen!' he declared in a voice that would carry to the far hills. 'The owner let me have it for a consideration.' He laughed and the waters rippled at the noise.

'What consideration?' enquired Joan, although I had already guessed.

'That I chopped off his head instead of disembowelling him.'

The crew of rowers sitting in his craft guffawed at that jest.

Hugo coughed. 'The king?'

'The king is well. Can we be fed now, Your Highnesses? It's hard work, rowing; we've been at it all night.'

'Yes, Oswald. Get your men off the vessel and follow me,' I said.

We sat them down in the guard hall, and Hugo went off to organise some food for about twenty men, well-muscled and jolly. Oswald and his steersman, Ældric, joined us, leaving the rest of the crew to entertain themselves by downing tankards as quickly as possible.

'How far have you rowed, Oswald?' asked Joan.

'About fifteen miles, Your Highness. The king has just passed Haifa.'

'But he has been gone nearly two weeks!'

'Yes, and they've fought off Saladin's cavalry all the way. It has been very difficult, as Saladin is determined to keep them away from the Holy City. He has devastated every field and orchard, and emptied every barn before them along the way, so the army is dependent upon supplies from the sea. Have there been any Saracens watching here?'

'There are a few sitting on the ridge a mile or so away. They've set up camp but do not come near,' said Stephen.

'Yes, most of them are following Richard. I doubt you will be bothered; Saladin seems to have given up on Akko.'

'Are there any messages for us?' asked Joan hopefully.

'Ah, almost forgot. Ældric of Winchester!' Oswald called, dragging him away from the wine-splashed table. 'The vellums, if you please.'

Ældric scrabbled about on the floor, where he had cast down a pouch when he joined us. He then produced three rolls, each bearing Richard's seal.

'Your Highnesses.' He handed one to Joan and one to me, then one to Stephen.

'This is for Stephen,' said Joan, handing him the correct roll. He then handed me mine, and I handed Joan's to her.

'Ældric can't read, Your Highness,' explained Oswald. 'He just steers where I tell him to.'

There was a silence while we read the scripts, which didn't take long.

'What does yours tell you, Joan?' I asked.

'Not a lot,' she replied. 'It says that they are making good progress and should reach the Holy City by the end of September, God willing. Yours?'

'The same.'

'Stephen?'

'He says to keep you safe and make certain that Lusignan keeps the supplies coming.'

'Do you have any reply, Your Highnesses?' asked Oswald.

'No,' said Joan shortly. 'When are you going back?'

'First light. We should find them somewhere near Caesarea, if they make good progress. There ought to be another galley on its way here; we should pass them mid-voyage.'

'Just tell the king that the city is safe. That's all.' Joan's message to her brother reflected my feelings, and I added naught.

Next morning, I was pleased to watch Oswald set off back to find the army, but I wondered why Richard couldn't find a few words of affection to set down in his progress report. Joan and I had received exactly the same message.

'Is that it: notes from a war?' I complained to her.

'Seems so. I'm not making excuses for him,' she responded.

'We'll have to wait it out until Jerusalem is taken.'

'You've known that for a while, my sweet sister,' she said, as we watched the tiny waves on the sand.

'I wonder why we bothered coming here,' muttered Alazne, splashing her toes in the warm water. Pavot stood near her, her kirtle hoisted.

'Back to work?' asked Joan.

'Yes, back to Hugo's lists. Another busy day to look forward to,' I said.

'Well, Alazne, lead on,' said Joan.

Making our way along the sands to the city, I wondered if there was any point in remaining. I was in a marriage of state, with all the trappings of gold and silver and crowns and feasts, but Richard and I were not in love. I could not see myself lasting very long in this relationship, and I resolved to discuss the issue with Joan when the time was right.

The following day, after a few, more cheerful words from Father Francis and a few bites to eat, I gave Joan a nod and she followed me out of the palace and up onto a sea-facing wall.

It was a calm and beautiful morning, with ships reflected on an azure sea and very little going on, apart from a single galley disturbing the surface. It was heading southwards to find Richard.

'There are plenty of ships in the harbour,' said Joan. 'You could go and become the Lady of Cyprus.'

'Hasn't Lusignan re-married?'

'I don't think so, but he has daughters: Alix and Maria.'

'Idle thoughts, Joan. Now that Richard has re-sold the island to Lusignan, I have no business in Cyprus.'

'You are right, and I have none in Sicily. There is too much squabbling over that island's future for a queen dowager to be involved.'

'You think that we should leave here? I've not been to England yet. I suppose it to be bigger than Cyprus.'

'What a jest: one queen and one queen dowager stuck on a wall, marooned on a Crusade in which we have no part. What should we do, Berengaria?'

'Richard has a long reach; we can do naught without permission, I suppose,' I said.

'No, I suppose not.'

'Good morrow, Your Highnesses.' Stephen had found us.

'Good morrow, Stephen. When will the king reach Jerusalem?' I asked.

'At his present rate of progress, not until October.'

'What can we do now apart from wait, Stephen?'

'Keep busy. The palace staff are integrating quite well with your households, Your Highnesses, and the locals who survived are pleased to have some direction. I suppose we should just get on with the business of managing a city.'

'And wait for the next galley?' asked Joan.

'Indeed, Your Highness, indeed.'

The next galley brought news of a skirmish south of Caesarea, in which Richard had been wounded. They were heading for the town of Arsuf.

'Is being wounded not of concern to one's wife, Joan?' I grumbled. There was no vellum from Richard, only a report from a scribe, which was mostly a list of supplies required. With it came some bedraggled wounded.

'I'll set up an infirmary, Your Highness,' said Stephen. 'A man from the Knights of Saint John has asked for somewhere to practise. We might as well prepare for more wounded to return.'

'Think about sending them over to Cyprus,' I said. 'They'll be a nuisance left here, and easy meat if the Saracens return.'

A week went by, then another. With things mostly under control in Akko, boredom set in once more. Our worries about Richard and his men came to the fore, and doing needlework while sitting on the wall became a frantic pastime.

'You are holding that needle as if it were a sword, Alazne,' I said.

Pavot laughed and replied, 'She doesn't really like these women's pastimes, Your Highness. I think she'd rather be down in the ward, practising swordplay with the guards.'

'I'd slash their gizzards open,' said Alazne with a snarl.

Visits to the wall became frequent now that we had everything running smoothly. Today was no different, save that Joan and the others were busy, and I was alone for a while until Stephen climbed up to join me.

'Morning, Your Highness,' he said.

'You already said that at Prime, Stephen,' I said, laughing.

I was becoming quite friendly with him. We had taken to swapping tales of home, he of a county known as Kent, in England, and I of Navarre.

'There isn't much to see today,' I began.

'Depends on what one's looking at,' he replied.

I realised that it was me upon whom his gaze rested. 'Don't.'

'Sorry, Your Highness. There is no fairer sight.'

'Speak not like that in this city; it contains too many eyes and ears.'

'Aye.'

He moved slightly and our arms touched on the wall. I withdrew, but looked at him. I was not minded to repulse him.

'You realise that what's in your mind could lose you your head?'

He laughed. 'You misread me, Your Highness. I've a wife, Edeline, and daughters named Alice, Mabel and Beatrice.'

'Oh! I'm sorry; I thought you had something else in mind. You enjoy the company of females?'

'Indeed. I'm sorry if I am too presumptuous. I'm here to preserve your person, Your Highness.'

I held out a hand and was relieved when he took it and held it for a moment in his warm grasp.

'I've just realised how much I miss my father,' I said. 'I so enjoyed his company. He was my chief support and haven.'

'I know about your mother's early death.'

'Yes, Father could not replace a mother's love, but he excelled in a father's position.' I sighed. 'Let us act with decorum, Stephen. I believe that I shall trust you. Perhaps you could advise me — as a daughter?'

'Perhaps I shall. Perhaps that might ease the hurt of distance — you from your family and me from mine. Ah, here is Hugo with the list. Full of things to do, I expect, Your Highness.'

It was nearly the middle of September before another messenger turned up, and once again we gathered on the beach to await the grounding of the galley. It was late in the evening and the last of the sun cast long shadows.

Just before the bow grounded, we heard the orders of, 'Up oars!' They came out of the water as one as the galley slithered up the sand and came to a halt.

'Your Highnesses!' The voice of Oswald rent the evening air as he beamed at us. 'Good news, Your Highnesses, very good news. I'll come down. Is there any food? We've rowed nearly seventy miles to reach here.'

'What about that sail?' I laughed. 'Did you forget about it?'

'Queen Berengaria, ever the jester. The wind only comes up in the afternoons. Sweat, sweat and more sweat; that's what brought us here.'

'News first, then food,' I said firmly.

'Should we talk as we walk across the sand, Your Highness?'

'Go on, then. Stephen, send someone ahead; these men want feeding.'

'Marvellous, Your Highness. Now then, there has been a great battle near a place called Arsuf, and Richard has roundly defeated Saladin. They had agreed on a meeting, but only Saladin's brother, Al-Adil, turned up, with a rejection of Richard's offer, so he readied for battle.'

'Here we are,' said Joan. 'Sit here in the late sunshine and tell all.'

We were in the citadel gardens. It was very pleasant, with the birds singing their final song of the day as the evening spread over us. We took our places to hear the rest of Oswald's story.

He remained standing, and with much throwing about of his arms and voice, he explained the battle of Arsuf.

'The sixth, it was — the sixth of September. The army had marched out of a thick forest to find Saladin's army stretched out before them across the plain; there was no way back. Richard had them organised on the march in such a way that they could deploy quickly to meet any threat. Is there any wine? I'm parched.'

'Sorry, Oswald; I should have thought,' I said, and I motioned for a steward to satisfy the man.

'At the fore were the Templars; then the Bretons and Angevins. King Guy had his Poitevins in the fourth division, then Richard's English and Normans were at the very side of him. The French were left guarding the baggage train and the Hospitallers kept the rear safe.'

Oswald's men were now joined by some of our garrison troops, and members of our new household gathered around us with other locals. A great circle formed to listen to this English raconteur; a troubadour could not have sung it any better.

With a deep draught from his cup, Oswald got to the battle itself. 'They stood tight, every man sticking to the side of his comrades, while the Saracens rode around them, firing arrows into the close-packed rank and file. Richard had ordered them to stand firm, and if they broke, the Saracen horsemen would be among them in a trice to pick them off as they stood or ran. All day they tried and could not break our men.'

'What was he waiting for?' I did not understand.

'Many must have died,' Joan added.

'And horses too. But the plan worked. Late in the afternoon, there came a great trumpet blast and the Knights Templar made ready to charge. Richard's infantry stood firm to the front and, as they'd been told, they pulled away from the middle, moving to the side and leaving a clear avenue in their centre.

'Now the enemy would see Richard at the head of his cavalry, his golden helm with its crown gleaming in the sunlight, his red surcoat with its three lions emblazoned, his sword held high and pointing at Saladin's centre.

'Then came the charge — a great shout as our horsemen broke into a gallop and aimed themselves at the Saracens, who were now riding without direction. Richard was soon into the melee and rolling over the tired enemy horsemen. They were short of arrows, and it was hand to hand, sword against sword, man and horse riding over Saladin's horsemen.' He paused for a glug of wine. 'Though they fought gallantly, Saladin's men were roundly trounced, and he had to withdraw them from the battlefield before they were all slaughtered. The battle of Arsuf was won in an afternoon, an outcome that Saladin could not have envisaged in his worst nightmare.'

I was quite breathless by the end of Oswald's telling. Joan had her hand over her mouth and everyone else was astounded at the great success thus recalled.

There followed a silence, during which Oswald drained his pot and held it out for a refill as spontaneous applause broke out from his audience. Grinning proudly, he answered questions from all and sundry.

'A day to remember,' said Joan.

'Indeed,' I responded. 'Perhaps we can find out where Richard is now.'

'Oswald, if you can spare some time from your storytelling, your food is ready in the castle. And do you know where the king will be?' asked Stephen.

'Thank you, my lord. The king is heading for Jaffa, despite rumours that Saladin has taken down the walls. The next galley to arrive should reassure you.'

'Thank you, Oswald. We can wait. There's little else to do,' I said without enthusiasm.

CHAPTER SEVEN

It was the end of September before the sail of our next messenger galley was spied. All other vessels entering the harbour were staging between Cyprus and somewhere along the coast. I was tempted to board one and go and visit my small domain, as Joan described it. Whether or not I would ever visit my larger realm of England was a matter for conjecture.

We dashed down to the beach, gathering up some fruit on the way and an escort of running guards whom we took by surprise at the gate. There was no Oswald this time; instead there was the shipmaster we'd named Old Misery because of his long face. Hubert of Zeebrugge was his proper name.

'Your Highnesses.' He swept a dolorous bow with an old, salt-stained hat. 'I bring news from Jaffa.' His tone was not exactly inspiring, but he did not seem distressed. 'The king is taking time to assess the situation and has sent a patrol galley out to reconnoitre Ashkelon from the sea. There are rumours that Saladin has wrecked the port, which would make it unsuitable as a base from which to attack Jerusalem.'

'So the king is in one piece?' I asked.

'Indeed, Your Highness.'

'And have you no missives for Queen Berengaria or me?' enquired Joan.

'Indeed not, Your Highness. No vellums were given to me, apart from lists. Who is responsible for the port?'

'I am,' responded Stephen, arriving in a timely fashion, as ever. Hubert handed over a roll and stood waiting silently for a response.

'Have you eaten?' asked Joan eventually.

'Not since leaving Jaffa, Your Highness,' was his reply.

'Take Hubert and his crew up to the halls and get them fed, Stephen. The queen and I will stay here for a while.'

It was growing colder, although we could still rely on sunshine most days. Talks about the winter weather evoked memories of the snowy peaks of the Pyrenees back home.

'Do you have snow in Sicily, Joan?' I asked, idly stitching a piece of fabric. Eirini was showing us some Byzantine designs.

'There is snow on Mount Etna. It's very odd: fire and ice on one mountain.'

'Why fire?' asked Eirini, not familiar with European islands.

'It is a volcano,' answered Joan. 'I've been up to the top, and it is very frightening to look down into the jaws of hell. It spews out fire, and in the winter it steams all the time.'

'Mad,' declared the little princess, and Amynta crossed herself.

'Is Stephen still in the privy hall, I wonder?'

'He may be,' answered Joan, 'or he may be prowling the walls and the main city gates. He takes his duties seriously.'

'I'm going to find him. I've thought of something to do tomorrow.'

'Nothing desperate, I pray,' said Joan. 'I'll come with you and you can reveal all.'

We found Stephen on top of the main gate, looking out across the debris of Richard's trenches and ditches, which had previously kept the army safe while they were hurling rocks at Akko.

'Come up, Your Highnesses; the guard sergeant will guide you,' he said.

It was a frightful sight; the earth had been disfigured by endless excavations, left-behind tents and other debris.

'Horrible,' I said.

'Some of those pits are middens, and others are full of uneaten food and not a few corpses, I shouldn't wonder. Some have filled up with water, and I dread to think of the stink come next spring,' said Stephen.

'Can't you do something about it?' I asked.

'Haven't got the manpower. I could send some of those old Akko men out, but they might fall in or be attacked by those Saracens watching from yonder hill.'

I changed the subject. 'You know the head cook, Ahmed the Syrian?' I asked.

'Ahmed, yes. Why?' said Stephen, looking at me.

'Go and find him. I want him to teach us how to cook in the Syrian style. I've quite enjoyed the food he has presented, and I intend to take him, or his recipes, to England with me.'

'Oh, my Lord!' said Joan, astonished. 'I think that I will join you; it should be fun.'

'I'll go and find him, Your Highness. He usually sleeps near the larder in the afternoons,' said Stephen. He sped off.

We traipsed along after him and stood hopefully near the kitchen door. After a few minutes, Stephen emerged, smiling.

'He agrees that if you help him, he will teach you. I said, "They are queens and everything in the kitchen is theirs."'

'And?' I probed.

'He said that if they own everything, then they can cook everything … without him.'

'Oh,' said Joan. 'What should we do, Berri? Stitch or help?'

'Help. I'm beginning to hate needles.'

'Tell him we will help.'

'Very well,' agreed Stephen, with a grin. 'Which means that we may, or may not, eat tomorrow evening.' And he disappeared into the smoke and steam, amid the rattle of crockery.

The next day dawned dull and misty. A stroll along the wall confirmed that the horizon could not be seen, and it was pointless trying to spot any approaching craft. So, after breakfast, we presented ourselves at the kitchen door, escorted by Stephen. Amynta, Eirini, Alya and Nabila accompanied us — mainly for their language skills, but they could help if directed.

Ahmed had clearly escaped most of the privations of a city under siege, and was showing no sign of the strict rationing that the ordinary citizens must have suffered. He was also quite personable and pleasant, but not entirely comprehensible, which was when Amynta and her girls came to the fore; they now conversed in a blend of Mediterranean languages.

Ahmed had evidently taken the matter seriously and, after inspecting our hands and ordering us to wash, he introduced an array of fruit, vegetables and spices lined up on a table together with some knives and dishes.

'Ask him if he has ever taught cooking, Amynta,' I said.

The reply came in the affirmative. He'd been seconded from Baghdad Palace by Saladin to accompany him on his journeys.

'Tell him that we are honoured.'

That pleased him, and he set off describing everything on the table before gathering the ingredients together for particular dishes.

'He says that we will make a small selection of dishes from Syria to begin with, if you please, Your Highnesses,' explained Amynta.

'First,' he told us through his interpreters, 'we will prepare some side dishes: *addas bi-husrem*, a thick lentil soup, and *mfarakit kusa*, a dip with fresh flatbread. Then a fish dish of *sayadieh*, *dawood basha*, meatballs in tomato sauce, and to finish, *baklava*, a butter and nut cake, and *tamria*, or caramelised dates.'

'He has suggested that you two,' said Amynta, looking at Alazne and Pavot, 'prepare the first dish, then the queens can attempt the main dishes. The youngsters can do the sweet dishes.'

'What can I do, Your Highness?' asked Stephen, surprising me.

Amynta said something to Ahmed, and his reply was to the effect that Stephen should get the hall servants together and help to prepare the refectory tables.

Thus dismissed, Stephen stomped off, muttering.

'The dishes,' beamed Ahmed, addressing Amynta, 'will be presented at the table this evening to whoever you care to invite, Your Highnesses.'

Amynta worked the hardest, being rushed back and forth all morning, interpreting, until we were done. Some dishes were taken down to a cool room, others were left in pots and cauldrons, and yet more were left simmering in the ovens.

It was a good morning's work, and I was pleased.

'Well done, Berri,' said Joan, her hair plastered in something sticky. 'Now I will have to dream of something else to keep us occupied.'

'I fancy coming back here, actually. I have enjoyed it very much. Amynta, thank Ahmed for us; we appreciate his time, and ask if we may return another day.'

'He says that it was a pleasure, and the girls remind him of his daughters back in Baghdad. Thank you, Your Highness.'

'I'm going up onto the wall to cool down, Berri,' said Joan as we emerged from the heat of the kitchens.

Soon after, we were lined up along the battlements, watching the harbour activities. Then Stephen climbed up, but remained away from us by the steps.

'I'm going to see if everything is ready,' I said. 'I'll be just a moment, Joan.'

I went and chatted to Stephen about how the supplies were moving, whether the ships were finding it easy, travelling back and forth to Cyprus and then on to Haifa and beyond, and importantly, whether they should not be going there directly from Cyprus as the army moved along the coast. There was warmth developing between us, and I looked back to see that we were being watched. Father figure or not, I was also enjoying his company as a man.

'Sails!' a sentry cried from a wall tower. 'Sails on the horizon.'

'Seems that we will need to discuss provisioning at another time, Stephen,' I said.

'Indeed, Your Highness. If this is the king, we may not get the chance until we discover his next intentions.' There was sadness in his eyes as he went to climb down the steps.

'Who is it, Joan? Are they Saracens?' I asked, reaching her side.

'Can't tell yet; they're still too far off in the shimmering air.'

Then there was a cry from a tower. 'The king, the king's galley is in the lead!'

'How many ships?' called out Alazne.

'Six, perhaps seven. It must be the king,' was the response.

My husband was nearing, but I felt nothing but unease. I now knew he was a man with a love for violence, to the exclusion of all else. The others felt more joy at Richard's return than I did; that was certain.

'Should we move off to the shore?' asked Joan, her excitement mounting.

'What, in these kitchen clothes?' I was less enthusiastic.

'Never mind them. He will be fresh from battle; we can at least show him that we are usefully engaged. Come on, ladies; the beach.'

I was left trailing in their wake. Stephen, who had been waiting at the bottom of the steps, wandered along behind me.

'Joan!' It was Richard, and he hailed from the ship. 'Berengaria, yes, yes.'

The large galley needed to drop anchor and stay in the deeper water offshore, but Richard's voice boomed across and no doubt could be heard by the watching Saracens.

We waited until a small galley reached the *Thor* to collect Richard. Joan had her shoes off and was up to her knees in the water, looking windswept and kitchen-stained, but happy to see her brother once more. I remained demure and dry at the edge of the water. I could hear Stephen breathing as he stood respectfully behind me.

Richard jumped into the waters as the small craft beached, and he seized his sister, holding her aloft and then carrying her onto the dry sand. Placing her down, he picked me up.

Then came a surprise. Holding me against his chest, eye to eye, he spluttered some remark about having been eager to get back and told us he was taking us to Jaffa. Then he dropped me before demanding Stephen's attention and engaging him in a conversation about supplies.

Joan watched as I was left on the beach, the forlorn expression on her face no doubt matching mine as she put her arm around my shoulders.

'That's the homecoming of a king, is it?' I mumbled into her arm.

'That's the homecoming of a blind man, Berengaria. I despair.'

Richard, evidently finished with Stephen, turned to us and shouted across the sand. 'Joan, Berengaria, can you be ready to sail in the morning?'

We looked at each other, astonished, but we agreed.

'Right, let's pack. At least we are wanted somewhere else,' I said.

'Stephen,' called Joan, 'you know what to do now.'

'I do,' he said, watching Richard striding up the sands towards the city gate, trailed by a couple of his commanders and a guard of twelve. 'Worry not, I'll send up some palace maids to help you pack.'

From his face, I judged he was not best pleased.

Later I established that Richard was in conference with his commanders in one of the Crusader halls. I marched in and surprised him with an invitation to join us at the evening meal.

The look of astonishment on his face, and those of his nearest advisors, was well worth the risk. I was determined to make a mark as the queen in charge of Akko Palace.

'Good Lord, what, what, a feast? How did you do that?' Richard asked.

'With organisation and hard work. Will you bring your friends, my lord?'

'Of course. Hear that, lords? A feast in among the rubble. Attend me, if you please; it would be good to have a meal at a proper table, yes, yes. Now then, Stephen,' he said, turning to my guardian, 'you believe that the supplies should move directly from Cyprus to further along the coast?'

'Yes, Your Highness, as the queen has suggested,' said Stephen, to my delight.

'The queen? Good Lord, Berengaria! You?'

'Me,' I declared, turning away and marching out of the hall. 'And don't be late. Stephen will tell you when.'

I stomped up to my chamber and flopped onto the bed. There was silence from Alazne. Then she went out and came back with Joan.

'What have you done, Berri?'

'I've invited the king to dine with us. Let's dress up for the occasion. I've invited him to bring along his friends.'

'If he has any left.'

'Quite.'

That evening, when we were as well prepared as we could be, given the uncertainties of our itinerant robe chests, Hugo and Stephen presented themselves to tell us that all was ready.

'We've got a surprise for you, Your Highnesses,' said Stephen.

'Really?' I said, already sharing his smile. 'And what can that be?'

'Good Lord!' he exclaimed, looking behind me.

Amynta, Eirini, Alya and Nabila were standing behind me, and they were stunning. Amynta, in her Greek dress, was outshone by the Eastern splendour of the Byzantine princess and her companions, all dressed in splendid, though baggy, pantaloons. Eirini wore a tight bodice, and her shining black hair was topped by a silver circlet, which I presumed Amynta had found somewhere in the city. But they did not outshine we two queens, both now in golden gowns with gold crowns, mine set upon my glossy black hair and Joan's atop her reddish-gold tresses.

'You like what you see, my lords?' asked Joan with an impish grin.

Hugo reddened, while Stephen spluttered, 'Very much.'

'Joan, do not tease so. You said that you had something to tell us, Stephen,' I said.

'Oh, yes. Camville has arrived from Cyprus; we are to be Richard's representatives to Lusignan. We will discuss sending the ships directly along the coast to wherever the army is.'

'Her Highness thought of it,' added Hugo.

'So she did; clever Berengaria,' said Joan.

'We've prepared a grand entrance for you when the king and his companions are settled,' said Hugo. 'I'll let you know when to come in.'

'My, my, how clever. No wonder the Queen of England is always singing your praises, Hugo,' said Joan.

'Wait for the trumpet blast,' said Stephen as he left.

I wondered if he was moving to Cyprus. I wouldn't want that.

Later, after some final preening, we set off down the staircase. Stephen was waiting at the bottom. Hugo rearranged the order of our little procession.

'The trumpets will sound, Your Highnesses, and that is the signal for the younger girls, with your tending ladies, to precede you. The girls will process along the hall to the table behind the throne. Then you, Queen Joan, will go directly to the throne to the right of your brother. Finally, the Queen of England — your throne is on the king's left. I'm sure that you will find it suitable. You will all be guided to your seats, Your Highnesses. Lord Stephen will take your arm. Queen Berengaria, do you think you could wait a few moments for the others to go to their places before you enter?'

'I'm to enter alone?'

'With Lord Stephen. I'll announce you. Make your queenly way with Stephen, and I shall walk behind you.'

'Why Stephen?'

'It was him or some hairy captain of the guard. We have no one else of sufficient rank here. You can enter on your own if you wish, Your Highness.'

'You've been reading my thoughts.'

'Everyone should know that England's star is in its ascendency,' said Stephen. 'Enter as yourself.'

'Jesu, Stephen,' said Joan. 'Ladle it on, what, what?'

He trotted across to the grand archway leading into the refectory and peered in. After a moment, he waved to someone and a trumpet blast that might have been heard in Jerusalem sounded out.

Eirini jumped out of her skin, but was granted no respite as Hugo gave Amynta a gentle shove to get things moving. I was left standing for a while until the ladies disappeared into the candlelit grandness of the refectory hall.

Stephen came back and stood behind me. Leaning across my shoulder, he asked gently, 'Are you ready, Your Highness?'

I half turned to find his face next to mine and instinctively gave him a peck on the cheek. 'Thank you, Stephen. This is perfect.'

He coughed, touched me on the back, and we were off.

When I entered the refectory hall, the trumpets sounded again and Stephen announced, 'Her Highness, Berengaria, Queen of England,' in tones that almost out-blasted the trumpets.

'Good Lord, what a noise,' said Richard. 'Berengaria, there you are — almost lost you in the crowd.' He stood, and his grin was mimicked by all the others in there — and suddenly I felt very, very small.

'Slower,' hissed Stephen. I had almost broken into a gallop before he reined me in. Nevertheless, I reached my throne without tripping, and some attendant pushed it in behind me.

The seat was well padded and seemed to be higher than normal; I could see across the table. *Thank you, Stephen*, I thought. My debt to my guardian was climbing by the moment.

'Berengaria, you look splendid.' Richard had taken a look at me, which was a rarity. 'I congratulate you. Splendid arrangements, are they not, my lords? The queen has a good grasp of things, wouldn't you say, what?'

His commanders, captains, and other military men gathered around, speaking in solid agreement.

'Sit, sit,' Richard said. 'No formality tonight, let us enjoy the queen's table and hospitality.'

'That was kind, Richard. Thank you.'

'True, true. Been busy, you know — Saladin and all that. Who's that behind us?' He gestured to where the ladies were sitting. 'That's not the Comnenus girl, is it?'

'Indeed she is, Richard. A fine hostage you have there; are you going to behead her too?' It just slipped out; it must have been in my thoughts. Now what had I done?

But Richard was in a different world to mine and burst out laughing. It sounded like the best jest he'd heard for many a day, and he even repeated it for the benefit of his guests.

Jesu, bones of the saints! What an idiot. He might think that I am like-minded.

Seeking a diversion from my silly remark, I took a look around the table. Joan was on Richard's right, so I couldn't easily talk to her. Opposite me, but at one end, I recognised Richard de Camville from Cyprus. He did not look away but half smiled, which caused me to hold my gaze a little. Joan had next to her Guilbert, master of the *Thor*, and we'd invited

Father Francis, who was opposite her. I judged that she had the best of it.

Camville was next to Stephen and now deep in conversation, I noted. Next to me was one whose face I remembered but not his name. I smiled at him and he introduced himself again.

'William des Barres, Your Highness,' he said.

Richard heard and cut in. 'Brought him along because he deserves it — stout warrior, first-rate, led many charges, scattered the Saracens. Wounded, he was, by God.'

William responded quickly, dismissing his own wound. 'Thank you, Your Highness, but no more than you.'

'Yes,' I said, 'you were reported as wounded, my lord. Why have you not mentioned it?'

'See, Will, I told you she'd be all concerned. It wasn't much, Berengaria, nothing.'

He dismissed the event, but I had seen that he was stiff on one side, and so had Joan, who was listening.

'Show us, brother. Let's see the damage,' she said firmly.

'God's beard,' said Richard. 'Women!'

He stood and pulled up his tabard and shirt, worn loose, as was the custom in the heat. There was a nasty red scar traversing the side of his ribs.

'Oh, my God,' gasped Joan.

'How did it happen?' I asked.

'Spear thrust. Mail diverted it, else I wouldn't be here.'

'I thought you were aiming for Ashkelon when you left here,' said Joan.

'I was. There was more fighting along the way than I expected — got a new problem now. Jaffa, which we hold, is forty miles north of Ashkelon, and they're both the same from Jerusalem: eighty. Saladin has wrecked Ashkelon harbour, so we can't use it. Now I need to regroup because of the supply lines; we need to ship them directly. Good thinking, Berengaria — probably was going to happen anyway. Are you a soothsayer, eh?' He burst into over-loud laughter again.

A touch of madness lay within this man. I needed to proceed with caution above all else, that I could see.

'Are we going to live in Jaffa?' I asked.

'Yes — nice place. You should be happy there until we get hold of Jerusalem. Good grub, this,' Richard added. 'Who's the cook?'

'We are,' Joan and I said together.

'What? Queens cooking? Is there not a cook left in the place?'

'Yes, there is,' I replied. 'He is named Ahmed, and he taught us. Do you like it?'

'Best I've had since leaving Cyprus,' commented Barres.

'And me,' said Richard, clearing his platter with some fresh bread. 'Stephen, load the cook on board in the morning. We'll have more of this, yes, yes.'

Stephen nodded agreement and looked at me with a warm smile. 'A queen unique among queens, Your Highness,' he said to Richard.

'I agree — quite unique. Must have more of this.'

Then he engaged with Stephen and Camville. A detailed discussion about Cyprus and replenishing the army followed, in which I was not invited to contribute. Both Stephen and Camville kept glancing at me, but I was annoyed at being excluded and spent the time questioning Barres about his home life again, as I'd spoken so much of Navarre the last time we had met.

This conversation came to an abrupt end when Richard declared, 'Need to talk to these men, Berengaria — things to do; early start in the morn. Can you leave us? God bless you all.'

He began to deliver the expected kiss on the top of my head — difficult, because I was wearing a crown, and my ear was attacked instead. Then off I went up to the bedchambers, along with the other ladies.

'Sent to bed, Berri! Haven't had that for a while,' said Joan, sitting next to me on the bed. 'Will he, or will he not?'

'Probably not.'

'I'll stay. If he comes up, I'll clear off.'

'I wouldn't expect him to, Joan. He hasn't touched me all night, even though we sat next to each other.'

'Dear God, he is driven by this mission to the exclusion of all else.'

We cosied up and sat quietly, enjoying each other's company until there was a cough outside the door. I heard Alazne questioning someone, and then she poked her head in.

'It is Lord Stephen, Your Highness.'

'Let him in.' When he was standing before me, I asked, 'What is it, Stephen? You've brought me bad news?'

He seemed uncertain. 'Pardon me, Your Highnesses. It might be busy until the morning, so I would like to say goodnight, and see you on the shore tomorrow. All your chests have been loaded, and you are ready to board.' He was twisting his hands.

'Is there more?'

'The king has missed my services; he considers me better suited for the task than those who replaced me, and he has tried to take me back. I complained that I was not fit, because of my knee. I didn't want to move back to Cyprus, so I suggested that I stay with you.' He fell silent and I waited hopefully for his next statement. 'He agreed, so I am staying with you — if you want me to, that is?'

I was struggling now, angry that my life was dictated by someone who was rarely present, yet glad that Stephen would be staying with us. I fought to bring myself under control while Joan questioned him.

'How can we repay you, Stephen? You have done so much. We will have you as our guardian without question, and that will be the king's loss.'

'Oh, come here,' I said, throwing caution to the wind and planting a kiss on his cheek. Joan completed his embarrassment by brushing the other one.

'Thank you, Your Highnesses,' he said, reddening, and disappeared out of the chamber.

'Oh well, Berengaria — my brother works his wiles again.'

'Aye, it is turning into a joust. Are you up for it?'

'I am; we'll stick together.'

Amynta came in. 'Are we moving?' she asked. 'What did Lord Stephen say, Your Highness?'

'Lots. We'll depart for Jaffa tomorrow.'

Leaving at midday the following day, watching a sad crowd waving goodbye on the sands, I wondered if we would ever see Akko again. We would stay overnight on the *Thor* and expect to sight Jaffa late the following afternoon.

Richard barely spoke, at least to any of us. He looked at Eirini so much that I sent her below deck out of spite. Then William des Barres came across and said quietly that the king should sleep.

'Despite his bravado, he is not fully recovered from his fevers, Your Highness. We should let him rest.'

'Can I see him?' asked Joan.

I knew that if she was refused, she would go into Richard's sleeping area anyway, so it was a relief when Barres offered his arm and she went inside. Not long after, she emerged from behind the canvas curtain.

'He sleeps, but he looks awful — drained.'

We held each other in comfort.

'This Crusade is too costly, Joan.'

'I am starting to agree with you, dear one. It is too costly by far.'

CHAPTER EIGHT

Jaffa was a wondrous sight, built on a ridge with unbroken views of the coastline and a well-sheltered harbour.

'Where shall we live, Richard?' asked Joan.

'The palace on the end of the ridge should keep you happy. Bring out Eirini — let her see it.'

I sighed. Richard seemed to think about her all the time.

'That surely seems to be big enough for your needs, Your Highness, let alone a Byzantine princess.' Stephen was close behind, and the last part of his sentence was for my ears only.

I sniffed. 'Bring Ahmed, Stephen. He can find out where his new kitchen will be.'

'And his kitchen staff. He seems to have brought them all from Akko, or perhaps they fancied a ride in the king's galley,' he replied.

There were walls, gates and gardens with sumptuous planting, even at this time of year. I wondered at the industry of the palace gardeners. By the time we reached the inner sanctum, we had passed through many layers of the palace. Then it was into a world of closed courtyards with fountains playing, and more plants.

Hugo and Stephen had stopped in front of us before an arched doorway. They were talking to a very large, dark-haired man who was wearing only breeches and carrying a great curved sword.

Hugo walked back, smiling. 'That's Abla. He's very nice, and it's his duty to guard the women of the palace. I told him that you were married to King Richard, Your Highness, and you were not, Lady Joan. He said he will prevent any men entering here. I told him that it is normal for you to receive visitors, so he is thinking on that.'

'*Lady Joan*, Hugo?' queried Joan.

He reddened and muttered, 'I heard…'

Joan took pity on him. 'I suppose the chance for me to rule over my previous realm is long gone now; Richard seems not to want to contest Tancred in the matter. "Lady Joan" will do — until I find a prince.' She laughed.

I was surprised that she would give up being a queen so easily, but I supposed neither of us had much influence in these matters. I was sure that most of our retinue would continue to call her "Your Highness" out of habit.

'My lady,' responded Hugo, clearly relieved to have the issue settled.

Joan returned to the immediate question. 'Is Abla alone? He is very big, but this palace is enormous.'

'No, he is not alone. He is the master of the women's apartments.'

'He is also very handsome. Is he to be trusted with all our women, Hugo?' I asked.

'He is not interested in women, Your Highness, and he has not the wherewithal to cause them any harm.'

'Oh, you mean —' gasped Joan.

'I mean precisely that, Your Highness. He is a eunuch. You may trust his presence entirely.'

'In we go,' I decided. 'Let's see what awaits us. Stephen, Hugo, help install Ahmed in his kitchen; we will enjoy his food tonight.'

Further in, the palace was dark and cool, with many sheer draperies about the place. Some of the rooms had indoor fountains, and the bedchambers that I glanced into had enormous beds. Some had reflecting ceilings, enough to make a maiden blush.

The women's enclave was arranged around an open courtyard with a garden, and most of the bedrooms faced into it, with garden doors for easy access. Emerging from one, I bumped into Joan.

'Dear God, this is a palace devoted to the pleasures of the flesh. Better not let Father Francis in here; he'll die of embarrassment,' she said.

'I doubt he'll get past Abla.'

'I wonder where the men's quarters are? I'll ask Hugo when he comes back.'

'Should we start arranging the chambers? I'd feel safer if we were all next to each other,' I suggested.

'Yes, and if my brother doesn't turn up, we can share again. Is that good?'

'If that's my best offer, Joan, I'll take it.' I said this lightly but with a heavy heart, and Joan did not press me on the matter.

We solved the matter of the too-stimulating bedchambers by closing the internal doors and drawing curtains on the outer ones, using a central chamber as a place for receiving guests.

Hugo brought Father Francis to visit in the afternoon two days after our arrival, and he soon settled down in the courtyard garden, quite at home and apparently unaware of the nature of the complex.

'What is the date today, Father Francis?' I asked. With all this travelling, it was difficult to keep track. He was sitting quietly in the shade, reading his Bible.

'The twelfth day of October, in the year of our Lord 1191, Your Highness. Tomorrow is the day to remember an English saint.'

'I recall there are many saints in England,' said Joan.

'Indeed, Your Highness, and the one we honour tomorrow is Edwin, king and saint of Deira. He died fighting the pagan Welsh in the sixth century.'

'Where's Deira?' I asked, woefully ignorant about my realm of England.

'In the north, Your Highness. It was one of the ancient kingdoms of the Saxons before King William the Norman took over. And the Welsh are a tribe outside England, from the west of the country.'

He returned to his studies while I pondered on learning more about England. Then, missing Stephen, I went to find him.

The place was a labyrinth, but I found him on a battlement with a good view of the sea, watching the comings and goings of Richard's fleet preparing to move further along the coast. Richard never visited to tell us himself, so we still relied on Hugo and Stephen to bring back morsels of information.

'Heard anything interesting lately, Stephen?' I asked, startling him.

'Ah, my queen; I was thinking about you.'

'Really? And I am of interest to you?'

'Yes, but not quite in a personal way,' he replied boldly. 'I have learned of something that will interest you.'

I stood beside him, leaning my arms on the top of the wall. 'Tell me, Stephen.'

'The king has opened negotiations with Saladin and they are seeking an honourable settlement.'

'They've tried that before.'

'Saladin seems to have altered somewhat. Rumours have it that his emirs have lost interest; it is costing them too much, and they want to go home. Richard thinks that it's time to give them a push — help them along a bit. Saladin is interested, and he has sent his brother, Al-Adil, with his secretary, Imad al-Din, to conduct the negotiations.'

My thoughts were busy with this while I spent the next moments enjoying the sights. There was a busy market near the walls, and we had a good view from up here.

'Is Ahmed settling down in his new kitchen?' I asked Stephen.

'Yes, I think so. Shall we go and see?'

I thought that we should. I was feeling quite warm with only Stephen for company, though we were on the windy battlement on a mild afternoon.

Father Francis had for two days been scouring the palace for a chamber suitable to use as a chapel, but for this morning he was content for us to gather in our reception chamber. To our surprise, Richard attended and came to kneel next to me.

'Good morning, my queen,' he whispered as he bent a knee. 'I have been busy, you understand, yes, yes?'

'As you wish, my lord. But you are here now. This is an English saint's day: Saint Edwin, who was also a king. Pay heed to Father Francis.'

He lapsed into silence, and I looked to my left to find Joan gazing open-mouthed at her brother. She raised an eyebrow, and then turned her attention back to Francis, who was prattling on about how far we had progressed in pursuit of our mission. I wondered if the words were directed at Richard, telling him to get on with it. Priests sometimes used Mass to say things that they wouldn't normally mention.

Afterwards, Richard took me by the hand and we sat on one of the many settles left behind by the former inhabitants. Joan joined us and kissed his cheek.

'How are you, dear Berengaria?' he asked. 'I have missed not coming to know you better.'

'We are well informed as to your doings, Richard. What do you know of ours?'

'Yes, brother, messengers are not the same as a note from your hand, or a visit.'

'Oh, don't combine against me. Let's be easy with each other. I have much to do. I do know about how you organised things in Akko, and I am most grateful for your support.'

'Will you be staying for long, husband?' I asked.

'Yes, we had almost forgotten what you looked like, Richard. Can you not attend us more often?'

'Ah!' He slapped his thigh. 'Attend you! Now then, yes, yes; I have some part for you to play.'

'In the war?' asked Joan, as amused as I was.

'Yes, yes. I am to receive emissaries from Saladin; we're trying to reach an agreement, you know. Can you get your cook to do something for them — to sweeten them up, you know?'

'We can do that, Richard,' I said. 'I am well used to organising palace receptions, and we have Hugo and Stephen to help. Yes, we would like to do that for you.'

'Good, good. Make sure that the Byzantine girl attends. Dress her as a proper princess, if you will. Got to go now; things to do. Reception tomorrow, if you please.'

After kissing the tops of our heads, he was gone.

'He was serious. Nothing matters except what he imagines,' said Joan.

'"Dress her as a proper princess." He has the feelings of a donkey, does your brother.' I was fuming. 'I'm going to find Stephen.'

'Look behind you,' said Joan.

'I heard, Your Highness.' Stephen was hovering. 'He accepted that I will be better employed here on the coast than in Cyprus. Lusignan and Camville can see to things there. We'd better get this reception organised.'

'We'll go and see if Hugo needs any help,' I responded, feeling pleased that Stephen wanted to remain here.

'I'll come with you,' said Joan.

Despite his bursts of violence, Richard did sometimes display an understanding of diplomacy, and today was one such occasion. The nature of his court had been altered; the lords selected to attend him had somehow found soft clothing among their baggage, and the women's apartments took on the appearance of a European court.

Richard was splendid in his white hose and scarlet coat, with his golden red locks topped by a crown. Similarly, the coats of arms of the kingdoms of northern Europe and those of the important lords with us on the Crusade were much in evidence. Richard's desire seemed to be to display Christendom as one kingdom in design and intent, despite the reality of the petty squabbling and manoeuvring for gain among the various factions.

Not in seagoing apparel today, both Joan and I were conducted to ornate golden chairs on Richard's left side. There was an empty chair on his right, but no explanation as to its purpose. Eirini was on one side of the chamber, flanked by Alya and Nabila and attended by Amynta.

Alazne had found a splendid crimson gown for me, the one least damaged by the predations of the sea air. With my hair captured in a golden net and topped by a golden crown, I was, for the first time, on display to outsiders as the queen of a monarch.

Joan wore a golden gown worked with intricate red and green embroidery, and no queen's crown adorned her hair, which was gathered in with a golden caul.

Richard was in good cheer and spent some time explaining who his visitors would be.

There came a trumpet blast from somewhere outside, but there were no shouted orders in here as the splendid guards took up their positions. Each had been chosen for his height, and they dwarfed everyone else in the chamber except for Richard.

'Your Highness,' called out Hugo, 'His Highness, Sultan Al-Malik Al-Adil.'

Al-Adil swept in with much rustling of garments: splendid green robes which trailed on the ground and a huge round hat in green and gold. His face was framed by a well-shaped beard, and a sort of smile was on his lips as he advanced on Richard. An entourage of gowned officials trailed in his wake.

Richard stood and stepped forward to greet him. They were joined by two others.

'Interpreters,' whispered Jo.

'Get Amynta to stand behind me,' I whispered in return.

Joan made a gesture, and Amynta moved behind us while Richard and the sultan were exchanging greetings.

Eventually Richard guided Saladin's brother to the chair next to his, and they began a conversation using the interpreters. Al-Adil became quite agitated from time to time and kept peering round in the directions of Eirini and Joan. At length, Richard stood and conducted the emissary out of the room, whispering to me, 'Stay here, Berengaria; got some delicate negotiations to do.'

I beckoned to Amynta and she leaned over between our chairs. 'What was that about, Amynta?' I asked.

'Something about marriage, I think. Eirini seemed to be involved, but my Arabic is not that good, so I am not entirely certain of the details. But King Richard wants something to happen which the Saracen is not authorised to agree to.'

An unpleasant thought entered my head. 'If he thinks that Eirini is to become a bargaining pawn, then he'll have me to deal with.'

Joan was not best pleased either. We waited for a while, but when Richard did not return, Joan stood. The chamber fell silent as she asked if I was coming. I agreed, and we left the lords to chatter among themselves and retired to the guard hall, where there was a buffet laid out with Hugo in attendance.

Stephen wandered in, accompanied by Hugo, later on in the evening. Everyone was tucking into the food quite nicely and I asked them to join us.

'I'm not that hungry. I ate out there,' replied Stephen.

'Well, we're hungry for news. Give it, you two, or I'll have you strung up on the battlements.'

'Yes,' agreed Joan, 'or we'll put you in the same state as Abla.'

'Oh no, not that — please, my lady!' Stephen pleaded with a laugh. Jesting aside, he told us all that he knew. Richard was now angling for access to the Holy City and had suggested a solution: all faiths would have access, including Saracens, but he wanted to retain the string of forts along the coast as a guarantee of pilgrims' rights and safe conduct. In addition, there should be a pact between the two faiths to become united in peace. 'And that's when they went into a privy conference.'

Joan nudged me. 'Why am I so uneasy, Berri? There's something of the dark arts in this; what are those two plotting?'

It got dark early at this time of year, and the palace servants had but a few moments ago been lighting the candles, of which there were many, when Richard strolled in.

'Sorry, got delayed — much to discuss, yes, yes.'

'Did you get an agreement, brother?'

'Nearly, yes, nearly. Got something to ask you, dear Joan.' He looked across the chamber to where Eirini was stitching with her little household. 'Is she ready for marriage yet?'

'She might be, but we have not got anyone in mind, so we've given the matter little thought. Why?'

'Thought that she might be going to the sultan's household — that's all.'

That remark met with silence, mostly because we could sense that he was not yet finished. We waited.

'And you, dear sister; have you thought about remarriage, what?'

'No — why?'

'Nothing much. Curious, that's all. You don't fancy another man in your bed, eh? Must be lonely.'

Joan's plate hit the floor and her eyes went cold. 'What? What have you done, Richard?'

Richard shuffled and seemed to shrink a little before the icy gaze of his sister. 'Just wondered. Saladin's brother — he's a nice fellow, and he took a fancy to you.'

'What?'

'Your marriage to him would solve a lot of problems, yes, yes.'

'No! You dunderhead; you deceitful plotter — you would sell your own sister? Wait until the Pope hears this; I'll —'

'Already written to him.'

'Then unwrite to him. It will never happen. Do you understand me, Richard? Never.'

Then a goblet went flying towards him, which he evaded, and a plate, which he did not. Then Joan stomped out of the hall, tearing tapestries off the wall and sending platters and ornaments crashing to the floor as she went.

'Oh. Gone amiss, I believe, what, what.' Richard's gaze crossed the chamber to where Eirini was sitting.

'Forget her,' I spat. 'Richard, that will make things worse. My God! You do yourself no favours. Will you have any friends left, or do you intend to assault the Holy City single-handedly?'

'Not quite. Must fly; got things to do.'

'I'm going to find Joan, and you, my lord, should stay away for a bit until your sister has calmed down. But note this, Richard, for your own good: the Pope will hear of this, and the consequences may just place your own soul in jeopardy. Ladies, attend me, please. I'm going to find Lady Joan.'

'She's by the city walls,' said Stephen gently as I passed him by. 'I'll stay in sight. Give me a wave if you need me, Your Highness.'

'Thank you, Stephen.'

We swept through an empty palace, the wise having made themselves scarce. I was left with an empty feeling; the king, my husband, would sacrifice his own sister in order to satisfy his obsession. God surely would not require that.

I let my ladies search ahead of me, eventually taking the steps up onto the wall. The moon was bright that night, but even so the way was well lit by braziers. As I reached the top step onto the battlement itself, there were a few soldiers keeping watch. Stephen was already there, standing apart from the soldiery.

My ladies approached along the wall from the opposite direction, and we converged on Stephen at the same time.

'What has Joan said?' asked Stephen.

'She sent us away,' Alazne said.

She pointed towards the far end of the wall, where it turned back into the town. A lone figure was leaning against the parapet, illuminated by a flickering brazier.

'Leave us now, please,' I commanded. 'I'll manage. Thank you.'

They turned to leave without comment, but Stephen stayed and trailed along behind as I set off to join the disquieted Joan. I was very sad.

'That was quite an evening, Joan. Full of surprises, eh?'

'Hold me, Berri. I feel ill. I thought that his behaviour towards you was without feeling. But to be used as a bargaining tool, to be sent to live in a harem as the prize exhibit, a Christian harlot! How has such obsession driven his mind to this foul depth? I'm his sister, his own flesh and blood. Is he mad?'

'He may be,' I said, holding her tight, 'but it cannot be God who is driving him; he is impelled by the devil, surely. Come, Joan; it is chilly up here. Let's go to bed; we will talk better in the morning when we are refreshed.'

The morning brought a little respite from our anger and anxiety. Torène entered my bedchamber to wake us.

'A little late this morning, Your Highnesses,' she said, drawing back the window drapes. 'Father Francis was asking if you are ill. I said that you were more disappointed than ill. Did I answer correctly?'

'You did, my sweet,' said Joan from the depths of the covers on the other side of the bed.

I sat up, bleary-eyed. 'Make sure that everyone attends Prime before breakfast this morning, Torène, and ensure that Stephen and Hugo come to see us afterwards. There are things to discuss, and we may not be here much longer.'

After Prime, we went along the corridor into the reception hall, which was laid out for breakfast. Richard was not there.

'Where is he?' demanded Joan.

'H-his Highness has left for the hills, Your H-highnesses,' stuttered Hugo.

Joan and I exchanged glances. Her lips were tight as she wrestled with her thoughts.

'Perhaps that is for the best, Joan. Come, Ahmed has set out some nice things for us. Look, your favourite: *riz bi haleeb*, fruits and some of that *maamoul bi ajwa*.'

Stephen walked in just as Joan was becoming interested in eating and took her attention away.

'Stephen,' I said, receiving a warm smile in return, 'where is the king? Do you know more than Hugo?'

'Yes. It is complex.'

'Have you eaten this morning?'

'No, Your Highness.'

'Then join us, and tell us all you know.'

He took a place next to me and we settled down, figs in hand, ready to hear of Richard's latest plans.

'He is planning to advance on Jerusalem, but he needs to safeguard the return route back here, where the army will be supplied from. To this end he is rebuilding certain castles along the chosen route, namely that of Yas'ur, and the one at Moyen, both considered key points from which to watch over the supply wagons and baggage trains.

'He will then establish a forward supply position nearer Jerusalem, which will be the final departure point for the siege and attack upon the Holy City. He expects Saladin to yield by this time and prays not to have to assault Jerusalem by this strategy.'

'And marriages, Stephen — any more nonsense about marriages?' demanded Joan.

'I've heard nothing, but even though he is planning to attack Jerusalem in the spring, he is still holding diplomatic channels open through Al-Adil. Saladin and Richard are playing the game with the highest stakes imaginable, and neither will concede any position yet.'

'So I'm still a hostage to fate?'

Stephen made no response to that remark for a while, and then said, 'The rains have begun. It makes for soggy warfare, so there will be no great confrontations, no mass army attacks and no sieges. Moving wagons will become difficult if not impossible.'

'Until springtime?' I mused.

Stephen, whose face was near to mine, nodded to confirm it. I found the meeting of our eyes uncomfortable.

'Expect the time from now forth to be taken up with preparations for a spring offensive. If the negotiations come to naught, that is — else we may have a treaty instead.'

I had a desire to grab and kiss him, but resisted for my dignity's sake.

'I suppose I'd be at the centre of any treaty,' spat Joan. 'Can you get us out of here, Stephen?'

'Oh, my lady, not without the king's permission. He'll have my head off.'

'I suppose he would. Sorry to put you in such a position. But will you take us away if I can get permission?'

Stephen's hand brushed against mine and I grabbed it, holding tight. Looking into his eyes, I added, 'I will stay with Queen Joan, so if we can get away, it will be the pair of us ... and our little household. Will you?'

I did not want him to take any unnecessary risks, but I wanted to get away from this place. Nothing made sense anymore.

'I will indeed, Your Highness. Be assured that I will always act in your best interests.'

He left then. I had a warm feeling that was not entirely welcome. I needed to pray.

After a week or so, when Joan's indignation at Richard's attempt at diplomacy through marriage had subsided, we sat together to see if we could discover a way out of our dilemma. Our eagerness to leave Jaffa, now more of a prison than a palace in my mind, was somewhat reduced when Hugo announced something half-expected about our ships.

'They have cancelled all voyages, Your Highnesses. The winter is upon us, and many ships will need to be careened out of the water for their annual maintenance.'

Stephen came in behind Hugo. Seeing our miserable faces, he thought to make further comment. 'It is true; all ships need attention. They have been kept busy and the wind and sea take a toll, summer or winter. Ropes become frayed and weakened by exposure to sun and sea, sails rot, wood weakens and the crews need a rest. All the stores which have been stockpiled in Jaffa will be taken inland — weather, wagon wheels and hostile Saracens permitting — and the supply voyages from Cyprus will recommence when the ships and the weather allow.'

'Ladies, get your needles out,' I said with a sigh. 'We are here until the spring.'

'And we might, or might not, see the king,' said Joan.

'If he knows what you are thinking, Your Highness,' said Alazne, 'he might feel safer up in the hills among those Saracen raiding parties that we hear about all the time.'

'Humph, he might,' agreed Joan.

I had never been so bored. Needlework had never been one of my main interests. At home in Olite I'd always been too busy, although I could admire the work of others. This enforced attention to thread, cloth and needles was enough to make me irritated beyond belief.

I enjoyed the language tutorials, and Eirini was turning into a fine woman, if at present one without a clear future. I was determined to find a path for her as soon as I was free to do so.

The few weeks leading up to Christmas passed by, interspersed by messages concerning Richard. As always, routine reports were followed by exciting combat reports, especially those where Richard was the main combatant. I often wondered how embellished they were, but all spoke of his bravery, or of his foolishness, depending on whether or not you cared much.

The rain was at its dreary worst that year, worse than anyone could remember, as Ahmed told me when we had the beginnings of conversational Arabic in our grasp.

Then, the week before Christmas, Stephen came into the receiving chamber with some news. 'The king wishes you to visit him at Ramla for Christmas, Your Highness. I have word that he is not very well and needs some rest. Perhaps you could cheer him a bit.'

An outsider might have expected some celebration at that news, but there was only silence, and then a cough from Hugo, who had been sitting with Amynta, trying out his Greek.

'Will I be going with you, Queen Berengaria?' he asked.

'Perhaps, but if he is ill then he should be allowed some peace.'

Joan gazed at me. 'You should go; your husband is unwell. Show the army your support.'

The army? Perhaps it needed a hale and hearty commander, but inside I was crying for myself. Still, I determined to go and see Richard. 'Will you come with me, Joan?'

'Of course. I might not speak to him, but I'll go with you.'

Stephen was having none of it. 'I will close the gates against you, Your Highness, if you so much as approach them.'

'We're going. Get used to the idea, Lord Stephen.'

My formal address cracked his resistance. 'If you are determined, then I will make arrangements. But be certain, Your Highness: when we go to Ramla, you will be wrapped up in so tight an escort you will scarcely have room to breathe, and there will be no room for all your women. It will be dangerous enough for the two of you. You will have to do without them for a few days.' He planted his feet and stood before me, defiant.

'You defy your queen?'

'I defend my queen. Allow me to do my duty, Your Highness.'

Shrugging my shoulders, I nodded assent. 'Don't try that in public, Stephen, or I'll be obliged to defend my position,' I scolded him. Looking about me, I planted a kiss on his cheek, and he blushed. 'Get us ready to go — however you wish.'

'Your Highness.' He smiled roguishly. 'Riding clothes, if you please.'

The weather was foul and wet, and the track was muddy. Soldiers were having trouble keeping the red disease off their weapons; most of the sheep's wool they usually used having been exhausted, so they resorted to olive oil, which was not as good and made everything sticky.

I was on a bedraggled horse, and Joan's wouldn't have commanded much of a price at the meat market. The best animals had gone to the cavalrymen — we were merely the objects in the convoy to be guarded.

The country was quite flat, and we could see a long way ahead until we came to a wooded region.

'This looks to be a dangerous area,' said Stephen, bringing his horse alongside mine and pointing ahead. 'I'll wait until the scouts return before we proceed.'

The track ahead pointed towards a gap in the trees, where it disappeared into the forest. A good place for an ambush, I thought, and bad ground for cavalry. I could see the need for caution. After a few moments, two figures appeared at the entrance to the trees and beckoned to us.

'Good. It is safe,' said Stephen, and he called for our column to advance. 'Forwards; keep a sharp lookout!'

I heard the slither of metal against leather as our horsemen loosened their swords from their sheaths. Lances were raised, and we set off.

'Stay close to me, Your Highnesses,' commanded Stephen. There was no place for argument here. There was something about the place, something threatening in the air.

'I'm scared, Joan,' I said.

'Me too; those trees seem evil.'

Entering the wood, we were hemmed in on either side, but, reassured by those beckoning figures ahead, we pressed on at a trot. Joan and I were in the middle of the column and we were making good progress when I spied a glimpse of open ground ahead of us. We were almost out, but then there was a shout and we came to an abrupt halt. The riders at the front had stopped.

A cry came back, repeated along the column. 'We've been tricked! Our scouts are lying at the trackside in bushes, with their throats cut.'

'Those scoundrels ahead are not our men!' shouted Stephen. 'Let's gallop through; we are trapped in here.'

Digging my heels in, I got my scruffy nag into a semblance of a gallop and did my best to keep up. I could hear Joan panting along behind. I knew we were slowing the column down. I was not reassured by the sight of two naked bodies as we raced by: our scouts, half concealed at the side of the track. They had been slaughtered, and their clothes had been taken to disguise the enemy.

They were waiting for us as we emerged from the cover of the trees. A dozen Saracen horsemen came at us from the right. Stephen shouted some orders, and two sergeants closed up on either side of me and Joan as Stephen pointed his lance at the oncoming Saracens and led the rest of the column into a counter-charge.

Watching the action playing out before me, I felt the most useless of creatures. Men were going to die to defend Joan and me. Then one of the sergeants at my side cried, 'Behind! Those two are at us.'

Spinning around, I saw that the two whose disguises had fooled us were heading straight for us. I was near extinction, or worse.

Growling and screaming, my sergeants got going and rushed towards the oncoming pair. They must not have expected that, because although they got two arrows off while standing tall in their saddles, they were immediately hit by lances with such ferocity that it threw them backwards onto the ground. My sergeants wheeled around and came back to finish the squirming Saracens off. As they pulled their lances from the men's chests, a great spurt of blood rose skywards, and my guardians gave guffaws of triumph.

Soon they were back at my side. 'Thank you, thank you!' I cried, grateful for their quick actions.

'My pleasure, Your Highness,' replied the ugliest and biggest, spitting on the ground. 'I enjoyed that. Look there — Lord Stephen is enjoying his day.'

I had forgotten the greatest threat. Stephen needed to win his battle. But then I heard the other sergeant curse, and as I turned to look, I saw him pulling at an arrow protruding from his chest.

I felt sick. His companion reined in alongside him and shouted at the stricken soldier. 'Is it in? Has it got through, Bada?'

'Nay, lad,' was the reply. 'The mail has held; it is but a scratch.' Then, ignoring the obvious pain, he began to clean his lance by dragging the tip through the desert scrubland.

Assured, I looked across at Stephen's tussle. It was not going well. It appeared that Stephen's initial charge had only been a partial success, and now the ascendancy was with the Saracens. There were bodies on the ground, true, but in the manner of Saladin's method of warfare the remainder had backed away and were riding past Stephen's men at a distance, loosing their deadly arrows from horseback. I began to take fright again.

One of my sergeants asked the other, 'Should we go in, Godric?'

'No, Bada, get ready to flee. The queens are our concern.'

'The scoundrels!' Bada spat into a nearby bush.

Then Godric shouted, 'Bada, look left! There are some of ours.'

I looked to where he was pointing and saw horsemen in the distance.

'Are you certain they are ours? Get ready to flee, Your Highnesses!' called Godric.

'There are banners; it must be a patrol.'

A shout came from where Stephen was still engaged, only a hundred paces away. One of the Saracens had spotted us and broken away from the melee, heading straight for me.

'Flee, Your Highnesses! Back into the trees!' shouted Godric as he kicked his horse into a gallop and sped off to meet the oncoming archer. His lance was still stuck in the ground as he had followed Bada's example of cleaning it, and he was now without his main weapon. Bada grabbed at my reins, but he missed when his steed suddenly took fright and sprang away, taking all his attention.

Godric was now near the onrushing warrior, who was aiming his bow. He loosed, and an arrow bounced off Godric's shield. He was standing in the saddle with his sword above his head. Realising the danger, the Saracen attempted to turn away, his light horse and armour being better for manoeuvring, but he was too late. Godric's blade cut through his shoulder in a downward slash and his arm fell off, showering Godric with blood.

There were shouts from my left as the oncoming patrol, now safely identified as our men, sped towards us at a full gallop.

The remaining Saracens, realising they were outnumbered, gathered together and sped off towards the distant hills, leaving their wounded and dead behind.

My insides churned. I watched, horrified, as the wounded Saracens were dealt a death-slash across the throat with knives as our men dismounted to finish them off.

Silence fell as the patrol eased off from the gallop and trotted towards us.

Then my body began to tremble and I slid off my horse, falling to my knees alongside the skittish mare. Joan was quickly by my side and we clung together like sheep abandoned to a wolf pack.

'Jesu, Berri. That was something I do not want to repeat.'

'No, there's not much of the past few months that I want to repeat, Joan.'

A shadow fell across me. 'Your Highness? You are not hurt?' It was Stephen.

I looked up, past his blood-drenched chest and into his concerned eyes. 'Apart from shivering and being desperate to relieve myself, I am quite well, Stephen.'

'Ah, the trembles: newly blooded warriors always have the trembles. It is the excitement, you see, Your Highness.'

'I see, and what about the other problem?'

'Ah, yes. There are bushes over there; drop in behind them, but hurry. I'll go and talk to the patrol commander.'

Joan and I both relieved ourselves then strode back to our horses.

Stephen returned, smiling from his conference with the patrol commander. 'That is Eric of Rouen. He is on his way to Jaffa to escort more supplies up to Ramla; it's lucky he was near. I thanked him, Your Highness, on your behalf.'

'Good. Call him over before he leaves.'

Eric of Rouen soon pulled up alongside me. With his helm removed and his mail coif pulled back, I could see that he was very handsome indeed. I took him to be the patrol commander.

'Your Highnesses, you are safe. I'm pleased that we could help,' he said.

'Yes, Eric of Rouen, your presence is timely. Thank you.'

'I thank you too,' added Joan. 'Even though our Lord Stephen was at his most valiant, we might not have survived the day.'

Eric gazed at us. 'Valiant Stephen may be, but not of good judgement to bring you out here...'

'I commanded him, Eric of Rouen,' I said. 'He did his duty.'

'I understand, but the king might not.'

'How is my brother?' asked Joan.

'The king is not well, Your Highness; he might not know you.'

'You may address me as "my lady". Sicily is no longer my realm. We should make haste. How far from his encampment are we?'

'Two miles, my lady. You're nearly there. You will be safe,' said Eric. 'Now, I have a duty to perform, so you may continue if you wish.'

'What do you need to do, Eric?' asked Joan.

'I must see to the bodies, my lady; it's better if we treat them with respect.'

'Of course. Do we have many casualties?'

'I meant the Saracen bodies, Your Highness. As honourable enemies, we should respect their valour. We will lay them out and cover their faces. Their brothers are waiting to collect them.'

Eric pointed towards the horizon far to our right, where figures could be seen faintly through the rain.

'They are the Saracens?' I asked, astonished.

'Indeed. They will appreciate our respect, and you can take our casualties back with you, along with the bodies. How many, Stephen?'

'Three dead, and two wounded.'

'Then take them back quickly for treatment. I must go. It was an honour to meet Your Highness, and my lady.'

Not waiting for a response, Eric spun his horse around and issued some orders. When the Saracen dead were suitably covered, he gathered his men together and headed into the wooded track on the way to Jaffa, followed by his men and some creaking wagons.

'What a strange war,' said Joan.

'Indeed — strange and frightening,' I answered. 'Stephen, get us to safety. I've seen enough for one day.'

Ramla was not much more than a stone curtain wall and some buildings in need of repair. Barracks and stores were housed in tents, and the whole area was miserable with constant rain.

Stephen, Joan and I were conducted to Richard's pavilion and led to his bedside.

My husband's face was ashen with patches of red skin, and heavily coated with sweat. There was a speck of blood on his lips. I was scared for him. I went to him, shocked as I looked into his normally clear eyes. They were yellowed, and he mumbled, trying to make sense.

'Shouldn't see me like this, no, no. Oh, dear God, free me from this.' He grabbed at my arm, trying to look at me. 'Berengaria? Berengaria, I am sorry that you see me in such poor spirits. My legs hurt, my arms hurt, and I have been ordered to bed by my physicians.'

Although any intimate feelings I'd had for Richard had diminished, I could not ignore my sympathy for one so cast down. 'Oh, Richard,' I said, 'let us take you to the coast, where you will be comforted. By your appearance, the physicians have acted properly in confining you in your illness, but when you are fit you must come with us.'

Joan was waiting behind me, and leaned down to give him a kiss on the cheek. His appearance seemed to have shocked her into silence. Eventually, she managed to say, 'Brother, let's make you more comfortable.'

Between us and two squires, we got him sitting up on the bed, then two men came into the bedchamber and announced themselves as the king's physicians.

I said that we should get the sweat-sodden garments off him, and sent the squires out while the physicians aided Joan and me in stripping Richard down to his small breeches.

As I pulled the covers over, he began to shiver. I lay on one side of him, and with Joan on the other he began to warm as the two medical men looked on anxiously.

Soon he fell asleep and we withdrew from the bed, covering his body with the fresh, dry blankets that I had ordered.

'As soon as he is cogent again, we will bring a warm tub in here and get him back into a civilised condition. He smells like something between a stables and a midden,' I declared.

'Yes,' said Joan, on the attack, 'you physicians should have more care for your king.'

'Caring for the king is similar to herding cats, Your Highness: a futile exercise,' declared one.

'Well,' responded Joan, not to be put down, 'if you are in charge of his health, you can do it properly now, by my command.' We swept out of the pavilion together, our duty fulfilled for now.

'Did you see their faces, Berri?'

'Yes; well put out at two women taking over.'

That kept us cheerful for a while, at least until we asked about sleeping arrangements. This caused some discussion among Richard's retainers, until I demanded two truckle beds be found and brought to the pavilion for our use. We set them up with concealing curtains and informed Richard's stewards that we forbade anyone from entering without Stephen's permission until the king recovered.

The pavilion door was quite busy for the next couple of days, with many people trying to see Richard, but Stephen had strict instructions about who should be admitted as the physicians tended to the ailing king.

Richard sat up a couple of times but did not recognise me when he opened his eyes. I resolved to remain in Ramla until he returned to normal. It was a worrying time.

Few incoming reports gave us any hope that we would ever enter, or even see, the Holy City. The closest we got was within twelve miles: a place named Beit Nuba. Stephen, against his better judgement, was coerced into taking us there, but before we reached it we were compelled to turn back for fear of ambush. Our scouts had reported movement in the area, and I did not want a repeat of our earlier encounter. It could have been a dangerous waste of time in the wet, but Stephen used it to gather some intelligence. It was not optimistic.

'All is not well with the army, Your Highness,' he said as we splashed along a muddy track, heading back to Richard's camp. 'The promised Germans have not appeared, Philip's departure has turned out to be less helpful than at first it seemed, and there are desertions and sicknesses. If Saladin is in trouble with his men, then so are we.'

'Thank you, Stephen. Very cheering, but what does it mean?'

'It means that we should pray that both generals are running out of options. The best that Richard and Saladin can hope for now is some kind of negotiated peace.'

'They could have achieved that without all this death and destruction.'

'Aye. If only that were the way of things.'

Among the many people wandering around Richard's encampment were a number of bishops. Praying for the capture of Jerusalem was their main purpose, but it meant that Christmas would not go by without suitable attention paid to its passing. Thus there was no shortage of celebrants as we gathered together for the special service held on Christmas Day in front of as many mud-stained soldiers as could be spared from their duties.

Given that it rained, the service was not long, but even so Richard was not able to attend. Bishop Jean of Evreux, the very same who had married us, accompanied Joan and me into Richard's pavilion. The king was given a shortened version of the service and blessed.

I thought he appreciated that, and he perked up enough for us to stay until he fell asleep once more.

'The best cure, Your Highnesses,' said one of his physicians by way of encouragement. 'And we have been advised to feed him fruit, for it seems that his condition is known by local physicians.'

'Of course,' replied Joan. 'Any advice will be useful, if it works.'

Joan was determined to remain in the ascendancy, and used every opportunity to discomfit these two learned men. Her brother's attitude seemed to have hardened her against men, and she was not alone in this.

We were now housed in a large tent nearby, set in a sea of mud, under constant drizzle. Our ears were assailed by the seemingly endless accompaniment of coughing soldiers, clergy and others, all of whom were suffering in this dreadful wetness.

Two days later, Richard sat up and demanded to be released from his 'prison', as he described it. The two physicians sent for a tub of hot water and eventually Richard appeared late that afternoon, all ready to return to his duties and go about his business.

Sending for his commanders and captains, he quickly assessed the situation and declared himself ready to go and fortify Latrun, wherever that was. Then, being shoved atop his horse, he departed, leaving us to our own devices once again.

The camp emptied, save for some cooks and servants, and the faithful Stephen.

'How long will we be stuck in this bog, Stephen?' I asked.

'Until your patience runs out, Your Highness. Or you succumb to this coughing malaise everyone else seems to have had.'

'A cheerful prospect, Stephen,' said Joan. 'Shall we go back, Berengaria?'

'What, back to the comfort of Jaffa? Do you dislike this damp hillside, sister?' I asked wryly.

'I hate the place. We are not required here, Berri. Stephen, have you enough soldiers to make the return journey safe?'

'No, but we can travel with Eric on his next supply mission.'

At least that was cheering. 'We still haven't glimpsed the Holy City, Joan,' I reminded her.

'We'll see it from heaven, Berri. It will always be there,' she replied, gazing into the distance.

We returned to Jaffa dismayed and resigned to a life of indifference.

'Back to the needles?' sniffed Joan once we were back in our apartments.

'Not entirely,' I responded, trying to be merry. 'There's learning Greek and cooking, and if the rain eases we might try a little horse-riding along the beach, perhaps.'

'Some hope,' muttered Stephen, who had entered the chamber. 'It's dangerous out there — a game of hit and run is at play. Neither Saladin nor Richard is ready to fully confront the other with an army and engage in battle, but skirmishes remain a great risk, and could result in your abduction. Be patient, Your Highness. I'll be ready to get you out of here as soon as the king grants you permission.'

I did not like Stephen's words, although I knew the truth of them. *Let spring come early this year*, I prayed. For warmth, I had to content myself with Stephen's presence, for apart from Joan's love it was all that I had for comfort in rainy Jaffa.

CHAPTER NINE

1192

March had come at last, and armies and diplomats were stirring.

'The first ship is leaving the harbour, Your Highnesses.' Hugo brought the expected news. 'Do you wish to go onto the wall?'

A walk along the city wall in the sunshine was a welcome offer, so I led the way.

'Hermes or Mars?' I mumbled, gazing at the Akko-bound ship.

'What?' said Joan.

'Diplomacy or war? That is the choice. If things keep on the way they have throughout the winter, Richard and Saladin will need to fight it out in single combat. They've lost so many men.'

'Yes,' agreed Joan. 'Saladin's emirs have run out of patience and money fighting his war, and if the rumours are true, they're for heading back to Syria.'

'It is in Richard's interests to agree to a treaty,' Stephen added. 'His men are wet and bored. Many of the French have retired to Akko; the fleshpots are active once more. Then there is squabbling among the Christian lords about who gets to be King of this and Lord of that. Richard is struggling to hold it all together. The idle winter has agitated idle minds into matters of self-interest.'

'It was ever thus,' said Father Francis. 'I believe the First Crusade was driven by self-interest. Men joined not merely to save their souls but to seize domains for themselves here on earth.'

'Quite,' I answered. 'But what of our dilemma, Stephen? Is it time to petition Richard to let us leave?'

'It might not be too difficult to achieve,' said Joan. 'I have learned something in a letter from Mother.'

'You said nothing,' I remarked. 'What does Eleanor have to say? Do tell.'

'It only arrived today. Mother says that matters in England have reached a sad state. My younger brother, John, is inept, but we all knew that — why he was left in charge I'll never know. But he is in dispute with Chancellor William Longchamp, who was sent to mentor him; indeed, he has dismissed Longchamp from office. And the country has fallen out of love with John, if it ever was enamoured of him. The land is in turmoil.'

'Richard might want to go back,' I said hopefully.

'He might be persuaded to send someone back to support Mother.'

'I've not noticed that Eleanor needs much support,' I retorted.

'She is not a young woman, Berri; it must be difficult for her. Anyway, there's something else. Mother says that the new Pope is incensed by Richard's idea of marrying me off to a Saracen. Pope Celestine may want to speak to him if he ever goes back home again.'

'Oh! God in heaven; how wonderful! That's you out of a disastrous match, Joan.'

'And well pleased, too. Does this alter things, Stephen?'

'Probably,' he smiled. 'As you are of little use anymore in his negotiations, he may well find you an encumbrance.'

I grasped her with both arms, kissing her on the cheek. 'Release! Release from this muddy hell.'

'We'll try him,' Joan said. 'We'll send a note out to him and see what his reaction is. Where is he, Stephen?'

'Ashkelon; they've set about repairing the wrecked harbour.'

'Come, Berri. Let us compose a love letter to Richard; it may beget our release from here.'

I went with her, but my thoughts were momentarily diverted. I was thinking about Stephen. Even while he engendered warm feelings in me, he was not dangerous to my honour, and I wondered if we could find a way to keep Stephen as our escort back across the sea. But first, we needed permission to leave.

Do what you wish, was the terse response from Richard in Ashkelon. *Move back to Akko if you like it not in Jaffa. I myself am going back to Akko to restore some discipline.*

There was to be movement once more, although the messenger also told us that Richard was ill again.

The enduring campaign had lasted far beyond his expectations, and his support was dwindling by the day. Indeed, there were more waiting in Akko for passage on a ship than remained in the field with the king; this Stephen reported with dismay.

'We can leave now?' Joan said with surprise.

'If we will be safe,' I replied. 'Perhaps we should. With all Richard's so-called allies deserting him, we should be safest near him and his loyal men. Staying here is not an option.'

Stephen nodded. 'If Richard's army is dwindling, there is a chance that Saladin might try to re-take this city, in which case we might be forced to flee. I doubt the king would want you two to fall into the hands of the Saracen soldiery; they've not got a reputation for kindness towards captured women.'

'Make the arrangements now,' I commanded. 'I'm not waiting around for fate to find me.'

It was a worrying time while Stephen put into place a plan for us to return to Akko, with few ships and fewer men. We had, of course, tarried too long.

The day we had dreaded arrived in July, when the alarm was raised by the sentries.

'What's amiss?' asked Joan, half awake.

'They're shouting something about an army.'

'Has Richard returned?'

'Don't know. Let's go and see.' I pulled down the cover and put my feet on the floor.

'Call Alazne; get her to bring in a drink.' Joan was now sitting with her feet on the floor on the opposite side of the bed. We were wearing little, it being warm at night.

There was a shout outside in the castle ward.

'They are here! Saladin's army is outside the walls!'

'Jesu! Joan, we're in trouble. Get dressed — sea attire.'

We were under siege. Richard had marched northwards back to Akko, where he hoped to persuade reluctant soldiers to return to arms. Here in Jaffa, we had only our troops within the garrison with which to defend the city.

Stephen burst in before we could move. 'Time to go, Your Highnesses,' he ordered. 'No time to lose now, dressed or not.'

I leaped off the bed, naked save for my netherwear, as did Joan. Next Alazne dashed in, wearing only small breeches as we grabbed our seagoing clothes.

'Give me a hand on with my rope sandals, Stephen, while I button up my shirt,' I said. 'Seen anything that you like?'

'Indeed, Your Highness,' he replied, looking up from where he knelt at my feet, a wry smile lighting up his face. 'Ready or not, come as you are,' he added as Eirini and her household rushed in.

'Jesu!' cried Joan. 'Give me a chance to cover my chest. I'll be exposed all the way down to the quayside like this.'

'It'll be worse if the Saracens catch you. Get a move on.' Stephen had cast aside etiquette; it was fast becoming a matter of survival.

Just as I echoed his call to hurry, a great ball of flame crashed into the wall and everyone fell to the floor.

'Jesu!' exclaimed Stephen. 'They've got Greek fire. Get out now!'

We scattered for the door. Abla was at his station and I called for him to follow, then Ahmed appeared with his kitchen staff. They were all dressed; rising early was the norm for them. Alya and Nabila appeared half clothed.

Amynta threw some bedding at them, shouting for them to join us.

'Run!' shouted Stephen.

'I am running,' responded Hugo, puffing and panting. 'Where's Father Francis?'

'Behind,' replied Stephen, and all we ladies hesitated just as another fusillade of Greek fire came over the wall.

'Hurry, Your Highnesses,' cried the gate sergeant. 'Go straight through; we'll hold them back.'

The steps were very steep, and I struggled to stay upright and not trip as I flung myself down to where our galleys lay. Stopping at the bottom, I urged my ladies to proceed with both speed and caution. Chaos was seizing my thoughts, and Joan touched my hand as she ran past. I urged my ladies on before me and was glad to see them all pass unscathed, though Amynta was weeping as she ran. I glanced along the jetty to see a galley alongside, and the crew already at their oars.

'Be careful; do not lose your step, priest,' called Stephen, looking behind me to where Father Francis was struggling with his skirts. He took my hand. 'Not the exit I had planned, Berengaria, but it will suffice.'

Glancing behind, I saw a soldier tumbling down the steps, and both he and Francis went over the side and landed in the water, disappearing beneath the surface.

'They've broken through the gate! Berengaria, for Christ's sake, run!' shouted Stephen. Grabbing me by the wrist, he dragged me into a gallop along the jetty.

'Father Francis!' I screamed.

'Gone. Run, my queen, run for your life.'

Crossbow bolts bounced off the paving by my feet and I almost passed Stephen. We arrived at the steps leading down to the galley together. I paused to look back, and my stomach churned as I saw two or three Saracens speeding down the steps.

Behind, Ahmed's staff were too slow, and two more went down in a vicious rain of bolts.

There was a shout from a galley some way out in the harbour, and arrows from the Saracens took out two seamen. A howl from the wall gate was accompanied by more crossbow missiles: we were in the middle of a cross-harbour battle.

'Get down the steps!' Stephen commanded.

'I think I have annoyed him,' I said to Joan as I fell into the bottom of the ship.

'Jesu,' she gasped, 'can you smell this boat?'

Alya and Nabila fell on top of me — followed by one of our seamen with a bolt in his chest, spurting blood.

'Joan,' I gasped, 'is this the end?'

'Not yet; we are moving now.'

I looked up; the rowers were indeed at their work, and I could see that we were underway at last.

'Quickly, or they will reach the end of the pier before us.' The ship's master was barking out orders now, and all I could do was cower in the stinking bilge water. With my head kept low, I could hear the sound of bow strings twanging as our three archers attempted to stop the Saracens reaching the end of the pier, from where they could shoot into our ship.

The oars swept back and forth as the rowers increased their speed, and I could feel the boat surging ahead.

'Stay down until we're out of the harbour,' the master commanded.

A few bolts thudded into oars, hull and mast. I suspected the sail was receiving its share too.

'Stephen!' I called. 'Are we all here?'

'Aye, Your Highness, except the priest, who's gone to heaven early, I believe. And two of your cooks, I'm afraid.'

'What does he mean?' asked Joan, alarmed.

'You didn't see? Father Francis went down with one of our brave men back at the gate steps. I'm so sorry, Joan. I know that you were fond of him.'

After a while, there were no more bolts thudding into the ship and no more cries of pain.

'You can get up now,' said the master. 'Come aft and we'll make you comfortable.'

We scrambled along the centre of the galley. Standing and rubbing our aching bones, I could see that we were in one of the smaller, faster boats. It had little room for passengers.

'My name is Isaac, and I'll get you ladies to Akko. Settle down back here and prepare for an overnight sail.'

'Was anyone wounded, Isaac?' I asked.

'Several killed, my lady, and some wounded. They're over there if you want to take a look.'

'Address her as "Your Highness", if you please, Isaac. The lady is a queen,' Stephen said. 'She is Queen Berengaria of England. And over there is Lady Joan of Sicily.'

'I'm well blessed. Welcome aboard, Your Highness and Your Ladyship. And I suppose that she is a queen, too,' he said, pointing at Eirini.

'No, that's Princess Eirini of Cyprus.'

'Jesu! It is a wonder that the craft doesn't sink beneath the weight of such royalty.'

I could see that Stephen's patience was wearing thin, but we were all a bit tense after our escape, so I laughed and said, 'Thank you, Master Isaac. You were very brave back there. Some would have left when the hostilities began.'

'I might have, but I was told that some important people would be joining the ship, along with a healthy purse. I did not expect such a cargo of beauty, that's for sure. You'd be worth a fortune in a market, without doubt.'

He grinned and Hugo was about to chide him when a cry from the mast reached us.

'Sail, a sail away to the north!'

'We'll head away from the shore. We can't be getting my precious cargo into bother, can we?' Isaac fixed me with a smile. He was quite a handsome man, and charming in a rough sort of way.

'Sails, master!' the lookout informed him. 'It is a fleet.'

It was indeed, and I strained to see it. It was hidden at first, as it was sailing close to the shoreline, but eventually flags and banners could be seen from aloft.

'It's King Richard, heading back to Jaffa!' shouted the lookout.

'Can we get closer, Master Isaac?' I asked.

'No, Your Highness, we are too far to seaward. If I turn towards them, they'll have gone past before we reach them.'

'What did he say, Berengaria?' called Joan from the other side of the craft.

'That's Richard's fleet, on the way to Jaffa. They'll soon have the city under control again.'

'Good. Are you sure we can't get even a little nearer?'

'I'll turn towards them,' said Isaac. 'Show your banner, my lord; then they'll know we're Christian.'

'What banner?' asked Stephen. 'We've got nothing more than what we're wearing.'

We got near enough to see Richard standing next to the steersman of his galley. He looked across as we passed but made no attempt to slow. I watched as he spoke to some other lord near him, but then he turned away and was lost to sight as his vessel ploughed on.

'We need to get to Akko,' I said. 'He isn't interested in us.'

'That's true,' Joan replied. 'We're on our own again.'

'Not quite,' said Stephen. 'There's me and Hugo; that and a few prayers should suffice, don't you think?'

'A limping soldier and a factotum for an army? Yes, we'll do very well, thank you,' I called.

'Don't forget the girls, the cook and the eunuch,' added Alazne, and we all fell about laughing, although it was very brittle laughter.

Akko was changed — safe, perhaps, but altered since we had left its anchorage. The shoreline was different; I could see that from the galley as we approached.

There was a patrol of horsemen near the water's edge, waiting for us to beach in front of them.

'Isaac,' called out their captain, 'did you have a good voyage?'

'Aye, Bertrand — valuable cargo, too. You'd better get them up to the castle before that drunken lot claps eyes on them.'

He pointed back up to the top of the tideline, where rows of tents were now neatly pitched. That was what was different.

'Who are they, Bert?' asked Isaac, looking at the encampment.

'Scroungers, malcontents and the wounded, surrounded by wine and harlots as they wait to ship out home. What's your cargo, then?'

'One queen, one princess and a lady. You'd better take good care of them, else Richard will have your head off.'

I stood up then, as did the rest of my party. Captain Bertrand sat with his mouth agape before swinging into action, dismounting and running to me.

'Upon my soul, Queen Berengaria! I believed you to be in Jaffa.'

'We were. It came under attack and we needed to escape.'

'Did you see the king's fleet on your way, Your Highness?'

'Yes, we passed it at sea. It was heading for Jaffa, we believe.'

'Ah, well, he'll have a hot reception when he arrives, but then King Richard likes that sort of thing.'

'He does. Are the Crusader halls of Akko safe, Bertrand?'

'They are; safer than out here with that collection of miscreants up by the beach. May I help you out, Your Highness?'

'Indeed.' I swung a leg over the gunwale, and he picked me up to put me down on dry sand.

'Thank you, Bertrand, though I won't melt if I get wet, you know. Is there a horse for me?'

'Aye, I'll walk you on mine.'

'And one for Lady Joan and one for the Princess of Cyprus, if you can manage it?'

'Lady Joan?' He looked at Joan. 'But you were a queen.'

'Of Sicily,' said Joan, 'but not anymore. I've resigned.' She gave a sardonic laugh.

'Oh, it's hard to keep up with all this change. Who's he?' Bertrand asked, spotting our giant eunuch.

'He's the guardian of the women's apartments.'

Not taking his eyes off Abla until he received a winning smile from him, Bertrand called out some orders. It did not take long to get us mounted and on our way up to the main gate of the city of Akko.

'We'll bring the rest, Your Highness,' called out Stephen as we trotted across the sand.

It was almost like a homecoming: there was my bedchamber, the privy hall, Ahmed back in his kitchen and Abla at the door, and we had passed my husband heading in the opposite direction along the way.

The first galley to reach us had news. Richard had indeed stemmed the assault against Jaffa, landing on the beach and personally leading the counterattack. He soon regained control of the city, and then the palace and castle.

Then, during the second week of August, we received the news that we had been waiting for.

Stephen, unusually excited, came rushing into our privy hall. 'We've won! Saladin is beaten, Your Highnesses.'

'Tell us more, Stephen, and then we can go home.' Joan was pleased, if not excited. I felt oddly deflated by the news.

'Richard held Jaffa for a few days and the Saracens seemed to have left, but then they were seen as they massed for a dawn assault. Richard went swiftly out to face them head-on. The

Saracens fought gallantly as usual, but he swept them aside with our heavy cavalry and they evaporated as water in the sand. Saladin is back at the negotiating game once more.'

'Without me as bait, I presume,' added Joan.

'Find us a ship, Stephen,' I said. 'One suitable to take us to Italy.'

'As you wish. For some reason, it has been made easy for me to leave. The king is sending his baggage back with my brother, Robert; he has orders to move it back to Barfleur. The king does not seem minded to remain in the Holy Land for much longer.'

'Is it coming to an end, this holy war?' I asked.

'And are we dismissed as baggage?' added Joan. 'How do you read it, Stephen?'

'With no certain instruction from the king, I shall, Your Highnesses, take my instructions from you.' Stephen shuffled and looked away, then went on, 'However, this could place me in a difficult position with the king; you are aware of that?'

'I am, but will you serve me as a member of my household?' I asked.

'It would be my privilege, Your Highness. I know not what after that; I'll just wait and see what else Richard has in store for me.'

'That I did not wish to hear, but I understand. Your first duty is to the king.'

He took my hand and kissed it, looking up into my eyes. 'You are the bravest of the brave, Your Highness. I couldn't think of a better way to do my duty.'

I thought of something. 'Ladies,' I said, looking at Amynta and her charges, 'would you like to take a trip to England, at some time in the future?'

'Ooh, yes,' was the response, in various languages.

'When will we leave, Your Highness?' asked Stephen, grinning — as well he might, for never had a man been blessed with such a collection of beauties to care for.

'As soon as we are loaded.'

'I agree. With no instructions to the contrary, do you give me permission to move away from Outremer?'

'I've had enough of crusading,' Joan said. 'It's not what I had in mind, Berri, when I agreed to join Richard at Messina. I'll come along with you, if you'll take me.'

'Oh, Joan,' I responded, embracing her, 'you can be with me for as long as you want.'

'We are taking all the young ladies, including Alya and Nabila?'

'Of course; why not?'

'Jesu!' muttered Stephen, loud enough for me to hear. 'A ship full of women and girls — wait until I tell the crew.'

'What is the date, Hugo?' I asked.

'The twenty-ninth of September, Your Highness.'

'Thank you, Hugo.'

I watched as Akko disappeared from view in the wake of our vessel. Stephen was standing behind me at the stern, breathing into my hair.

'The king is not travelling with Your Highnesses?' Master Isaac had us safely in his vessel.

'No, he sent word that he had business elsewhere, and would not be returning with us.'

'Then we wasted those weeks waiting for him to return to Akko.'

'Fret not, Master Isaac; *we* have spent two years waiting for him to gain access to the Holy City,' said Joan, with some venom.

'And we are going to Italy?' he asked.

'Indeed,' I replied. 'I will seek an audience with His Holiness, and Lady Joan has questions regarding Sicily. It is rumoured that he wants to keep the German emperor out of there.'

'Life is never dull around you, Your Highness,' said Stephen.

I turned to gaze at him, wondering. 'Does that bother you, Stephen?'

'Quite the reverse, Your Highness. I look forward to a new adventure every day. I've not been to Rome before.'

We looked at each other until a gentle cough from Joan brought us back from where we had been.

'Careful, you two. The Church's ears reach everywhere.'

Stephen looked down and smiled at me, and I returned his smile. I then threw an arm around Joan.

'Where will we first make land, Stephen?' I asked, staring at the mountains of Outremer as they faded into the distance astern.

'I wondered if you wanted to call at Cyprus, but then I thought not.'

Joan snorted. 'Seeing as how she was the Lady of Cyprus for only a few days before Richard sold it to the Hospitallers.'

'Quite, and then to Lusignan,' said Stephen. 'I suppose having one island at a time is quite enough. We'll head for Crete.'

Four days later, in gusting winds and intermittent rain, we spied the mountains of Crete on the horizon.

'We'll drop anchor on the north side of the island for a while,' said Isaac. 'There we'll rest the crew and go ashore for fresh water.'

'Can we go on land for a walk?' I asked hopefully.

'Best wait until we spy out the situation,' said Stephen. 'Crete is still in Byzantine hands; at least, it was last time I heard.'

By the end of the day, we were safely at anchor in a small bay and I watched as a small rowing boat was hoisted over the side to set off for the shore, laden with empty water barrels.

It was dusk when it returned safely, so there would be no walks today.

'It is reported as friendly,' Stephen informed us. 'We'll take a walk in the morning, if it pleases Your Highness and my lady.'

'It does,' Joan and I chorused together. We then went into our shelter to discuss what to wear.

It was diverting to walk on the sand, and Joan and I watched as the others frolicked at the water's edge.

After a while, I could not resist. 'Sandals off!' I cried.

'Sandals off,' responded Joan, and we dashed into the water, not caring if our breeches got wet or not. I heard Stephen groaning as his men cheered loudly; not often would they have seen two queens besporting themselves in such a brazen fashion.

Far too soon, Stephen called, 'Back in the boat, Your Highnesses.' He was pointing at the hills behind the beach.

'Look, Joan — horsemen.' I saw them lined up on the near horizon. I did not know who they were, and I was not inclined to wait and find out. The four seamen rowing the small boat had already begun to push it off the sand as we came rushing along and helped them to scramble it into the water.

Keeping out of their way, we watched as they made ready with the oars and propelled us away from danger.

The patrol of horsemen had galloped down from the hill and were lining up along the water's edge. One or two had jumped off their horses and were aiming what looked like crossbows at us.

'Who are you?' shouted one of the riders.

'Crusaders, homeward bound!' bellowed Stephen.

The crossbowmen lowered their weapons and the patrol went into a huddle, the spokesman gesticulating and wading his steed into the water.

'Crusading women?' he shouted.

'Of King Richard's household, on their way to Rome.'

Another consultation ensued.

'God bless you, and go in peace.'

'Thank you; God bless you.'

It was turning dark by the time we cleared the island and headed out into the gloom. The last visible light on the shore soon disappeared, leaving us reliant on the master's knowledge.

'There's a storm somewhere out there, Stephen,' I heard Isaac say as I climbed up onto the aftercastle to join them.

'What's that, Master Isaac?' I asked.

'The waves and the wind tell me things, Your Highness. The sea is restless, and somewhere out of our view it is disturbed.'

'Will it affect us?'

'It might. I am not a soothsayer, but it is likely that we will meet it at some point. We will stay within sheltered waters as much as possible and hopefully round the toe of Italy safely. If we head into the storm, be prepared to move around to stay sheltered from the worst of the weather. Stay safe and do not be tempted to go out onto the open deck; it is dangerous if the wind increases in force.'

I went to sit next to Joan. Her eyes were wide in the dim glow of our one swinging oil lamp as I gave out Isaac's instructions, and she pulled in closer to me.

Isaac's foretelling was accurate, and the tossing of the ship increased as the night wore on. Beneath our canvas shelter, we all shifted closer together. The sea was coming at us from ahead, but it also slapped the sides of the ship, casting great dollops of water onto the canvas above our heads. There was no comfort that night, and the wind was so noisy it hurt my ears.

Stephen pushed his head through the canvas flap at one point; he was soaked through. 'How are you, ladies?' he asked, seeing us awake and all huddled together. 'It will soon be dawn.'

'Why is the ship tossing about so much?' asked Joan.

'Because the wind keeps shifting and altering in strength; it mostly blows from Italy in these parts. Progress can be slow, but today it is odd — these are not good conditions. Master Isaac says that we would be safest running before it.' Stephen lowered his voice. 'I'm thinking that we need to sight land before Isaac will know exactly where we are, but stay cheery. We are safe.' Then he withdrew his head.

Another five days in a restless sea saw us round Italy into the Messina strait, a welcome relief. With the wind coming from the side now, I knew we should make good progress. But first we paused at Bagnara Monastery for reflection, and to visit the brothers and thank them for their earlier hospitality on our journey nearly two years previously.

'We'll wait here for my brother Robert,' Stephen proposed.

'And my husband too?' I suggested.

'Of course, if those inconstant winds haven't blown them off course. But Richard may have gone to Cyprus to see Lusignan.'

'Well, I'm here for prayers, fresh water and steady ground beneath my feet,' said Joan.

'And a wash in their caldarium,' I added, sitting on the side of the jetty. 'This is where we had our first conversation, Joan.'

'It seems like decades ago, my sweet.'

'Ladies, who are you?' called a voice from the sand. I turned; it was a monk. He was eyeing our ladies and girls playing in the water; he did not seem impressed.

We stood. 'I am Queen Berengaria of England, and this is Lady Joan.'

He stood still, a light dawning in his eyes. 'Of course.' Then he turned and fled up the hill to the monastery.

Stephen laughed. 'That should get a result, Your Highnesses. I think I'll pull off these boots and join your ladies. We might be about to have a meal up yonder hill.'

'We've tried that,' I said. 'It's not above ship's food.'

'Oh,' he said, crestfallen. 'That bad?'

'That bad,' I replied.

'Never mind, Stephen. At least it will be well blessed,' said Joan, chuckling.

It was not long before we were awash with visitors. A gaggle of monks came tumbling down the hill at the same time as Isaac called out, 'Galley, Stephen, galley!'

Stephen ran back along the jetty to board our ship, no doubt seeing to its defences. This left me to deal with the monks: six in all, including the earlier messenger who'd run off.

'*Altezza*,' said the leader. 'Welcome. We were not expecting you.'

'No, Brother, but we are on our way north. Perhaps you can render some assistance? Travelling by sea is very tiring at times, especially in poor weather. Where is Brother Michel?'

The brothers crossed themselves.

'Alas, you have missed him by a mere two weeks; the good Lord called him. I am Brother Matheus, newly elected to be Brother Abbot.'

'God bless you, Brother Abbot. Who is in yonder galley, I wonder?'

'The flag is that of the master of the harbour of Messina. They think to squeeze some money from all who travel through here, and they have noticed that you've stopped.'

'Do you ask for money?'

'Not from queens, usually. Although a donation would be appreciated, *altezza*.'

'Oh, we have nothing. We escaped from Jaffa with our lives in danger.'

'God bless you. But how long will you stay here?'

'I'm not sure. Our guardian thinks to wait here for King Richard to catch up. He has money.'

'The wealth of England — I've heard of that.'

'It might not be such a pile; he has found crusading an expensive affair.'

'I see. Are your guardians engaged with the galley master now?'

I looked towards the end of the jetty, where Stephen and Hugo were talking to another man. 'Yes, that's them.'

'What is Outremer like, *altezza*?' asked Brother Matheus.

I looked him in the eye; he was not going to like my reply. 'Bloody; confused and bloody. It is a contest of gods with men as their sacrifice.'

He was shocked, and images ran across my mind. Silently and before God's servant, I began to weep.

Turning away from him, I watched through teary eyes as Stephen came back along the jetty and the galley set off across the water.

'Your Highness, what's amiss? What has that monk said?' He glared at the discomforted cleric.

'Nothing, Stephen, nothing. It is merely a remembrance of things past. I feel so much more free here. I have not felt so light for a long time.'

'Ah, I too.'

I leaned against his chest and heard the monks take a sharp breath. Stephen felt good, comforting. Joan coughed.

Composing myself, I turned back towards the brother. 'You are kind, Brother Matheus; forgive me for my moment of sadness. Shall we hear what Lord Stephen has gleaned from yonder departing galley?'

Stephen stood behind me and explained his encounter with the harbour master. 'He wondered if we would rather drop anchor in his harbour, his master being your old friend Tancred, Lady Joan.' He grinned at her as she coloured up and spluttered.

'He will inform Tancred of our arrival, no doubt,' she said without joy.

'No doubt,' I added. 'Should we make use of it?'

'I told him that we'd prefer to be in Italy while we decide our next move, Your Highness,' said Stephen.

'Yes, of course,' I replied. 'Brother Matheus, is there any accommodation available?'

'There are a few cells; travellers are few at this time of year. You're welcome to stay for a few days.' He stopped and began to count the girls frolicking in the water, and Amynta watching from the sand. 'Are all of you staying?'

'And perhaps a few of Lord Stephen's men from the ship?'

'Men? That's not a problem. Give me some time and I'll go and organise a cell block for you.'

Gathering his skirts and his monks, Matheus scampered off up the hill.

We sat in the sunshine for a while, waiting for Robert or Richard to arrive. The waters were alive with boats of all sizes.

'How many of those heading north are returning Crusaders, Stephen?' I mused.

'Quite a few, I suppose. Do you think that you could get those girls dried off before any monks come past?' He nodded at Eirini, Alya and Nabila, still frolicking in the water.

'Yes,' laughed Joan. 'I'll go and get them out and sit them on the sand to dry.'

Sun-dried and demure, we did not need to wait long before a pair of monks arrived to escort us up the hill and into the refectory, where Brother Matheus was waiting with a buffet of fruits, bread and drinks.

'Please help yourselves, ladies. We should talk; your chambers are being prepared. I think that you know the rules and how you are expected to behave?'

'Indeed, Brother Matheus. We'll intrude as little as possible,' I answered, meaning to brief my retinue as soon as possible.

'We have a plan for you, if you will permit. We are expecting a regular *messaggero*, a Benedictine courier. We will send him back to Rome to inform them of your presence, and you may stay for as long as it takes. Lord Stephen can tie up at the jetty and await the arrival of King Richard, and then your next move will be his decision. It is the end of the harvest and we have enough to feed you all, there being few pilgrims passing through this year. I fear that the wars in Outremer have put many off travellers.'

'I see. King Richard and Saladin have reached an agreement: pilgrims will soon be able to cross the sea from here, or Messina, directly to Ashkelon.'

'Oh! That is good news. We should prepare for that next year.'

'Indeed,' said Stephen. 'Queen Berengaria, do you agree to Brother Matheus sending to Rome?'

'Yes, it is peaceful here. We shall enjoy your beach, Brother Matheus, while we wait, if you permit.'

'Indeed, indeed. It will take about two weeks for any response from Rome. Enjoy our location as much as you wish.'

'Shall I donate some money, Brother Matheus? I'm sure that no pilgrims means no money,' said Stephen, to my astonishment.

'You have money? I told Brother Matheus that we had none.'

'Of course, Your Highness. The treasury chest came aboard at Akko. It has not seemed worth remarking upon until now; forgive me.'

I turned back to the monk. 'See, Brother Matheus, I am so well served that I need not be informed about it.' Then I had another thought. 'I remember the Roman baths here; are they available?'

'Indeed, *altezza*. You wish to use them?'

'If you wouldn't mind. We have been immersed in salt for weeks.'

'The water will be heated overnight, *altezza*, and ready for you in the morning,' said Brother Matheus.

'Oh well, another night in salt-encrusted clothes. Is there anything else for us to wear on that ship of yours, Stephen?'

'I'll ask Isaac. I'm not certain what was loaded in Jaffa.'

A day of calm followed as we watched the rest of the world sail by. Outremer must have been emptying of Christians, at least until the springtime, when Brother Matheus could look forward to more pilgrim cash in his treasury. The nights in my cell were cold and lonely, filled with terrifying dreams of blood and heads detached from bodies. Sometimes visions of a wedding flashed across my mind, and Richard's faceless body. It always woke me in a sweat.

One morning, Joan shook me out of my disturbed sleep. 'Berengaria, Berri, there's a messenger, a galley floating near Master Isaac's. Get dressed. I'll help you.'

Soon the cell was crowded with my friends helping me into my well-worn clothing.

A mad procession followed me as we dashed down the hill to see the new arrival. When we were near enough to see their banners, Joan called a halt.

'It's that harbour official again.'

Indeed it was. The craft was offshore and near Master Isaac's cog, and I could see Stephen engaged in loud conversation. We ventured onto the jetty and Stephen walked back to meet us.

'He said that he is to deliver a message to the queen.'

'Me?' I said.

'Or me?' asked Joan.

'Let's find out,' I said, leading the others to the end of the jetty.

The recent storm was well past us by now, and the waters between us and the island were calm and sparkling. Seabirds whirled overhead and plucked things off the surface.

We lined up along the end of the jetty and waited to see what would happen.

The fellow in charge stood and called out in Italian that he had a message for Queen Joan.

'There is no Queen Joan,' she replied disinterestedly.

'I recognise you, Queen Joan. Please listen. My overlord, His Highness, Tancred, would like to invite you ashore. He has a feast prepared.'

'*His Highness*? How dare he!' Joan glared at the vessel.

'Should I answer, my sweet?' I asked.

'Your Highness,' said Stephen, concerned, 'it would be unwise. Perhaps send an emissary to find out what Tancred wants.'

'Good idea. Where's Hugo?' I asked, looking around. He was paddling on the shore with Brother Matheus.

'We can't send him alone,' said Stephen.

'Perhaps Matheus can help,' said Joan. 'Anyway, I don't want to see Tancred again; I'll leave him to the designs of Mother Church.'

It was less of a bother than Stephen expected. Brother Matheus summoned two monks, and they boarded the Sicilian craft with Hugo and were soon speeding across the strait to Messina.

'That was a short discussion,' said Stephen. 'I trust that they are safe.'

'Mother Church will guard them,' said Brother Matheus confidently.

'Yes,' answered Joan. 'Since my husband died and the upstart Tancred seized the throne of Sicily, he has depended upon the support of Rome; they *will* be safe, else Rome will remove him.'

'He might want you back as the dowager queen to give him some extra credence,' I said mischievously.

'Berengaria, don't; he's already tried that. Richard saved me from occupying *that* bed,' she answered with passion.

'Sibylla of Acerra is the lady in that role,' said Brother Matheus.

'I would like to see his queen, Joan,' I said. 'She cannot light the earth in the way that you do.'

'Flatterer! I shall not be lighting anything around here. When is the galley from Rome expected, Brother Matheus?' she asked, blushing.

'Any day; it changes with the weather. I thought that Constance should inherit the throne, as a descendant of the kings of Sicily, but here we are. What's done is done.'

'Why did she not?' I asked.

'She's not married, but I heard rumours from Rome that there may well be a marriage in the offing.'

'To whom?'

'Emperor Heinrich.'

'But does His Holiness want a German in Sicily?'

'I think not,' replied Matheus.

'Then that won't improve Constance's chances,' I said. 'Queenships are easily come by and easily lost.'

Joan laughed and Matheus looked across the strait, but Hugo and Matheus's two brothers were well out of sight.

Gathering her kirtles around her, Joan set off back up the hill faster than she had descended, leaving Alazne, Pavot and Torène trailing in her dust. Eirini, Alya and Nabila stayed open-mouthed, trying to work out what the exchange had meant. Amynta was probably still abed.

'A goodly response, Your Highness,' said Stephen.

'Shall we enjoy the morning sunshine for a while, Stephen? The monastery's wrinkly apples are not calling me at present.'

'Nor its smelly cheese. Yes, we'll watch God's world go by for a while, Your Highness — no harm in that.'

Thus I whiled away the day, wondering how Hugo and his protecting monks fared. I finally left Stephen's company when I entered the women's cell block. I still had mixed feelings about him, unsure if I saw him as a companion, a father figure, or something else.

That night I did not sleep alone, for Joan came to me and we comforted one another with our warmth.

After another three days of indolence and prayer, a new sail in the strait brought excitement to the beach.

'Your Highness, Your Highness!' called Eirini, whose sharp young eyes had spotted Tancred's galley heading our way.

'Hugo's back, Joan!' I said.

'Should we go down?'

'Yes, let's interrogate him on the sand.'

'Stephen, the jetty — Hugo's here!' Joan shouted across the abbey courtyard, where Stephen was in conversation with Matheus.

'Very well, Your Highness. Let's hear his news.'

We scampered down the steep hill and across the sand.

'Hugo, welcome back,' I greeted him as the harbour master's galley slid alongside the jetty opposite Master Isaac's ship.

Hugo jumped ashore while the monks gathered their robes about them so as not to become entangled and fall between the galley and the jetty.

'Did you meet Tancred?' asked Joan.

'Oh, yes. Let's see this fellow off and I'll tell you about His Highness Tancred,' said Hugo, waving at the galley master.

Joan sniffed, but I kept a straight face.

Soon the craft was splashing its way back to Messina, and Hugo breathed out a sigh of relief. 'Phew, that was interesting. Lady Joan, he was expecting to see you; he wants your support.'

'Why, has he a broken leg?' asked Joan bitterly.

'Not that I noticed, but he is determined to retain favour with His Holiness. He believes that you can help him in that regard.'

Brother Matheus was with us now, and he listened intently.

'Tancred has a short memory, Hugo. Is he ill?'

'No. He is sharp; he misses naught.'

'Why does he believe that having detained me against my will until Richard paid him a visit, I owe him any favours?'

'He has put the circumstances of Richard's visit to the back of his mind and thinks that the pair of you owe him for the ships and money he donated to the Crusade.'

I laughed. 'Then he is delusional; those donations were the price for detaining Queen Joan.'

Stephen was half listening, half watching his men, who were gradually losing their clothing as they tumbled boisterously in the water. Then something else attracted his attention. Standing and shading his eyes, he called out, 'A galley, another galley, from the north! Out of the water and get dressed — we have another visitor.'

His men scrambled to obey and were soon properly dressed, armed and lined up along the jetty.

'The galley has Crusader banners, Your Highness!' Stephen shouted.

'This will be the messenger from Rome,' said Brother Matheus.

'Joan,' I said, 'it must be for us; Matheus's courier was successful. His Holiness must know that we are here.'

Joan started to dance on the sand and was soon joined by all the other girls and women except for Amynta, who merely clucked and crossed herself at the sight of the Crusader flags.

One showed a red cross on a white background and the other a red cross on a black background.

The galley dropped its sail, and oars brought the vessel alongside the jetty on the side opposite Master Isaac's cog — a contrast in elegance if ever there was one.

In the galley, the oarsmen were all clad in matching uniforms, and there was little noise save for the commands of the master as the craft eased up to the jetty. The men were silent as they disembarked with ropes to tie the vessel up. Looking at the stern of the craft, I identified the master, and standing beside him was a seemingly important figure.

'A cardinal, Your Highness: we are blessed,' said Matheus with some reverence.

'A papal nuncio, Joan,' I said, impressed. 'We are about to learn how highly regarded we are in Rome.'

'A cardinal, Berri?' said Joan, somewhat surprised.

'So it seems, my sweet. Are we dressed as queens?'

'No, we look like sea urchins.'

'Too late. Here he comes.'

The tall figure gathered his robe about him and stepped onto the jetty. He had a friendly face and was smiling — a good sign. He approached us, holding out his hands.

'Your Highnesses, I am Cardinal Melior, sent to escort you to Rome.'

'Welcome, Your Eminence, Cardinal Melior. We are pleased to welcome you. I am Berengaria of England, and this is Lady Joan, formerly of Sicily.'

'This is a great pleasure. I am privileged for this duty.' He looked at Joan. 'Lady Giovanna, I see.' He was no doubt wondering how to proceed if she had relinquished her title already; perhaps it solved some of Rome's diplomatic problems. 'You are expected in Rome; His Holiness is looking

229

forward to meeting you and hearing about the Crusade. And he wishes to learn about your experience with Tancred, Lady Giovanna.'

I wondered about that: the position of Sicily had become a serious matter for the Church. The German Holy Roman Emperor's desire for it to be handed over to him was well known now. I wondered what part the Pope had in mind for its dowager queen.

'May I introduce my escort, Your Eminence? This is Lord Stephen, and he is on his way to Normandy.'

While the pair were chatting, the noise of running monks echoed down the sides of the ravine leading down from the abbey. News of a papal envoy had clearly reached them.

We eventually found ourselves back in the refectory, gathered to discuss our further journeying.

'I cannot leave you, Your Highness,' said Stephen. 'No matter what, our prime duty is your welfare.' He gestured towards Guy de Bernez and Stephen Longchamp, who were standing quietly to one side.

'Then leave Master Isaac here with his cog to await Richard and Robert, and we'll go to Rome with Cardinal Melior.' I turned to the cardinal. 'Your Eminence, how many can you accommodate on your fine vessel?'

'Not many. It's more for show. How many do you want to bring with you?'

'All my ladies. Stephen?'

'I'll come with you and bring Bernez and Longchamp. I'll leave the two sergeants here with the men and they can follow on when my brother Robert arrives, or His Highness — they'll take such orders as he issues. Do you need Hugo, or should he return to the king's side?'

'Yes, Richard should know of our progress. Perhaps we'll meet again in Rome. When can we leave, Your Eminence?' I asked.

'Now, Your Highness. Is that soon enough?' He grinned. 'I came here directly from Napoli, where I received word of your presence. It is only a day and one night from here. Rome will be a three-day voyage and accommodation is fairly limited, although we can shuffle things around to suit you and your ladies.'

'Let us go, then,' I said. After some hurried farewells, including an unexpected hug from Hugo, I whispered instructions to Stephen. 'Leave the abbot some money, please.' I then wandered back down to the jetty.

'Is it not too late to be setting sail, Your Eminence?' asked Joan.

The pair chatted as they walked behind me, becoming friends now.

'It matters not, *altezza*; we sail all night anyway. The dark does not stop sail or oar. We will be off the river Tiber in three days.'

Joan decided to clear matters with the cardinal. 'I've given up "*altezza*"; I'm Lady Joan now. Being a dowager queen does not suit me at my age. I'm too young.'

'Of course, Lady Joan. It suits you,' he responded gallantly.

'Will we sail up to Rome?' I asked.

'No, the river is blocked to ships such as ours; there's too much mud in it. We'll disembark at Ostia. It is still a busy port, but alas, the river up to Rome is now unusable for large ships. There will be carriages waiting for us; it is a mere fifteen miles to the city. I despatched riders to Rome from Napoli to prepare for your reception. You have voyaged before — that I know.'

'Your Eminence, we have spent many miserable days — weeks — at sea since we left our mounts behind at Genoa, and we will be pleased to see once again the backs of horses' heads.'

We gathered what we could from Isaac's fat slug of a cog ship and climbed aboard Melior's elegant galley. It was not better for accommodation, though; we were once again in a canvas tent rigged up at the back. I noticed that all the rowers sitting at their benches had a pile of arms and armour stacked near them — not merely rowers, but marine soldiers as well. At least we should be safe with Stephen's two men and a few dozen soldiers from Rome by our sides.

'Have you seen them?' asked Joan as we entered our tent.

'Yes, Joan, and they took a close interest in us, so stay in here as much as possible.'

'Eirini is all flustered, but I'm going out for a good look at them when we get going. Such muscles!'

I laughed. 'You are impossible, Joan. I'll come and keep you safe.'

CHAPTER TEN

Almost three more boring days passed at sea, watching the mountains of Italy pass by to our right. We looked into many a small harbour, and many curious fishermen watched our passage, waving and shouting greetings to returning Crusaders.

By the time that we reached our destination, Cardinal Melior would know what we knew, as Joan and I made certain that he understood the consequences of holy war.

In return, he made sure that Joan knew about the tussle between His Holiness and Heinrich IV, who was simultaneously the king of the Germans and the Holy Roman Emperor. He now wished to claim Sicily for his family, but His Holiness was not prepared to see an enclave of Germans so near to the mainland of Italy.

The winds were kind and we sped north, soon to arrive off the coast near Ostia, where the crew pulled down the sails while the oarsmen gathered together their arms and began to dress in their mail.

'Are we expecting trouble, Your Eminence?' I asked.

No, *altezza*, they are preparing to escort you along the jetty, as befits a visiting queen.'

'Oh, I see. How kind.'

We watched as they extended the oars, ready to pull up to the jetty, and I marvelled as the oars were shipped and stowed neatly away.

'Ostia, *altezza*,' said Cardinal Melior as we touched the side and ropes were run out to secure the papal galley.

Then the marine soldiers disembarked swiftly to line up along the side of the jetty, as the cardinal had predicted.

Crowding the rail, we observed an excited crowd gathered at the end of the jetty, with soldiers holding them back. Beyond them, a train of carriages were lined up.

'What is the fuss, Your Eminence? Are they expecting someone?' I asked.

'*Sí, altezza*: you.'

Joan laughed. 'How did they know to bring carriages?'

With a kind and knowing smile, Melior explained, 'Everyone knew that you were on your way home, and originally they were also expecting King Richard. But when we received the message from Bagnara Monastery, we knew to expect you without the king, and I despatched horsemen from Napoli to arrange things differently for your arrival. As for the crowd, look yonder at the Pharos.' He pointed into the distance where the lighthouse stood. 'The lookout would have signalled when our sails became visible on the horizon; the rest is merely good organisation.'

'Jesu!' exclaimed Stephen.

'So, *altezza*, if you gather your things, we will be off to Roma, where accommodation awaits you.'

There followed a walk along a windy jetty. We were watched with eager anticipation by the crowd, who showed no signs of moving. Being so closely observed in salt-encrusted and distinctly worse-for-wear clothing was not ideal, but we decided to make the best of it.

'Head up and smile, Joan. Stephen, get our knights out in front and stay close to us so that they don't see what urchins we are, and keep our girls closely guarded. They can do without groping hands.'

Bernez and Longchamp were outnumbered, but help arrived in the form of some knights, who rode up, dismounted and reinforced the soldiers who were struggling through the throng to clear the way. We were then able to scamper towards the waiting carriages.

Then I heard Cardinal Melior calling for the coachmen to help us climb in. The steps were very high and I struggled to get a foot onto the first one. I then felt a hand grasp my rump, and whoever the ungracious fellow was more or less threw me in.

Joan, tight behind me, said, 'Don't even think about it, Stephen. I'll manage myself.' She leaped in beside me, and I looked down to where Stephen stood, shameless, with a big grin on his face.

'Stay with the girls and Amynta,' I instructed him. 'She does not like this throng.'

'Bernez and Longchamp have them safe, I can see.'

'And keep their hands in view!' called Joan.

Stephen stood aside as Melior arrived, out of breath. He climbed in to sit opposite us on the well-padded cushions.

The coach was well appointed, with open sides and a canvas roof, and it rolled about a bit when we moved.

'You are very popular, *Regine*; you will enjoy your stay with us, I'm certain. Welcome to Rome.'

'*Grazie, Cardinale*, we are looking forward to it,' I replied.

'Will we be in a hostel, Your Eminence?' asked Joan.

The horrified expression on Melior's face put paid to that suggestion. '*Santa Maria!* No, no. We have a villa at your disposal. You are our guests, and we are responsible for your safekeeping. The villa has servants, and an armed guard will be there at all times. If you wish to go out and explore, they will accompany you. You two queens — er, queen and lady — are at the very centre of European politics, and until King Richard turns up it is our responsibility to take good care of you.'

'Why?' asked Joan.

Melior coughed and prepared another speech. 'We need stability in England, and between Richard and Philip of France. Tancred gave himself a title.' He looked at Joan. 'This might suit His Holiness, but Emperor Heinrich disagrees with it. There is much to discuss.'

'Why is England not stable?' I asked.

'John causes confusion,' Melior replied tersely. 'At times His Holiness is minded to excommunicate him. The prospect of John becoming King of England is something we should avoid.'

'And Sicily?' asked Joan.

'Emperor Heinrich claims the island as an old family holding; he wants Tancred gone. You, of course, are the country's dowager queen.'

'Are we pawns in this game, Your Eminence?' I asked directly.

'No, *altezza*. You are a queen, much more valuable than a pawn, but you, Lady Joan, are in a mix which we are on our way to clearing, if you are not holding any more ambitions towards Sicily?'

'No, Your Eminence. That is in the past.'

'I'll inform His Holiness. Thank you.'

I looked at Joan, her stiff jaw hinting at her turbulent thoughts. 'Where is this villa you speak of, Your Eminence?' I asked.

'Ah,' he said, more comfortable with this subject. 'It is on the *Collis Esquilinus*, the Esquiline Hill. It is where some of the best families in Rome have their dwellings. Nearby is the *Basilica di Santa Maria Maggiore*, which you may wish to visit; it is very beautiful and peaceful. You can walk there in a little while. Then, about a mile away is the residence of His Holiness, *Basilica di San Giovanni* in Laterano. It is also very beautiful, but a carriage will be provided for you. There are other vistas from the hill: *il Colosseo* lies at the bottom. We will take you to all the ancient places you might want to visit.'

'And is His Holiness well?' asked Joan, something I had forgotten about.

'Pope Celestine is well enough for a sixty-year-old,' Melior replied. 'He is looking forward to meeting you.'

'I pray for him. He seems to be carrying all the disputes of Europe on his shoulders,' I said, not yet certain of my part in this squabbling of nations.

'That is true, *altezza*. I, too, pray for guidance; times are difficult. We are near now.'

The carriage had begun to climb and swayed from side to side, nearly as bad as a ship.

'Why are we swaying, Your Eminence?' asked Joan.

'The carriage is suspended on leather straps, to make the journey more comfortable.'

'I feel ill.'

'We'll soon be there,' he replied, comforting her.

The ostlers were urging their animals on. As we climbed, the air became sweeter and the road was lined by trees, some with and some without leaves. Given the lateness of the year, it was very pleasant, and I thought that we should be content up here.

We stopped suddenly, swaying backwards and forwards now instead of side to side. Joan was ashen.

'We are here.' I made my way to the back and fell down the steps, to be caught by Stephen. He helped me down onto the ground, his eyes less than a finger width from mine. I was very tempted to take hold of him, but I resisted.

'How was your journey, Your Highness?' he asked, his eyes full of mischief.

'Long enough. Catch Lady Joan.' I went to the second carriage, which was full of unhappy ladies. 'This is it. You can come down now.'

'Huh!' I heard Amynta say. 'I shall walk in future.'

'Did you not enjoy it, Amynta?' I asked, suppressing a laugh.

'No! And those men tried to get in with us.' She pointed at Stephen, Bernez and Longchamp, who were stretching their legs and stamping on the ground. 'But we sent them to that rear wagon.'

The third carriage did not have a cover. I knew that Amynta had been thinking of her young charges' honour when she had dismissed the men.

'Look at that! Are we going in there?' asked Guy de Bernez. He was pointing at a splendid building next to where we had halted.

'*Sí, signor*,' answered the cardinal. 'Ladies, go inside. Soldiers, go around the back.'

That settled that. I'd been wondering what to do with them.

'Come, *altezza*, meet your household,' Melior went on.

There was a portico over the entrance gate and a driveway leading to the house. It was lined with soldiers, and nearer the house, by servants. At the centre of the entrance stood a formidable lady, immaculately dressed in plain work clothes.

'Allow me to introduce *Signora* Hortensia. She is your housekeeper.'

Hortensia curtsied and I held out a hand, which surprised her, but nonetheless we touched. If I was to form a relationship with her, we needed to get off to a good start.

'*Signora* Hortensia, you are expecting us.'

'Indeed, *altezza*, we care for all of His Holiness's guests, including many *Inglese*.'

'But none so poorly dressed, I'll warrant,' said Joan.

'Ah, but so widely travelled.' Hortensia was observant. 'Please step this way and we can discuss what to do next.'

The entry hall was indeed grand, with marble floors, marble walls and marble pillars leading to a marble stairway. Most of the statues lining the chamber were quite explicit, with both men and women wearing very little, if anything. I heard the girls suppressing squeals as we progressed upwards to the next floor. We entered a grand reception hall, where the air was thick with incense.

Melior came in behind us and issued some instructions to Hortensia. 'Please take the queen's ladies to their quarters, show them where the queen's apartments are, and have some refreshments served here. I need to explain some things to our *Regina*.'

'Your Eminence,' I interrupted, 'one of those ladies is a princess.'

'Oh, pardon, of course. *Signora* Hortensia, take special care of the Princess of Cyprus, if you please.'

'And her companions,' I added.

Hortensia smiled and left, waving for our ladies, Amynta and the girls to follow.

Melior led us across to a marble table and gestured for us to sit down. Within an eye-blink, servants appeared with glasses of lemon drink and set them down before us.

'Please bring another,' the cardinal instructed them.

'You are expecting someone else, Your Eminence?' enquired Joan.

'Indeed. Someone you know, *altezza*,' he said, looking at me. '*Cardinale* Benedetto.'

'Ah, yes. Eleanor and I met him at Lodi, when we were on our way to Sicily.' I turned to Joan to explain. 'Back when we were chasing Richard across Europe, your mother and I met

239

the cardinal to discuss matters concerning the Holy Roman Emperor.'

'You met Emperor Heinrich?'

'Yes — a formidable figure.'

'He remains so, *altezza*. A difficult man to deal with,' said Melior.

We heard the sound of a carriage and horses outside, as well as shouts and trampling feet.

'This will be him,' said Melior.

Cardinal Benedetto soon appeared, accompanied by several priests. He made a magisterial entrance, huffing and puffing up the marble staircase and into the grand hall.

'My word!' he boomed. 'God bless you, Queen Berengaria. You have survived and you are more beautiful than ever.' He crossed the floor like a ship in full sail and held out his hand with the ring on it. I kissed it and he took the chair next to mine.

Melior coughed, as if to remind him that there were others present.

'Alberto, *buongiorno*. You are surrounded by beauty. Is this *la Regina Vedova Giovanna*?' he asked, eyeing Joan.

'Not any longer,' she answered. 'I am Lady Joan, and pleased to have Sicily out of my sight.'

Benedetto stood and sailed around the table to offer his ring to my astonished companion. '*Grazie*, Lady Joan, *grazie*; you understand our politics.' He turned his attention to Melior. 'The lady has decided for us, Alberto. His Holiness will find grace in this, I'm certain. You have reported this?'

'Not yet. Shall we do it together?'

'Of course, together.'

Joan seemed somewhat overwhelmed by this spontaneous conclave, and I wondered which of them would gain the

Pope's ear first. She only relaxed when Benedetto had made his way back to my side.

'Our friend, Heinrich, is at it again,' he said.

'He wants Sicily,' said Joan without preamble.

'He has a case,' said Benedetto. 'Your husband, King William, acknowledged Constance as his rightful heir before he died. She is in the direct line of descent from the Norman kings of Sicily, and her husband Heinrich VI is claiming her right of ascent.'

'And I agreed,' said Joan. 'Constance is Queen Regnant of Sicily — the Normans of the south keep it in the family Hauteville.'

'Quite. She would become ruler of Sicily with her husband's right of marriage.'

'So where does that place Tancred?' I asked.

'Self-promoting. He's the illegitimate son of Roger III, Duke of Apulia — more southern Normans,' replied Joan.

'He is the grandson of King Roger of Sicily. He has a case, and is popular among the ruling elite of Sicily and supported by the late Pope Clement III.'

'But the Church wants stability and is willing to negotiate for it between Tancred and Heinrich?' I asked, looking at Benedetto.

'You have a sharp wit,' he said, 'but I'll not put it more gently. Essentially it is a dispute between the Norman Hautevilles and the German Hohenstaufens.'

'As I have decided it leaves me out of it, Your Eminence,' said Joan with a sniff.

'If we are speaking honestly, you're in reserve. If aught goes wrong we can resurrect you, find you a suitable husband and get you back to Sicily … suitably grateful, I pray.'

'So, Joan, there you have it,' I said. 'Nearly married off to a Saracen by your brother, and now the Church wants you for a bride. How fortunate to be in such demand.' We stared at each other. I could tell she would never let this plan go ahead, but we said naught. I turned back to Benedetto. 'And what are my plans, Your Eminence?'

'Get together with your husband and produce an heir for England. Forgive me for asking, but was there a wedding night in Cyprus…?'

I gave a noncommittal answer. 'The king has given his all to the Crusade, Your Eminence; there'll be time enough for other matters.'

'Ah, well, we'll pray for you.' He beckoned over one of his accompanying priests and spoke to him while Cardinal Melior changed the subject.

'Is the villa to your liking, *altezza*?' he asked. The conversation was heading in a direction he was uncomfortable with, I supposed.

'We've seen the entrance hall and this chamber, and a lot of statues,' chirped Joan, referring to the naked effigies and adding to his discomfort. I wondered if he was one of those churchmen who found the company of women difficult.

Benedetto returned to the conversation. 'I'll leave you now, *altezza*, and return in the morning. His Holiness is expecting you before midday.'

'He will see us tomorrow?' I had not expected an audience so soon.

'Of course. Pope Celestine is eager to hear about your experiences. In the absence of King Richard himself, who better to relate the story?'

Benedetto's tone suggested that Richard was still remembered for not visiting Rome on his way to Sicily. I hoped that he would visit on his way back.

'And I would like to introduce Father Edwin.' Benedetto waved at one of the priests in his entourage and the man stepped forward and smiled.

'English?' I asked. 'From his name.'

'Indeed, one of many we have here in Rome. He will be your intermediary between us.'

'Thank you, Your Eminence. Between *Signora* Hortensia and Father Edwin, we shall be well served. *Grazie, molto grazie.* Welcome, Father Edwin.'

The cardinals stood, and I joined them to say farewell. With much kissing and touching hands, we went with them to the door and watched as they sped off down the hill into the afternoon dust and heat of Rome.

Joan and I looked at each other, then, prompted by the same thought, cried out, 'What are we going to wear?'

'*Altezza.*' It was Hortensia. 'I can escort you to your chambers, if you wish.'

As we passed him by, I said to Father Edwin, 'Join us this evening, Father; we will talk.'

'As you wish, Your Highness,' he answered pleasantly.

'No one's mentioned Richard much,' said Joan as we followed Hortensia up the next flight of stairs.

'Richard does what Richard does. He can answer for himself when he turns up.'

'Aye, he's managed to upset most of Europe. That's a lot to answer for.'

When we arrived at my chamber, Hortensia proudly invited me in.

'This is nice,' I said as I passed her.

Joan followed me in. 'Goodness, look at those wall hangings.'

Dragging my eyes from the enormous bed to the walls, I was a little shocked by the depictions. They showed men sitting with half-naked women, pushing grapes into each other's mouths, and satyrs with enormous … 'Oh my Lord! Who is invited to live here, Hortensia?'

'All sorts,' she replied. 'Sometimes we pull drapes across, if we feel that our guests might be offended.' She grabbed a half-hidden drape hanging from a pole fixed to the wall and pulled it along. By the time she had repeated the move, all the walls were hidden. It immediately felt cosier and did not echo so much.

'Are we sharing, Hortensia?' asked Joan.

'*No, mia signora*, your chamber is the next one. I'll show you.'

I heard Joan's voice echoing along the corridor as they left.

'And where are our ladies?' she asked. 'Where is Lord Stephen?'

'First, I'll take you to your chamber, then all will be revealed,' Hortensia replied.

I jumped onto the bed; it was very inviting and did not move about. I thought about taking a nap, but Joan and Hortensia were back.

'The chambers are both the same,' said Joan. 'Hortensia has some fresh clothing for us, and the villa has its own baths.'

'*Sì, altezza*. The water is warm for you.'

'I knew I liked this place, Joan. Lead us to the water, *Signora* Hortensia, and fetch my ladies down. Where are my men?'

'At the rear of the house above the stables. You don't want them in your bath, do you?'

'No, women only, but thank you for the idea,' said Joan, wistfully.

'You have horses?' I asked.

'You wish to ride out?'

'Of course,' said Joan. 'Carriages are the same as ships: uncomfortable.'

Hortensia led us through the villa and outside to another building. 'Ah, here are the bathing chambers; this should comfort you after your journey.' Her voice echoed through the marble halls, and we could hear dripping and gurgling water.

'I'm going to like this, Joan. Off with these salty rags.'

Everything was there: hot and cold water, steam, the aroma of unguents and towels. There were no men, only some near-naked young women whom we were informed would be massaging us when we came out of the water.

The interlude passed pleasurably. When I had sighed for the last time, I was helped into a simple chemise, and a towel was wrapped about my head. Spying Joan on the marble bench across the chamber, I grinned.

'Better than life on a boat, Joan?'

'Better than life almost anywhere.'

'What about the girls, Hortensia?' I asked.

'We will bring them down now that you have finished, *altezza*.'

Hortensia was very attentive to us, but I decided I would discuss this distinction with Joan shortly. We and our ladies had suffered together, and I didn't see why we shouldn't be pampered together.

There was a robing chamber opposite our bedchambers, and Hortensia waved us in with a sweep of her arm. Laid out on a platform was a selection of the most appealing gowns, chemises and ladies' netherwear, together with accessories and other decorative pieces, some of which I had not seen before.

'Oh, heavens!' cried Joan. 'Can we choose?'

'They are all for you both, *altezza*, and there is a seamstress waiting to ensure that they fit.'

'What are they for? Some are very different,' said Joan, picking up a very ornate and expensive-looking gown.

'That is a court gown, for formal occasions. Here is something a little less cumbersome. This plain one is for everyday use. Perhaps you will walk out, go to the market and see the ancient buildings of Rome.'

'And for riding?'

'We will make up some split kirtles and silk netherwear.'

'What shall we wear in the morning, when we visit His Holiness?' I asked.

'The middle one,' said Hortensia without hesitation, 'but for now let the seamstress attend to you. We will serve food when you are ready. Who do you want at your table, *altezza*?'

'All our ladies, the girls and the Lady Amynta. Bring in my guardians from the stables and ask Father Edwin; we will have prayers first.'

'I shall arrange it for you.'

And off she went, leaving me, Joan and a seamstress named Gabrielle to pick and choose in a chamber of delights.

When we were reunited with our ladies and girls in our quarters, they were all fresh-smelling and dressed in their new day gowns, which Gabrielle had prepared while Joan and I were relaxing in the baths.

'Are we eating?' asked Eirini.

'I forgot about that. Amynta, explain to Alya and Nabila that they will be expected to join Hortensia's staff and help with the food,' I said. 'Alazne, Pavot and Torène can help too. We're missing Hugo already, but ensure that there will be a table set aside for you, Amynta, with the two knights.'

We set off down the marble stairway. When we reached the dining hall, we were greeted by a marvellous display of food: meats and fruit, breads and cheeses, and some sweetmeats similar to those from Syria that we had eaten in Outremer. However, the wine had been replaced by water.

'That was a wise move, Your Highness,' said Father Edwin, sitting next to me at the head of the long table.

Joan was on my left, and next to her was Stephen, opposite Eirini. Everyone else had settled down at their own tables, and they were being attended to by Hortensia's staff.

'Yes, the wine would be too red and mellow for young palates, Father. Tell me about how you came to Rome, and especially tell me about the land of which I am queen.'

He gladly obliged, and soon I was immersed in tales of England and of the journey undertaken by the English to walk all the way to Rome, and indeed to cross the sea to Outremer and visit Jerusalem. It was very informative, but as he droned on I felt my eyelids drooping. The long day was taking its toll.

'Father, our day began before sunrise,' I said eventually. 'Can we continue tomorrow?'

'Of course, Your Highness. I am to escort you to the Basilica di San Giovanni in Laterano myself.'

'Oh, good. Tell me, Father, is this gown suitable?'

He took a good look. I wore a long white linen cotte with a leather belt, covered by a blue gown that reached the floor and opened at the front to show the cotte. The gown was laced across my chest with golden string, and it covered my shoulders. The long sleeves flared out at the wrists.

'I have a caul to cover my hair, which shall be braided.'

'Splendid, splendid. And Lady Joan, another regal sight in green. I congratulate you; Rome will not recover from such a vision for quite a while.'

'Please thank *Governante* Hortensia and her seamstress Gabrielle,' I said. 'They have worked hard to make it so.'

'*Buono*. Well made and well worn.'

Bidding all goodnight, I stood and took Joan by the hand, and we made our weary way up the stairs together.

'I'll come in with you,' she said. 'We can chat a while about the morn.'

'Aye. Oh, look: there is a flagon of wine on the side table,' I replied.

Soon we were propped up against the pillows at the top of my bed, filled goblets in hand.

'What're we going to tell His Holiness, Berri?'

'I'm going to let him lead and seek an opportunity to move the conversation.'

She held my hand and took a slurp of wine. 'You know more about diplomacy than your husband.'

'That wouldn't cover much vellum.'

She spluttered into her goblet. 'I mustn't spill this. It is very good — have you tried it?'

I took a sip. 'Mmm, very good; so smooth that I can hardly feel it going down.'

In the morning, my mouth was dry as a desert. The last thing I remembered was holding the empty goblet.

'Your Highness,' said Alazne. 'The dawn is here.'

I heard her go to the door as I struggled to get my eyes focused.

'She's here, Pavot,' she called along the corridor. 'They are together.' Alazne turned back to me. 'Your Highness! Look at the state of you! Out of those clothes; you have to wear that gown later.'

'What?'

'Your chemise, Berri,' said Joan. 'It is now wine-coloured.'

I looked; there were red dribbles all down the front.

'Off with the gown; it seems untouched,' demanded Alazne.

'Yes, off with it. I'll inspect it properly.' Amynta had emerged to join this jolly throng, all trying to undress a queen. Soon I was only in my wine-spattered chemise, being directed to a *komuna* at the end of the corridor, where Alazne took off the rest of my clothes and proceeded to wash me down from shoulders to toes.

'Don't wet my hair. Gabrielle is going to braid it in the Italian style later.'

'I see. Basque style not good enough now, *altezza*?' she said, hurling a pot of cold water down my back.

'No, but when in Rome…'

'Insult your ladies.'

And that was the end of that conversation. I made my way back to my bedchamber and met Joan on her way to the *komuna*, escorted by Pavot.

'Watch your back, Joan, and don't say anything.'

'Pardon?' she mumbled as we passed.

Amynta had new clothes ready for me, and after much grumbling, she pronounced the gown fit to wear. I breathed a sigh of relief and wondered how long I should wait before putting in an appearance downstairs. It was mid-morning — time for some lemon juice.

'Try this, Your Highness,' suggested Amynta, handing me a goblet of water. 'It will clear your mouth.'

An apple went down along with more water, and I began to feel better.

'The carriage is outside, *altezza*,' Hortensia called up the stairway.

'Is Father Edwin ready?' I asked.

Alazne shouted my query down the stairway.

'Yes, Your Highnesses. I am ready,' came the calm response, echoing around the building.

'Joan, a Pope awaits us,' I said, as we set off down the stairs.

It was a very noisy affair: the carriage shook and bounced all the way down the hill as the ostlers wrestled with the beasts, holding them back on the slope.

'How are you this morning, Your Highnesses?' asked Father Edwin politely, sitting with Stephen opposite me and Joan.

'Fine,' I replied.

'A little nervous,' added Joan, more honestly.

'Indeed; most are the first time, and the *basilica* is magnificent. But be assured: His Holiness is looking forward to meeting you and is a very good listener. You will enjoy the experience.'

'Am I allowed in, Father?' asked Stephen.

'Of course; everyone can enter the *basilica*. Just remove your weapons; your queen will be well guarded. But the audience with His Holiness is for the ladies alone. His Holiness believes that everyone should speak for themselves, and he receives people in private when there are certain matters to discuss.'

'Such as kingdoms?' said Joan boldly.

'We'll stick to diplomacy, Joan,' I said. 'No need to force things at present; we'll see how the world is viewed from Rome.'

'With all the latest intelligence, Your Highness, there is not much that Rome does not know — sometimes before it happens. Ah, here we are. Look, there is a guard lined up to receive you.'

We came to a halt at the end of the line of soldiers. I managed to step down from the carriage with dignity, as some sharp-eyed person — Hortensia, perhaps — had made a stool available to help me climb in and out.

Cardinal Melior greeted us. '*Altezza*, we are honoured and pleased to have you here. Please come with me; His Holiness awaits. Did you sleep well?' he asked as we processed between the lines of soldiers. 'How is the villa? Is everything to your satisfaction?'

'*Governante* Hortensia has made us very welcome, and we want for nothing,' I replied as we entered the *basilica*.

It became quiet as we left the street, so quiet I could almost feel the weight of it. A cough from the other side of the church seemed far away as it echoed around the walls.

'Perhaps a few moments of prayer before we go in to meet His Holiness,' suggested Melior. He gestured, and a man came out of the gloom to be introduced as Father Edgar, another English priest. I wondered how many there were in Rome. He soon had us kneeling on prie-dieux for a little contemplation, and there was no time for questions.

A cough and a stirring by the cardinal had us up and heading towards a small door at the side of the altar. It was opened by another priest, then we traversed along a narrow corridor to be faced by another door, which likewise was attended by a priest. On the other side was Cardinal Benedetto. He stood before a table, sitting at which, attended by two more cardinals, was Pope Celestine.

He was not how I would have imagined an eighty-six-year-old. He was bright-eyed, smiling and welcoming — mischievous, even.

We curtsied, and he waved at the chairs placed before him, so we sat as bidden.

'Queen Berengaria, Lady Joan. Visions of beauty before me — visions of the blessed Maria. Welcome, welcome.'

'We thank you, Your Holiness, for seeing us. It is something we have prayed for,' I said.

'Indeed, my daughters, and we have prayed too, for your safe return from Outremer.'

'Alas, not with the desired outcome, Your Holiness.'

'No, it was not God's desire this time. I expect that we shall return. But tell me what you have witnessed; your husband has not yet returned, and we would question him.'

'Something that I too would welcome, Your Holiness.'

He grinned at that remark; a sense of humour was present. 'We hear that he has been afflicted by some ill humours. Perhaps it has delayed him.'

'It comes and goes, Your Holiness. It's not a certain event, but not uncommon across the sea.'

'Yes, some ailments occur across the sea and affect those from the north more than the local inhabitants, so we shall pray for his recovery.' He turned his attention to Joan. 'The dowager queen of Sicily. We too suffered from your predicament, but I understand that you have taken it upon yourself to solve the problem and leave your title behind you.'

'Do you agree, Your Holiness? One can outstay a welcome, or become uncomfortable with one.'

'If that is your desire, Lady Joan?'

'My former position holds no attraction for me. No doubt you have been acquainted with the doings of my former husband: a secret harem in the grounds of our palace.'

He looked at her for a while and sighed. 'What would you have us do for you, Lady Joan? What shall we do to ease your pain?'

'I seek your prayers, Holy Father, and your understanding. Nothing more. My problems will be eased by time.'

This conversation was more open than I had anticipated. Joan wanted to give up this game of realms, and His Holiness was pleased to accept that she had taken herself off the table, as it were. He could now insist on Tancred as *de facto* King of Sicily and reject Heinrich's demands for Constance to become the queen regent on the island. I wondered if it would remain settled for very long.

'It seems to me, Your Holiness, that one thing that realms can do without is spare queens,' said Joan. 'As Tancred is married and I am not his wife, what is the point of my presence? I have no wish to be an obstacle to peace in Sicily.'

'We respect your maturity. Some might have tried to gain advantage from the situation, but you are indeed a paragon of virtue. We shall pray for you to have a happy life from here onward. God bless you, my daughter. *Graziosa Giovanna.*'

He left it there and spoke gently to one of his attending cardinals. Benedetto smiled as if to reassure us. Then His Holiness turned back to us.

'*Altezza*, I am most interested in your story, and time is pressing. May we speak in private?'

I nodded. 'That is a privilege, Holy Father, for which we would be eternally grateful.'

He smiled and said to one of his attending cardinals, 'Guido, leave us for a while, if you will. I would speak with Queen Berengaria.'

'As you wish, Your Holiness.'

The chamber emptied and we were left facing the Pope alone.

'Akko!' he said after a while. 'You witnessed the events there?'

I began to tell him what had happened. He remained silent, his eyebrows rising from time to time.

When I had finished describing the slaughter, he said, 'That was a mistake; the matter might have been settled by diplomacy, but we are where we are, I suppose. I would welcome the opportunity to discuss the campaign with King Richard, but we'll have to wait for that.' Sitting up in his chair, he looked at me and coughed delicately. 'You married in Cyprus, my daughter — a beautiful island, I hear.'

'It is very beautiful, Your Holiness. You should visit.'

'Now that it is clear of the Byzantine Church I might find the time, but my duties here are many.' His next question was much more direct. 'Are you looking forward to continuing the line of kings of England?'

I smiled. 'No doubt, Holy Father, no doubt.'

'Ah, but not for a while, I suppose.'

'Kings are astonishingly busy during times of war, Your Holiness. There is little time for other matters.'

'Of course; our spiritual duties and goals sometimes take up our attention, even while we have other things we need attend to. But you became separated from Richard at times?'

'More than we were together, Your Holiness. However, as you say, time is the great decider.'

He seemed content with that and asked if we were to remain in Rome. I confirmed that we would until Richard caught up with us.

'Good. We pray for an early reunion.'

'And then we can seek some peace in our lives, Your Holiness.'

'Perhaps, but we need to see how true are the promises of the Saracens before we can truly rest. Now, shall we send for a little refreshment? Perhaps my cardinals can rejoin us?'

'We are old friends, Cardinal Benedetto and I, and Cardinal Melior has been most attentive.'

The Pope chuckled. 'You are most fortunate, ladies; not many get two attentive cardinals to guide them.'

Wine glasses and a decanter appeared on the table, and we began describing life at sea and the grandeur of the architecture all along the coast of the Holy Land.

Eventually, the cardinals' meaningful coughs brought the conversation to an end. Observing some gestures from Benedetto, we stood and curtsied before taking our leave.

'God bless you, my children,' said Pope Celestine. 'We shall pray for you and welcome your return to our side soon.'

We stepped back into the corridor, under Father Edwin's care. Benedetto came after us as we reached the church nave.

'Well done, *altezza*, well done. He likes you. Expect more invitations.'

'*Grazie*, Your Eminence. I'm sure His Holiness was well primed, thank you.'

'No problem, *altezza*. We will support you until Richard puts in an appearance.' He turned his attention to Joan. 'Lady Joan, you too have helped the Holy Father in his deliberations; he is most grateful.'

'I am free to remarry?'

'As His Holiness said, if it is your choice to walk away from Sicily…'

'I see no future in staying.'

I looked at her. 'Shall we search diligently for your next spouse?'

'We'll make a better pass at it than Mother did, that's for sure.'

We embraced and left the *basilica* in queenly dignity.

The sun held some late-year warmth, and I felt better on the journey back to the villa. Joan, sitting beside me and holding my hand, hummed happily.

'I think that we might enjoy Rome,' I said.

'Yes, we'll make the most of it while we're waiting for your husband to appear.'

'However long that may be.'

'There'll be news soon. Wherever he lands in Italy, we'll soon know about it.'

'So I pray. Now that we have left the carnage behind, I can look forward to setting foot on the soil of England and a new adventure,' I said hopefully.

A NOTE TO THE READER

Dear Reader,

I would be very grateful if you manage to find time to leave a review on **Amazon** or **Goodreads**. Reviews are the author's lifeblood.

More details about my writing can be found on my website: **www.history-reimagined.co.uk.**

Thank you.

Austin Hernon

Sapere Books is an exciting new publisher of brilliant fiction and popular history.

To find out more about our latest releases and our monthly bargain books visit our website: **saperebooks.com**